Julie Bozza

Homosapien

... a fantasy about
pro wrestling

LIBRAtiger

Revised edition published by LIBRAtiger 2018

ISBN: 978-1-925869-24-8

First published by Homosapien Books 2003, and by Manifold Press 2010

Homosapien
Words & Music by Pete Shelley
© Copyright 2009 Complete Music Ltd.
Administered by Universal Music Publishing Limited.
All Rights Reserved. International Copyright Secured.
Used by permission of Music Sales Limited.

libra-tiger.com | juliebozza.com

Homosapien

And I think of your eyes in the dark and I see the star …

How it began

Patrick It would make a great book – all the controversy, all the what's real and what isn't. Never mind the star–crossed lovers stuff.
David Not my thing.
Patrick It'd be a best–seller!
David So … *you* write it.

I looked at him. David smiled, a bit smug, like he had better things to be doing right now. Which I suppose he did.

So I sat down where he used to sit, and opened a new file on his laptop, and here we are.

I wasn't there for some of this story I'm gonna tell you, but someone told it to me. (Anyway, the dues on my artistic license are fully paid up.) Some of this story happened on national TV, and maybe you saw it. But like the title says, this is a fantasy, and the names and locations have been changed to protect the guilty – so if you think you know who's who, well, all I can say is you're entitled to your fantasies too.

Are you ready to *rumble … ?* If so, you'd better grab a mocha, put your feet up, and wind the clock back a year to more innocent times – back when men were men, women were women, and (most importantly) pro wrestling was real.

Whatever. It happened like this … Kind of.

How it really began

The mid January snows were biting deep and I was late to work that morning. Nothing new about any of that. David was used to my tardiness by now, so he just let out a big theatrical sigh and shook his head, not even looking up from the screen of his itty bitty laptop. He was pecking away at the keys, working on yet another draft of The Great American Navel–Gazing Novel. A lot of people don't realize this, but David Vigil is a dreamer. It's about the only thing we have in common, and because a lot of people are clueless about him, they have no idea how we put up with each other day in and day out.

We work together at the Q4 bookstore on Whitman, just off Mass Ave. Any queer who's been to Boston knows Q4, because we're right in the heart of the unofficial Queer Street. (OK, yeah, I know that Massachusetts Avenue is in Cambridge, not Boston. But names have been changed, this is a fantasy, yadda yadda yadda, don't expect me to be real literal about things like street names.) I should at least be clear about the bookstore, though – *I* work there and David owns the place. Built it up from nothing, from before this street was queered. No one can say he's not savvy–smart.

Anyway, there he was in his usual place on a stool behind the front counter, tap–tapping away with the frown on his face that had become a permanent feature. On the wall above him there are posters, but not the sort you usually find in queer bookstores – these were literary ones, of Shakespeare and Marlowe (not the private dick). Also some Romantic Poets I can't remember the names of right now, but they all lived fast and died young in Italy, leaving pretty corpses. Also a soldier from the First World War, looking rather dapper. The only modern poster is of a Derek Jarman film, but it was based on an old play about one of the King Edwards, and honestly I barely understood one word in ten. (Gaveston sure was cute, though, with his I'm–a–guttersnipe–and–the–king–loves–me sneer.)

Down on the back wall, by the storeroom and little kitchenette, that's where I have *my* posters and let me tell you they're far more appreciated by our customers than David's. We have a little reading nook back there, with a couple of worn old sofas and racks of newspapers and magazines going back ten years or more. People tend to hang out at Apollo's and the cafés down the street instead now, drinking latté, but David keeps our nook for the sake of tradition. To hear him tell it, these very sofas were A Hotbed Of Queer Revolt back in The Good Old Days. Me, I figure the only big deal is that he lost his virginity on one of them. Or maybe both.

I have a poster of *him* on the back wall. The pro wrestler, Homosapien. His poster's in, like, *the* place of honor, and everyone who comes back here drools over him, including me, which is why I had it laminated at the copy shop round the corner.

So I knew who he was the moment he walked in the door that morning.

It was about ten–thirty. A couple of customers were browsing the shelves, David was frowning at his laptop, I was taking my time unpacking a box of new books and checking them against the invoice. And Homosapien walked in.

I just gaped. The man was even more gorgeous in Real Life than in the wrestling ring. Tall, but not too tall – a tad over 6 foot. Built like an angel would be if only God were into body–building. And so damn handsome in the almost–*too*–delicious way of fashion ads.

He stood there just inside the store, letting the door swing closed behind him, looking around like he was a bit lost, his winter coat exaggerating his beautiful bulk. The customers were gaping now. And finally David sensed the hush and looked up from his writing. Of course David recognized him too, partly because of my poster of Homosapien, and partly because no one who spends any time in the vicinity of me and a video player escapes from being shown Homosapien's matches. Mind you, David only watches under protest and has never once let a mention of wrestling go by without dissing it. But he immediately knew who Homosapien was.

A moment passed. I kept gaping. Homosapien kept looking lost. If I didn't know better I'd think he was one of those closeted suburban gay boys who's ventured into Queer Street for the very first time. Surely that wasn't the case here.

As the silence stretched on, David's face grew darker and darker. "What are *you* doing here?" he finally snarled.

No reply. The lost look became a bit taken aback. Yeah, exactly like a Queer Street virgin.

"I asked what you're doing here!" David was standing up and getting angrier.

I should add that the store's front counter is five feet high, and there's steps and a platform behind it, so David – who's slim but 6 feet tall – was towering over this guy who could have beaten us all to a pulp. Homosapien was staring up at him, lost and taken aback and confused, and then quickly becoming very very blank.

"Where are the cameras?" David demanded, making a big show of peering out through the front window, looking up and down the street. "Is this a publicity stunt?"

"No."

"Then what the hell are you doing here? Research for this overblown queer crap you play at … ?"

"No."

"Because you just don't have a clue, do you? Pretending to be gay – it's nothing more than an angle you're exploiting. So, you go with the stereotype, you take the easiest path. Like the token gay best friend in the movies. It's bullshit! It doesn't *mean* anything."

Homosapien looked as if he were about to try arguing or explaining something, but then he shrugged. He just gave it up. A glance around at me and the customers, a quick nod of farewell, and he turned and walked right back out again.

Silence. Me, gaping at the closed front door. Me, gaping at David. The customers scratching their heads, then returning to their browsing. I walked up to the counter – and I'm only 5 feet 4, so all David would have seen was my adamant little upturned face. It was my turn to be demanding. "What did you do that for?"

"What?"

"Where do you get off, being so rude?"

David had the grace to look a bit sheepish. "Well, that guy gets insulted by professionals at least twice a week on national television. You think *I'm* gonna hurt his feelings … ?"

I give him my best *duh* look. "Sure looked like you did. Didn't it?"

The glare returned. "Go get me a coffee."

"Like, you haven't had enough already today?" But I swiftly recalled that there were times when it wasn't wise to sass the boss. "Yes, ma'am," I meekly agreed before donning hat, scarf, coat and gloves then sashaying off up the street without even taking his money. It would be my treat.

Well, of course you know what I found when I got to Apollo's … There he was – beautiful big butch Homosapien, crying in his cappuccino … Well, all right, it was an Americano, and he was just sitting there huddled over its meager warmth, looking like he'd gotten yet another dent in his armor – but that doesn't sound as good. He'd already sogged up a whole plate of biscotti, but the management didn't mind because he was a regular customer …

Scratch that last flight of fancy. Homosapien was sitting there all on his own, amidst the relative safety of a generic Apollo's coffee shop, oblivious to the few stares from other caffeine addicts. My soft old heart just crumbled. I've been on the wrong end of David's tirades a time or two myself, equally undeserved.

I bought myself a hazelnut latté (dollop of foam, to go) and headed back to Q4.

"Where the hell's mine?" David is flabbergasted. I had rebelled before, of course, but never about anything as serious as coffee.

"I think you'd better go get it yourself. And drink it there. And say a kind word or two to a certain pro wrestler."

"What?"

I glared up at the man with all the Righteousness of a Noble Cause. "Just do it!"

"You have *got* to be kidding me."

"Anyone else looking that lost, you'd never have chased them out. Admit it."

David glanced away for a moment, pondering.

"So, you go make it better. Or else!" And I meant it.

Of course, David's been around me long enough to know that I don't get serious real often, and when I do he'd better pay attention. "Well, I'll just get my coffee," he muttered before at last grabbing his jacket and sloping off up the street with his hands jammed into his pockets.

The bookstore was nice and quiet for half an hour. I sold a book or two, and flirted with a cute, bashful farm boy who signed up for our newsletter and catalogue on the understanding that it was mailed in a plain brown envelope. Finally David returned. He was looking sort of thoughtful. He didn't say anything. Just settled on the stool and opened up the latest draft on the laptop.

But then he did nothing more than sit there gazing at it, and I swear he didn't type a single word or even a letter for the rest of the morning.

So, what happened at Apollo's?

Consider this a dramatic reconstruction based on forensic evidence and the sworn testimony of witnesses …

Actually, writing this scene is kind of hard. David wouldn't have had much to say under the circumstances and I learned later that Homosapien is far more articulate in his wrestling persona than when speaking for himself. This pair of characters is going to be just *too* difficult to work with. They are such very different people and yet somehow now they managed to connect. How to explain that?

I can imagine David standing there by the Apollo's counter, doppio in hand (he got it to go, just in case), wondering whether to head over there and talk to the guy or not. And Homosapien looks up at just the right moment, and their eyes meet, and David is when–push–comes–to–shove a bit too polite to turn his back and walk away.

Homosapien gestures to the chair opposite him. David sits, leaning back and turned half away, one leg crossed over the other, trying to appear casual. He doesn't bother taking off his jacket.

"Uh," David begins, "I shouldn't have done that. That was harsh. It's not my habit to chase customers out of my store …"

"Not good for business," Homosapien observes.

"Yeah." David takes a deep breath. "Was there something in particular you wanted?"

Homosapien shakes his head. No.

The conversation stalls.

David sips at his coffee, but it's still too hot. Finally he asks, "So, what are you doing in Boston?"

"We have a show tonight. At the Garden."

"Ah, yes. Wrestling."

"You ever been?"

"To the *wrestling?*" David asks incredulously. "No." He smiles, shaking his head. How unlikely is that? "No."

They sit there for a while. David never seems to realize that intellectual snobs put a damper on the talk of regular folk. Homosapien looks like he wishes he could think of something reasonable to say. The silence stretches.

Finally David gulps down the last of his doppio, and gets up too quickly – his head is buzzing with a double espresso high and anyway no one can remain *totally* unaffected by Homosapien's gorgeousness. "Well," says David, "break a leg tonight."

"Thanks." Homosapien grimaces, for lots of reasons that he can't put into words. People aren't meant to think of wrestlers as actors – they're athletes.

"See you later."

That was only meant to be a generic farewell, but Homosapien takes him literally. Seizes the opportunity with both hands. "Yeah, that'd be good. We come through here every six weeks."

David pauses to consider the man. Certainly not totally unaffected. Oddly enough it seems that Homosapien isn't completely unaffected by my boss either. Must be one of those attraction–of–opposites things. "All right," David eventually says. "All right, I'll see you then." And at last he turns away and walks out. Thoughtful. Very thoughtful indeed.

A night at the wrestling

Do you know the opening number on Neil Diamond's *Hot August Night* concert album … ? A lone violin quietly starts the tune. The crowd is talking and laughing, paying more attention to their dates and friends than to the stage. The tune builds and another violin joins the first. Sweetness and yearning. The simple gradually becomes complex. Other instruments pick up the tune. People are growing hushed, beginning to anticipate. The yearning becomes a need, never quite frustrated, always full of hope. Then a keyboard chord holds, holds, holds. The wait would be unbearable if you didn't know they'll soon be giving you what you want. A strummed guitar takes up the tune. The drums kick in and the tune really starts to rock. Other strings join in, then an electric guitar. The crowd is ready to burst. The tune builds even further. And at last *He* appears and the crowd explodes, the guitar sings their joy. A night of tension and fulfillment and more tension begins.

I always imagine that the start of a wrestling show is set to the same music – except of course there are no violins in wrestling, and the audience *pops* (it doesn't explode).

Setting up a show in one of the stadiums must be like raising the big top of a circus … The fans gather and queue, wearing their favorite's latest t-shirt, carrying their signs, buying merchandise from the stalls, getting more and more buzzed. Once the seats are full, the cameramen and photographers, all dressed in black, begin circling the ring in the centre of the stadium. The commentators and the referee and the ring announcer take their places.

And at last the show begins.

There are a few federations in pro wrestling, but the one that manages to lead the ratings for 50 weeks of every year is World Wide Wrestling. I'm sure it was named for the sake of the acronym WWW. That's a mouthful to say, so it's fondly known as 'da Dub Dub Dub'.

The WWW's Ultimate Bad Guy is the first to appear tonight. As soon as his music is heard – the powerful, edgy opening to *Kashmir* (or *Come With Me*, for us funksters) – the crowd is on their feet, making a noise. They know this will be big. A blinding wall of red and gold fireworks goes off, and Lucifer appears with his valet. (I'm just glad they don't bother with a sulfur smell as well …)

Lucifer is a big, muscly, mean–looking dude, dressed all in black leather. The valet, known only as M, is tall and well–built herself. It's obvious that she works out as much as the wrestler does. She is also dressed in black leather, though not very much of it. The crowd – who are almost all young men, and definitely all rednecks – yell their appreciation of her. She remains poker–faced, despite the provocations and propositions, as the two of them walk down the ramp to the ring.

Then the music plays for someone *I* appreciate. The opening notes of a rocked–up version of Pete Shelley's *Homosapien*. The original has been my anthem for years. Homosapien appears without any other fanfare – and as usual he's dancing to the music, thrusting those hips, swaying that butt. Think of Elvis Presley in his heyday, when they'd only broadcast him from the waist up … Well, imagine Elvis the Pelvis with to–die–for muscle definition. Gorgeous. And dressed in nothing more than form–fitting purple lycra leggings and matching purple boots.

The fans hardly know how to react to Homosapien. He'd be a Good Guy if it weren't for the fact that his persona is gay. He's decent, and he never cheats, and he helps other Good Guys if they're in a fix. But he's gay. The audience of rednecks don't know what to make of him. There's some support and cool amusement, but there's also some resentment and outright hostility. There's even a guy holding up a sign that screams *LYNCH THE QUEER*.

Homosapien ignores all this. He's always happy and up–beat, and he never *ever ever* insults the fans, no matter what they say to him. That's another Good Guy thing.

As he dances, Homosapien also sings along. "I'm the cruiser / You're the loser," he taunts Lucifer, who is now pacing angrily around the ring. "Me and you, sir / Homosapien too."

Now, I'm the first to admit that I don't know all the technical terms of wrestling. So I'll hand over to the announcer and the commentators (Terry and Rumbler) for the match itself …

announcer	This match is scheduled for one fall only.
	Weighing in at 300 pounds, from Hell's Kitchen, New York City, and accompanied by M, please welcome *Lucifer!*
	And the contender, all the way from San Francisco, California, at a weight of 243 pounds, put your hands together for *Homosapien!*
Terry	OK, the referee's signaled for the bell to sound, but the two men are just circling each other warily –
Rumbler	Yeah, if I was Lucifer, I'd be *real* wary of letting *him* get a hold of me …
Terry	Isn't it about time you grew up? Homosapien is a professional. He's here to wrestle.
Rumbler	Is *that* what they're calling it these days?
Terry	Ah! They're locked up, each man struggling to gain the advantage – and Homosapien's managed to trip Lucifer and send him toppling! As the big man gets to his feet, Homosapien bounces off the ropes and drops him again with a Clothesline.
	This young man has had a wonderful year, and I predict that he has a great future in wrestling.
Rumbler	Oh, *please.* He's disgusting. What *I* want to know is – who did he sleep with to get this contract? The WWW used to be reserved for Real Men only, but I figure there's more than one fairy around now.
Terry	You sound like my great–great–grandfather.
Rumbler	Yeah, he was a Real Man too.

Terry	Returning to the match – Homosapien has pinned Lucifer, and the referee starts the count – one – two – but Lucifer twists out of the hold.
Rumbler	The day the WWW becomes politically correct is the day I quit.
Terry	I'm looking forward to that.
Rumbler	Which?
Terry	Both.

Patrick here. Let me fast–forward for a moment … The two wrestlers hit each other, throw each other around, grab and grapple …

Terry	… and Homosapien has Lucifer in a classic submission hold. Few people can withstand the Chinlock for long. The pressure on Lucifer's neck and spine must be horrendous.
Rumbler	Oh, *do* be careful, Homo! You might break a nail!
Terry	Lucifer's gonna have to give in and tap out soon. But wait! M is calling the referee's attention to the fact that Lucifer has one foot on the ropes! Homosapien will be forced to release the hold … Yes. And he's not happy about that, but he's never been one to argue with the ref.
Rumbler	Yeah, right. What a gentleman. *This is wrestling, for God's sake!* A Real Man would be mad as a cut snake.
Terry	He's still shaking his head. Can we get a replay on that? There it is! Look at that! M actually shifted Lucifer's foot over to the ropes while the referee wasn't looking! Oh my God, and now Lucifer has taken advantage of this last–minute reprieve, and is hammering Homosapien with a series of blows to the stomach.
	The smaller man is dazed, I don't think he knows *where* he is. Lucifer's going for his finishing move – the New York Pile Driver.
Rumbler	Sends them straight to Hell! Do not pass Go! Do not collect $200!
Terry	I think it's all over, folks. Lucifer's got the pin – one, two, three. Yes, it's over.

Lucifer's theme music blasts over the speakers. The referee declares him the winner, and lifts up his arm in victory. The crowd are cheering. Poor

Homosapien is left lying there on the mat, stunned. No one helps him. As Lucifer and M make their way up the ramp to the backstage area, the referee finally goes to check on Homosapien. After a moment, the wrestler manages to drag himself up, and he heads off up the ramp. Alone. The crowd jeers.

He's always alone.

Backstage

With one exception – in Real Life, Homosapien has a best friend, and that best friend is M, Lucifer's valet. They even share a dressing room, which is usually a spare bathroom or a janitor's closet or a storeroom. The stadiums have two big dressing rooms, which the Good Guy and Bad Guy wrestlers occupy *en masse* – but as the only female athlete, M is grudgingly given her own facilities. (The bimbo valets tend to dress and preen back at their hotels rather than risk the low–rent stadiums.) Homosapien shares the inadequate room with M as a gesture of support.

That night, as Homosapien watches M complete her transformation back into a regular woman, there is a knock at the door and Lucifer bursts in without waiting for an invitation.

"Hey, Lucy," Homosapien drawls. "I just can't figure out whether it's M you want to catch naked, or me."

Lucifer pointedly ignores him. "Emma, a few of us are heading off for a drink. D'you wanna come along?"

"Sure, Michael." She makes a point of turning to Homosapien. "What about you?"

"No. Thanks, anyway. I'll get an early night."

M sighs, and reaches to pat him on the shoulder. Then she says to Lucifer, "As long as it's nowhere fancy. I've only got these jeans and a sweater with me."

"That's fine," he replies. "You look great, Emma." And then the big burly man colors up, and promptly disappears, almost slamming the door behind him.

"Somebody likes you …" Homosapien teases in a singsong voice.

"Maybe," M says, pretending she doesn't care. She sits down again at the makeshift mirror, and hauls out her make–up kit. "Michael's all right. He can even be sweet. But he thinks you and I are an item. Well, half an item."

Homosapien snorts. "If they only knew … Do you want me to clear that up with him?"

"Nah. I ain't wanting to rush into anything. Let them all assume … You know they all assume we're sort of together, don't you?"

"I figured, yeah."

"Well, I guess that suits both of us right now. Protective camouflage."

"Yeah, OK," Homosapien agrees, a bit lamely. "Look, uh … about the camouflage thing …"

M turns to him, wondering. "What? What is it?"

But he's still too confused to be able to say, so he shrugs it off. "Never mind. Guess I'll head back to the hotel. See you in the morning."

But just as he heads for the door, someone else bursts through it, this time without even knocking. The owner of da Dub Dub Dub, the booker, the man who writes the checks … Mr. Jack Dynes.

Instead of protesting their privacy again, Homosapien and M remain dumb.

"Good match with Lucifer tonight," Dynes says in his usual rush. "You're earning respect. I think we're ready to take it a step further."

"What do you have in mind?" M asks when her friend remains silent.

Dynes announces to Homosapien, "You can challenge Porn ☆ for the championship belt."

M almost squeals in delight, and jumps up to hug Homosapien. Legitimacy at last. The wrestler just nods, and says, "Thanks." Dynes returns the nod, and rushes off again.

"This is wonderful!" M declares. "You deserve this."

"It's only a shot. Not a win. Not yet."

"Quit playing it cool! You know this is great!"

Finally Homosapien smiles, just a little. "Yeah, it's great."

"So, come have a drink with us."

"Your Lucy will get mad."

"Who cares? Let's celebrate!"

"All right," he says, ducking his head to hide a broader smile. "All right."

M squeals again, and hugs him some more. Friends. Mates, buddies. They're more precious than anything else in this life. Almost.

Kids, don't try this at home

"Ow–ow–ow–*ouch!*"

We are at the bookstore watching a tape of last month's pay–per–view wrestling on the little TV we keep behind the counter –

"*Jeez* … us."

– and David is madly empathizing with Homosapien, who is getting pounded every which way by Brute, one of the heftier Bad Guys.

"Christ! What is he *doing?* That must have **hurt!**"

"Ah," I opine, "there's nothing finer than watching two big beefy guys throwing each other around. If you're really lucky, you get to see them hugging each other afterwards too …"

David flatly retorts, "That guy is *not* going to be hugging our guy."

"You think?" I laugh. "You're really starting to get into this, aren't you?"

"No."

"After abusing me unmercifully every time I raised the topic, you're finally lowering yourself to my level …"

"What the hell do you know?" he snaps.

I learned long ago just to be silent when David does that. Unless it's over something worth arguing about.

Eventually David confesses, "I guess I'm interested to see what they do with this gay angle." A moment drags past. David casts a glance my way. "It *is* just an angle, right?"

"Right." I nod sagely.

"*Ouch!*" David flinches, but can't make himself turn away. "They could *kill* each other doing that!"

"Yeah."

Silence. Homosapien loses the match, but he's fought well and looks gorgeous, and the crowd applaud his exit. Once he's off–screen, David goes back to sorting through the distributors' accounts. "Um …" he begins, busy rustling paper.

"Yeah?"

"Well, um, what's his name? His real name?"

I grin to myself. "Adam O'Connor."

"Adam," David thoughtfully repeats. Yeah, he's doing that thoughtful thing again. Not the old intellectual thing, but the new thoughtful thing. It suits him.

Interlude

I meet someone. Mr. Tall, Dark & Intense. The sex is good; he makes me laugh.

You'd have thought that was a good thing, wouldn't you?

True Blue

The driving rhythm of the *Blues Brothers* music thumps out of the speakers, and the crowd pops! They pop like they've never popped before. This is, of course, the most classic introduction music you could ever find, and it announces the arrival of the WWW's Ultimate Good Guy.

Known only as Blue, this gorgeous man cultivates an air of mystery, which is kind of odd for a Good Guy. He makes his appearance in the midst of smoke and sparks, all back–lit with bright blue. He wears black boots and trunks, patterned with blue swirls. He obviously has mixed ancestry, because his face is intriguingly unusual and his skin is a warm terracotta that makes me blush in response, but he's not at all forthcoming about his background. If it wasn't for our Homosapien, Blue would be my favorite. Most of wrestling's Good Guys are a bit bland, but these two are exceptions.

Tonight Blue is wrestling Homosapien, and I wouldn't miss it for the world. Actually, I have to admit that I'm even taping it for posterity, or at least for my own future provocation. Though I have plenty of excuses – it's not just that the two must scrumptious guys in wrestling are going to be grasping and grappling each other all round the ring – it's also that Blue is a very technical wrestler, and if he's wrestling someone he respects, then it's always a good show.

announcer   This match is scheduled for one fall only. Weighing in at
            249 pounds, from the WWW's home of Chicago, Illinois,
            please welcome the most popular wrestler in world
            history … *Blue … !*

Blue struts around the squared circle for a while, soaking up the crowd's
appreciation. They adore him. There are more signs for him than for all the
other wrestlers put together; his range of t–shirts outsells all the other
WWW merchandise. He's in the middle of a love affair with pretty much
the whole of America.

Once the smoke has faded away, the rocked–up *Homosapien* blasts from
the speakers and our hero appears. He always has a genuinely happy smile
on his face as if he loves being there, even though the crowd's welcome is
rather ambivalent.

My own reaction to him is more straightforward … Ah, those thrusting
hips, that tight muscled butt … The way this man dances just blows me
away. He moves so freely that you just *know* he knows what to do with it
all … For the first time in, like, *forever,* I am jealous of David. My boss and
I usually have very different tastes, but somehow he managed to spark an
interest within Homosapien, and all I can do is wish I'd gotten there first.

announcer   And from San Francisco in California, weighing in at
            243 pounds, here's *Homosapien!*

The two wrestlers circle each other, sizing each other up. They are
perfect. Purple leggings over cool marble, and black and blue trunks over
warm terracotta. Handsome faces, incredible physiques. When they finally
get their hands on each other, it's like harmony and conflict all in one
delicious mix …

But I should probably hand over to the commentators, and let them tell
you about the actual wrestling.

Terry   They've locked up, each trying for leverage on the other, but
            Homosapien and Blue are very evenly matched. I'm
            expecting a real showcase match from these two men
            tonight.

Rumbler   You'll be lucky. The kind of show that Homo puts on – well,
            he shouldn't be in a wrestling ring, he should be on
            Broadway!

Terry   Homosapien does have many talents, that's true.

Rumbler   And how do you know *that* … ?

Terry   Exactly what are you insinuating? Can't a man be admired for his God–given skills, without you bringing sex into everything? His private life is private, and so is mine.

Rumbler   All right, all right! Don't get your panties in a twist.

The mostly–serious commentator shoots a glare at his colleague that even David could learn from, and then manfully returns to the wrestling.

Terry   Blue has managed to spin Homosapien around, and is attempting to apply a Sleeper Hold. If he's successful, this could be a very short match.

No, Homosapien manages to turn it around, and locks Blue up with an Armbar. Blue is grimacing in pain, and I'm not surprised – the pressure that hold can put on your elbow is brutal. Homosapien is shifting closer, maintaining that pressure with his body now. And he adds a Nerve Hold to the equation, gripping Blue's jugular in a ferocious pinch! Blue has fallen to one knee!

Rumbler   If there's a Real Man in the ring, will he please stand up?

Terry   Blue is stretching back and away from Homosapien, I don't know why, he only seems to be making it worse for himself – but, no, he's used Homosapien's hold against him, by suddenly slipping head–over–heels, and forcing Homosapien to fall head–over–heels after him.

As they come up for air – well, I hate to contradict myself, but actually Blue is the only one coming up for air. He's got Homosapien in another Sleeper Hold, which as you'd know makes it damned hard to breathe, let alone the fact it constricts the flow of blood to the head. Homosapien is gasping, trying to reach back for Blue, but Blue has him too well–placed for that, there's nothing he can grab …

Rumbler   Oh, puh–*lease*. The thought of what that sorry excuse for a man wants to grab –

Terry   Would you mind trying to keep your mind on the wrestling? Look at that! Homosapien has broken the hold! How the hell did he do that? Will you quit distracting me? No one's broken Blue's Sleeper Hold for as long as I can remember!

Patrick here, interrupting a blatant exaggeration if not an actual lie, unless the commentator's memory does actually only go back as far as June.

But this is where the match gets really interesting. Homosapien spins Blue around, and pins him. The two men – who have been in constant contact with each other ever since they locked up – are caught up together on the mat. How can I explain it? Homosapien is kneeling over Blue, holding his shoulders down, with one arm hooked around Blue's bent legs. They almost make a sphere.

The referee drops to the mat and starts counting. One! Two!

But Blue kicks out. In fact, he doesn't just kick out – he forces Homosapien onto his back, so that the hold is reversed.

The referee tries again. One!

Homosapien kicks out. And, for a few lovely long moments, Homosapien and Blue are tumbling one over the other, holding and then reversing the hold, pinning and then being pinned. It's incredible. Well, OK, I like to watch. And there's nothing finer to watch than two gorgeous guys tumbling over and under each other. But the main thing is the wrestling – the athleticism and the strategy of it. Honest!

<table>
<tr><td>Terry</td><td>They break apart at last. Homosapien is just lying there, he seems winded. Blue isn't trying to pin him, though – he's running, bouncing off the ropes, getting as much momentum as he can. Homosapien is getting to his feet. He's a bit dazed, but he's gonna be a whole lot more dazed real soon …

Oh my God! I don't know how Homosapien managed it, but at the last possible moment he deflected Blue, and sent him crashing right into the turnbuckle.</td></tr>
</table>

The two of them slingshot themselves and each other from the ropes, each trying to lay out his opponent with Clotheslines or just plain punches or with full-body Splashes. And then they're climbing the ropes, leaping on each other from the turnbuckles.

And the thing is, it's a really even match, and it's lasted for over fifteen minutes. Lower-ranked wrestlers like Homosapien don't usually do real well when they're pitted against the Ultimate Good Guy. Sometimes they can cause an upset and defeat the champ, but usually that's by cheating in some way, playing dirty, or taking some kind of unfair advantage. For a while I am sitting there praying that Homosapien won't suddenly turn; won't cheat to win and thereby become a Bad Guy, a heel. But, no, he's wrestling fair and he's wrestling well, and the crowd are even starting to cheer his successes almost as much as Blue's. There is something significant happening here.

Rumbler   For God's sake, someone put me out of my misery. Blue should have won by now! Blue should have mopped the floor with this guy! Talk about having an off–night.

Terry   I have to disagree with you there – I think they're both having *on*–nights. It's a long while since I saw such a technically proficient match. I think these are two of the WWW's best.

Rumbler   Lord save us! What's the world coming to?

Terry   You might not like this, but the fans are enjoying themselves. Good grief! I think Blue is suffering from one too many Splashes – he's stirring, but he's not getting up. Homosapien is putting a Chinlock on him, bending him back … I've never seen Blue look so spent, not even after that title match with Lucifer.

Rumbler   Come on, Blue! Get with the program! You're out there to win!

Terry   He's giving in! He can't take any more! BLUE IS TAPPING OUT! I've never seen anything like it. This young man, this Homosapien, he has a bright future ahead of him, that's for sure.

There's nothing but muffled groans and the odd retching sound from the color commentator, who has dropped his head to the desk in disgust.

The referee lifts Homosapien's arm in victory. The crowd are mostly cheering and applauding – though nowhere near as enthusiastically as they would have if Blue had won, and there is some booing mixed in there. Homosapien doesn't mind, though. He's grinning happily, proud of himself and of what he's achieved. He's beautiful, he really is beautiful.

Blue finally gets himself up to his feet, and begins tactfully withdrawing, leaving Homosapien to enjoy the victory he's earned. But Homosapien doesn't let him go; offers to shake hands with him; and they do, looking at each other with respect.

Rumbler   Oh, now I'm *really* gonna be sick …

Homosapien lifts Blue's arm, sharing the victory. The crowd love it. Ah, doesn't it warm the cockles of your heart … ?

The all–too–realistic retching sounds from the commentary desk are the only thing to spoil the moment.

Chez Lui

"Q4 bookstore," I cheerily singsong into the phone.

The caller pauses a moment to gather together a few scraps of courage, as they sometimes do, poor things. Finally: "Uh, can I speak to David?"

I know who it is; I've been expecting his call. David must have been expecting it too, because he'd been on edge – even more on edge than usual – for a week now. The World Wide Wrestling is back in town and have a show that night at the Boston Garden.

"Sure," I reply, and I holler for the boss: "David! Guess who!"

He comes to the phone, shooting me the darkest look he's ever managed. "Yeah?" he says into the receiver, turning his back on me as if I'd actually take the hint to disappear.

I can't hear the other end of the conversation, but David is silent for what seems like the longest while and I imagine Homosapien stumbling through a few disjointed sentences. Finally David exclaims, "Tonight?!" as if slightly panicked. "What, you mean after the show?"

Another moment drags by. "OK, yeah. But it's Friday; Patrick and I had plans." First I'd heard about them, of course. "We're heading for Chez Lui. It's a nightclub two blocks from here on Whitman." Another pause before David clarifies, "Yeah, it's a *gay* nightclub." But apparently Homosapien rises to the challenge, because David's shoulders sag. "Of course you won't be in the way. We'll see you then. Sure. Yeah." And he hangs up.

It's a moment before David turns around to face me. The boss needs a favor and he knows I am going to milk this for all it's worth.

"You are free tonight, aren't you?" David says. He doesn't know about Mr. Tall, Dark & Intense, so he thinks it's a safe assumption.

"Oh, I don't know … It's a school night, after all, and my teacher said if I'm late in on *one* more Saturday morning, he'll paddle my ass *so* hard. Of course, I think he's just been *dying* for an excuse …"

David calls my bluff. "Well, if you don't want to go clubbing with The Great White Queer, I'll give him your excuses. He'll understand that you missed your last penicillin shot."

We take a moment to glare at each other. Then I say, "You're not brave enough to go meet him on your own."

"So, you're not gonna be there?"

"You know I will be."

"All right."

"Bitch."

"Cow."

We part ways, shoulders huffy, mission accomplished. It's a date.

Later that day, though, David mutters to me, "Um, you know, Homosapien – he said he's never really been to a gay nightclub before."

"Oh." This takes me aback.

"What do you think *that* means?"

"I don't know." We exchange confused glances. I remember that Homosapien seemed like a Queer Street virgin when he first walked into the bookstore. I don't say anything to David, but it sure makes me wonder.

Chez Lui is full and the mood is hyped, almost as if they were expecting a celebrity to drop by – though no doubt this is only due to the fact that Friday night is the night for displaying our most alluring feathers, especially now that the worst of winter is over and baring a bit of skin doesn't automatically lead to hypothermia.

A booth just along from the front door is vacated as we get there. David sullenly slides into it. Usually it would be too far from the dance floor for me, but tonight it seems perfect. I head off to say hello to the DJ (he's a friend of mine), and to buy a round of drinks. Then I slide in next to David and settle down to wait. He's so anxious that we're here an hour early.

Music, mayhem, gossip, glitter. David too busy scowling to provide any conversation.

Then finally *he* arrives. Homosapien, standing in the doorway, taking a moment to look about. I see him first and I wave at the DJ, who obligingly switches mid–track to the rocked–up *Homosapien*. The big tough wrestler wilts a little as he hears his theme music pound out over the speakers, though he still seems somewhat more confident than when he came to Q4. With the music as a clue, the people around Homosapien suddenly realize who he is and a wave of recognition ripples through the crowd. It's rather amusing to watch, actually. Like running a finger across one of those frames full of iron filings and everything falls into alignment along your path – only this was the other way round, of course. Never mind.

David, who's been scowling so ferociously into his Manhattan that he didn't hear the music, lifts his head as he hears applause. He tracks everyone's gazes back to the centre of attention. He gapes a little.

Homosapien begins making his way through as best he can. I wave at him so he knows where to head for. But no one will let him go by without a word, an autograph, a handshake, a kiss. By this time David is gaping a lot because he had *no* idea that Homosapien actually has a lot of gay fans. A *lot*. David often assumes that the whole gay community likes what he likes and disses what he disses, but right now he's being proved very wrong.

"That man is looking *hot* tonight," I observe. And it's true – Homosapien is in faded denims that show off his butt, and a white muscle shirt (having shrugged off a black leather jacket), with a simple silver chain around his neck. A thick black belt and rugged black boots. Clean and fresh and perfectly groomed. "Delicious. I think he wants to make an impression."

David just grunts at me.

Even though Homosapien has reached our booth and is trying to say hello, his fans aren't done with him yet. Some young stud wants an autograph on the rear pocket of his jeans and Homosapien obliges, unfazed by the provocatively posed curves he's scribbling on. "If you're looking for anything or, well, any*one* to do while you're in town," the stud gushes, totally blowing his cool, "you can almost always find me here."

"Thank you," the wrestler politely replies, as if accepting best wishes on his mother's behalf. "You're very kind."

Finally it's just the three of us. "Sit down," I say. "Take a load off. What are you drinking?"

"I'll have a beer, thanks, Patrick."

I wink at him for remembering my name, slide out of the booth, and somehow manage to totally ignore David's beseeching expression. Honestly, he must be the only guy in the entire district who doesn't want to be left alone with this gorgeous man.

Of course, I am immediately swooped on by the Terminally Curious – that is, everyone in Chez Lui. "How come he's with you two?"

"Homosapien," I assure them, "has an impeccable social radar."

"Where's he know you from?"

"He spends half his salary at the bookstore." I wasn't above a shameless little plug or two. "He's our best customer."

"I don't believe it! Where'd you first meet?"

"Oh, we grew up together. Known him since we were *this* high …"

"What?" One of my oldest and not–so–dear friends was obviously in Sarcasm Mode tonight. "All of a sudden, Patrick, you grew up in Tulsa, Oklahoma?"

Momentary confusion. "I thought he was from San Francisco?"

"Aren't we all, darling? Aren't we all."

When I get back to the booth with drinks in hand, I find that my boss is making the most of this wonderful opportunity for small talk. "Yeah, you should give it a try," David is saying. "It starts in Boston Common, and you follow this red–painted line through all the old landmarks – Paul Revere's house, site of the Boston Massacre, that sort of thing …" David trails off when he sees me standing there taking my turn at gaping.

"Remind me to help you polish up your rather tarnished repartee," I say to him.

"Give it a rest, Patrick."

"Actually, it sounds interesting," Homosapien says. "We travel a lot, but we're always on the move. Never in one place long enough to do the tourist stuff."

I roll my eyes. Maybe they're doing all right after all.

"Um, well," says an unusually uncool David, "so, next time you're in town …"

"Sure." Homosapien smiles at him. They each take a large swig of their drinks. Then Homosapien confesses, "Last few years, seems like all I've done is wrestle. I mean, the travelling eats up a heap of time, and then there's training and working out, preparing for the shows. And I wouldn't have made it this far if I hadn't put the rest of my life on hold. But that's gotta change. It's time for a change."

David watches him solemnly through this. When he's done, David nods. "I know what you mean." And of course he does. What with the hours that the bookstore is open, David has no life either. The business is a success, but at what cost?

We're just starting a second round of drinks when some college boy sways up to our table and offers his hand to Homosapien. "Care to dance?"

The wrestler smiles, oddly gentle. "I'm just wanting to drink my beer."

"Oh." Did anyone *ever* look attractive while pouting … ?

"But I'm real flattered you asked."

"Oh!" A little brighter now. "Maybe later?"

Homosapien shrugs, still with a smile. "Maybe." I guess he's had a lot of practice in turning people down …

David is frowning, having been given a few things to think about tonight. The three of us manage to converse for a while about topics slightly hipper than the Freedom Trail. Meanwhile, Homosapien graciously autographs anything he's presented with.

But then my friend the DJ decides that it's time for a few slow dances. And the first one he plays, of course, is what I like to think of as the *How Soon is Now?* version of *Homosapien*. It's, like, Pete Shelley and Morrissey got together and had a lovechild … Anyway, there's an expectation here. Everyone in Chez Lui turns to see what the wrestler will do. Without pausing for breath or thought, the college boy is heading our way, hoping for that dance.

Homosapien stands, and turns to David. "Would you … ?"

"Sure." David is surprised at himself, but he stands, and they walk out onto the dance floor hand in hand. And they slow–dance. I watch them for a while. Strange, how well they fit together. They're of a height, and they're already moving in each other's arms like they belong there. Adam and David. Who'd have thought?

Mr. TDI shows up – that's Mr. Tall, Dark & Intense, of course, which is too long to type all the time. Mr. TDI shows up, and immediately leaves again with me in tow. We need somewhere private. And, anyway, my job here is done.

All the gory details

The next morning, as expected, David looks as if his sack time didn't include much sleep time …

Patrick	Honey, I don't think those bags are what they mean when they sing about Bedroom Eyes, you know?
David	Coffee. Go get me a doppio. In fact, get me two.

He props himself on a stool behind the counter. And he's so out of it that he thrusts a ten–dollar bill at me; more than enough to also cover my hazelnut latté (dollop of foam, to go).

Patrick	No way. I'm not going anywhere until you tell me all the gories.
David	Caffeine, or I'm not telling you anything.

Brief interlude while I dash up to Apollo's. Just hum amongst yourselves for a while.

OK, I'm back. David takes the lid off one of the doppios, and his eyes drift dreamily shut while he inhales the aroma – which would be enough in itself to give anyone else a caffeine high. I'm decent enough to wait while he takes a mouthful and lets it kick in. Then he looks up at me standing there beside him.

David	Patrick, I just wanted to say – your repartee only sparkles because it's draped in cheap tinsel.
Patrick	It took you this long to come up with a retort?
David	No, I just didn't want to descend to your level in public.
Patrick	You mean, in front of *him* …

David shakes his head, and looks down at the floor for a moment.

David	So, you want to know what happened?
Patrick	Duh! Yeah.
David	Nothing. Nothing happened.
Patrick	What?!
David	Nothing happened.
Patrick	You're kidding me.
David	We danced a bit; we talked; we called it a night. He had an early plane to catch; I had to be here. That's all.

David is looking a bit defensive. I figure he must be certifiable.

Patrick   Without *one kiss?*

David   Well, what would he want with me, anyway?

Patrick   I don't know – why don't you ask him? He obviously wants something.

There's no answer to that. David grabs his second coffee and turns away. I shake my head and go find some dusting to do. I'd been happily imagining all kinds of weird shit going on last night – but nothing weirder than that! How the *hell* could nothing have happened … ???

Interview 1

Between wrestling matches, as you'd know, they screen interviews with the wrestlers and managers and valets, etc. This one is being conducted by Terry, the mostly–serious commentator. And the interviewee is our very own Homosapien. They are in a stadium locker room, and it looks like Homosapien is the last wrestler to leave after a long long night. He is sitting there on a bench with his bag at his feet, looking a tad dejected.

Terry   Homosapien, you've been doing terrifically in recent times. That match against Blue was superb, and you deserved the win.

Homosapien   Thanks, Terry, I appreciate it.

Terry   But it looks as if you have something on your mind right now.

Homosapien   Yeah, I do.

Terry has to prompt and even push him a little to tell us what it is. Finally:

Homosapien   I've put a lot of work and effort into my career with the WWW, Terry. I've taken a lot of knocks, a lot of hits. I've done it hard.

Terry   That's all true.

Homosapien   But I'm not asking for sympathy, I'm just asking for what's fair. I think it's time that I got the chance to move it on up another level.

Terry   In what way?

Homosapien turns to look directly into the camera.

Homosapien   Mr. Dynes, if you're watching this, I just wanna say that I'm ready for a title shot. Porn ☆ doesn't do any credit to the WWW as our champion. He's low–life. Give me a chance, Mr. Dynes, and I'll do you proud.

And they end on that shot of his determined, sincere, handsome face.

Interview 2

Porn ☆   I'm low–life?! *I'm* low–life??!! Exactly who does that loser think he is … ?

Terry tries to answer this rhetorical question, or maybe ask something himself, but Porn ☆ will not be interrupted.

Porn ☆   I am the best Goddamned champion this federation has ever seen! And I can tell you that *no one* wants that two–bit fairy wearing *my* gold around his waist.

They are standing in a corridor somewhere. It looks as if Porn ☆ happened to see Terry passing by, and insisted on having his say – or his shout, if you wanna be real literal. The wrestler pushes his face right up close to the camera.

Porn ☆   You better listen up, faggot. You better get smart. You talk about levels – well, you try to rise above that bottom–feeder level where you belong, I'm gonna be there to kick you right back down again. And that's all there is to say about that.

Again, Terry opens his mouth to speak – but Porn ☆ couldn't care less. He's done. He turns his back and walks away, outraged anger in every line of his body.

Terry watches him go, then turns back to the camera scratching his head. After a moment, he shrugs.

Terry   Cut.

Interview 3

It's Terry and Homosapien again, sitting there in a formal interview situation, like the two civilized guys they are.

Terry	As you know, Homosapien, there's a lot of hostility around here about you and your … lifestyle.
Homosapien	It's not a lifestyle, Terry, it was never something I had a choice about. Being gay came with the plumbing.
Terry	I see.
Homosapien	But Porn ☆ is a fine one to talk about lifestyles – he's obviously made some choices in his life that other people wouldn't understand. Earning his money through the porn industry, that's not a career–choice that a lot of Americans can really respect. I bet he's come up against discrimination, trying to jump tracks and make it in pro wrestling instead. He should understand where I'm coming from.
Terry	Are you saying that you've been discriminated against?

Homosapien takes a moment to consider this, and when he replies he's talking slow as if he's trying to figure it all out as he goes.

Homosapien	No. No, I'm not saying that. There's other guys here who've paid their dues – some of us make it to the next level, and some of us don't. It's frustrating, that's all I'm saying. It's frustrating when it seems to have more to do with luck than merit.
Terry	Thank you for your time, Homosapien. I'm sure we all wish you well in your bid for the title belt. Now, it's back to Rumbler for the next match …

Misfire

The phone rings, and I pick it up. "Q4 bookstore / chains, whips and thrills galore." (Me, a writer? Hell, I'm a poet!)

"Hey, Patrick. Is David there?" It's Homosapien, of course.

"Sure, honey. Is he ever anywhere else?"

He laughs. "No. He won't give me his home number, but he says that's because he's only ever there to sleep."

"Alas, it's true; he has no life."

"And he says we have nothing in common."

"Well, that's at least two things, isn't it?" But I really shouldn't flirt with the boss's Romantic Interest. "Hold on." I put the receiver down, and holler, "David! Phone! You know who!"

David's given up trying to exclude me from their conversations, especially if it's just about wrestling. And, frankly, I think he still wants an excuse not to indulge in small talk, even now. What is *with* David and his Major League Reluctance? He knows by now that there's more to Adam than his gorgeousness (though that in itself would be enough for most people). David has figured out by now that Adam O'Connor is one of the most decent people he's ever met. So I just don't get why this is taking so long.

Anyway, David comes to the phone, and says, "Hey, Adam."

"Hey."

"Um, Patrick's been playing me the tapes. D'you think they'll give you that title shot?"

"Yeah."

"Yeah? Just like that?" David is surprised – and when he gets over that, he's happy for our hero. "That's great! I thought it was still all up in the air."

Homosapien clears his throat. "Well, yeah, I guess it is. I'm just feeling like it's my turn, you know?"

"Finally, yeah. Hey, and I was thinking."

"Oh, no," the wrestler says flatly. "You know I can't keep up when you do that."

David laughs as if this is merely a joke. "I was thinking that you should do an interview with *Kinsey 6*. I'm sure they'd go for it. You're becoming a real role model."

"What's *Kinsey 6?*"

"You know – the gay rag. They're based right here in Boston; I know most of them; I could set it all up for you."

"Oh." There's a long silence. Finally Homosapien says, "People like you need to take me seriously, first."

"I *do* now – OK? I *do* take you seriously. And it sounds like the WWW is starting to take you seriously too. You've really got the chance to do some good now."

Homosapien lets out a frustrated sigh. "Well, don't go pushing it, David. It's kinda complicated."

"Like, how?"

"I can't say."

David is getting irritated. Real irritated. He glances at me, and I shake my head, but that's not gonna stop him. "You think I *won't* understand or I *can't* understand?"

Another silence before Homosapien says, "I can't talk about it."

"Fine. Well, call me when you can."

And David slams down the phone. I can't believe it. David actually hangs up on this guy who is, let's face it, God's Gift. I shake my head again. I just don't get it.

The State of the Federation

Every couple of months, Terry gets to interview Mr. Jack Dynes Himself about whatever the current issues are in the WWW. This time round, of course, one of those issues is our hero and his bid for the championship belt.

Terry   Mr. Dynes, Homosapien seems like a very deserving young man. What do you think is holding him back?

Dynes pauses for a moment – though, when he answers, it's obvious he's already thought about this.

Dynes   He's gotta want it; he's gotta earn it.

Terry   I've spoken with him at length, Mr. Dynes, and I can assure you that Homosapien wants a shot at the title.

Dynes   But not enough. He doesn't want it badly enough. Not yet.

There's a hard–hitting question coming up. You can tell that from the frown on Terry's face, and the way he leans forward.

Terry   Is this about him being gay?

Dynes   No, sir, not at all. I'll admit it – that's not something that I like or even understand, but it's got nothing to do with his worth as a wrestler.

Terry   Well, I'm sure we'll all be watching the next phase of Homosapien's career with a great deal of interest.

Misfit

There's a wrestling match. Homosapien might have a hundred things to complain about while working for da Dub Dub Dub, but his current exposure is not one of them. He's in a match every week, along with interviews and other bits and pieces. The audiences, while not exactly rejoicing in his every appearance, enjoy seeing him make a contribution.

Tonight he's wrestling Brute again – yes, the old 'Brute by name and brute by nature' guy. But it's a different Homosapien we're seeing. This one isn't happy and smiling – he's deadly serious and over–determined. He even seemed a bit sullen when he first climbed into the ring.

I wonder if there's more going on behind the scenes than the frustrations of the title thing. David looks a bit guilty, but even he's not vain enough to imagine that a brief disagreement on the phone with him is enough to make Homosapien sulk on national television.

The match is a tough one, with neither man giving anything away to the other. Homosapien loses, of course, but he has worked so damned hard that the crowd stand in moderate awe while he makes his exit, dignified but crumpled a little with the pain. It's quite something.

"Uh," says David in a hushed kind of voice, "was that about him wanting it badly enough?"

"I don't know."

Later in the night's show, David is relieved to see that Homosapien is at least still mobile. After his new buddy Blue decisively won a match against Jay Caesar, Blue is set upon by Brute and Caesar, while the referee tries in vain to stop them. We all know what sore losers Bad Guys are, right? But Homosapien runs out to the ring, surprising and scattering the pair with the mere threat of his presence. It's quite a coup.

"He's, uh …" David frowns, and tries again. "He's really earning their respect, isn't he?"

"Yes, he is," I say very firmly. "What about yours?"

But David's gaze is fixed on the screen.

Homosapien and Blue, both rather the worse for wear by this stage, stagger up the ramp in each other's arms and disappear backstage. It's lovely.

Quite the stuff of fantasy, despite me knowing someone who has a prior claim to our guy.

It seems obvious that Homosapien is becoming more and more of a fixture in the WWW. But to what end? How is he ever going to really fit into the hierarchy of wrestlers?

Well, I guess if I knew the answer to that, I'd be running da Dub Dub Dub, and Jack Dynes would be blessed with running up to Apollo's to fetch David a doppio.

Working out

Chicago, Illinois, home town of the WWW. Homosapien and his friend M are working out in the WWW's gym. Grunts and thuds and cries of pain echo through from the next room, where Sam (aka Saddam) is training the latest batch of wannabe wrestlers. Sam's voice is always loud and harsh and challenging, based on the theory that if the new guys can't deal with him here, they're never going to cope with younger, beefier wrestlers in front of 10,000 screaming fans.

The memories stirred up by the sounds of training provoke some winces and wry smiles from M and Homosapien. When one of the new guys lets out something close to a sob, M murmurs, "Say uncle, kid," but otherwise our pair are silent.

It's only when Homosapien and M are alone in the gym – warming down, striding beside each other on the treadmills – that M raises the topic that's been bothering her for days.

"Adam. Maybe Jack Dynes is right."

Homosapien glances at her. "About what?"

"About you."

"Why – what's he been saying now?"

"I mean that interview he did with Terry." Still striding along tirelessly, as if she'd never have to stop if she didn't want to, M takes a moment to towel the sweat off her face. Then she looks across at her friend. "You know you've got the skills and the strength, Adam, you're a real athlete. You've got the looks and the charisma. You've got a character that gets people interested, even if they're not sure whether they like you. You've got determination, otherwise you wouldn't have made it this far. But maybe you don't have the passion to take it further."

Homosapien is staring at the far wall, and M can't tell if he's really listening. Finally he says flatly, "You think I'm missing out on passion."

"Maybe – that's all I'm saying. Maybe Mr. Dynes knows what he's talking about, and maybe you should listen."

They both stride on for a few more minutes. Then Homosapien stops, and lets the treadmill's belt deposit him back on the floor. He grabs his towel, and rubs at his face. Then he walks over, takes M's hand in one of his, and lifts it for a kiss. No hard feelings. Gratitude, even, for a friend's honesty.

A blond–mopped head pokes around the door of the training room. M notices him first, and then Homosapien turns to see him. It's a kid of about 19 or 20, apparently awe–struck to find himself in the presence of Genuine Wrestling Celebrities. He even mouths a "Wow!"

"Hey, kid," M says, "don't let Sam catch you slacking off."

A nervous glance back into the training room, even though the kid is already explaining, "No, it's OK, we're on a break, he went to take a phone call."

"Well, come over here, then." M hops down off the treadmill, collects her towel. "What's your name?"

The kid cautiously approaches – then he tries to put on a show, puffing up his chest and announcing, "I'm Cougar – I'm a bad–ass wild–cat from the Badlands, South Dakota."

Homosapien snorts with laughter. "Maybe we can help you work on that intro, kid."

The offer totally mitigates the unkindness. "Wow, thanks!"

M is musing, "Do they even *have* pumas in the Badlands … ?"

"Well, I figured they did, ma'am. Maybe I'm wrong about that."

Homosapien attempts a rescue from this dawning uncertainty. "So, you wanna be a wrestler, Cougar."

"Yes, *sir!* I've been to your shows, sir, whenever you're in town, and I haven't missed anything of yours on the TV, not since I was –"

"– a cub?" M supplies.

Cougar gets even more bashful. "Well, not since I was a kid, sir. I always wanted to be like you."

"What, gay?"

The bashfulness becomes a fully–fledged bright–red blush. "No, sir." And Cougar, almost despite himself, looks M up and down. "*No,* sir."

M laughs. Homosapien manages to hide a smile, then blusters at Cougar – "Are you looking at my woman, kid?"

"No, sir!"

"Keep your filthy eyes to yourself!" Homosapien is advancing on him. "Just because your mom mated with a mountain lion – that don't make you scary, it don't make you sexy, it don't make you strong, and it sure as hell don't make you smart."

Cougar is terrified. He backs away.

Homosapien suddenly rushes him, sweeps him up, and then dumps him down hard on his back. The larger man lands on Cougar, and begins pummeling him.

It takes a few moments, but Cougar belatedly realizes that they're on a pile of mats and Homosapien is pulling his punches like the old pro he is, and the kid finally realizes this is just for fun. The two of them stage an impromptu wrestling match, which isn't entirely one–sided, until Cougar taps out of Homosapien's Chinlock.

M and the two guys are all happily chuckling by now.

But they are interrupted by a roar from the training room. "Cougar! Little Johnny Cougar! Where the hell have you gotten to?!"

Cougar scrambles up from the mats, terrified again.

Sam is standing in the doorway. "I thought I told you not to bother your betters, Johnny."

"Yes, sir – sorry, sir."

As Cougar scrambles through the gym and off into the training room, M offers, "He wasn't a bother, Coach."

Sam winks at her, but continues roaring as he turns away. "I know what a pest this boy can be, Emma. I'll teach him a lesson he won't soon forget." And the doors swing shut behind him with an ominous clunk. Sam can still be clearly heard, though. "What did you think you were doing? *Little Johnny …* You're not fit to lick that woman's boots. You're not fit to breathe the same air as her … Oh, so it's like *that*, is it? Start thinking with your *big* head, boy!"

Homosapien and M chuckle all the way to the showers.

Phone calls

Mr. Tall, Dark & Intense calls. He can't survive another minute without having my hot little bod, despite the fact that he makes me laugh at the most inappropriate moments. I strongly suggest that he holds out for another ninety–six minutes at least, when I quit work for the day.

Mr. TDI	Can't you leave early?
Patrick	Not if I wanna still be employed tomorrow.
Mr. TDI	I'll come pick you up.
Patrick	Oh, no, you won't.
Mr. TDI	You still haven't told them about me? You're ashamed of me.
Patrick	Well, and so I should be.

I manage to hang up before David reappears. When the phone rings again, I'm not quick enough to answer it, but my fears are proved groundless – it's A Certain Wrestler.

David	Q4 bookstore.
Homosapien	Hey, David.
David	God, are you all right?
Homosapien	Uh, yeah …
David	You don't sound too sure.
Homosapien	It's just – well, why wouldn't I be?
David	You've got to be kidding. That match against Brute? You walked off like you'd aged 50 years in 10 minutes. And Caesar ambushing you like that – I figured you must have at least broken a rib.
Homosapien	I'm fine, David. Just a bit bruised. They train us how to fall properly, how to take care of ourselves.

David is silent for a long moment. Knowing how to fall properly doesn't explain how a man can have a steel chair slammed into his ribcage without suffering more than a bit of bruising. But the subject is changed.

Homosapien	Hey, we're gonna be in Boston again, week after next.
David	I know. Saturday night.
Homosapien	Well, can I come see you?
David	Yeah, sure. You know where to find me.

Homosapien That nightclub?

David No. No, I think you'd better come here to the store. As soon as you get into town. OK?

The most pregnant pause I've ever heard stretches on and on. David looks deadly serious, but I am grinning like an idiot. So the two of them is finally gonna happen. Something must have finally clicked with David, some button must have finally been pressed. When Homosapien replies, his voice is kind of husky.

Homosapien Yeah, all right, David. Yeah. I'll see you then.

And I picture him hanging up gently, gingerly, as if he can't bear to disturb the moment and its sudden possibilities.

Training

Homosapien and M are the only two wrestlers in da Dub Dub Dub who still train regularly with Sam even though they've already made it to the Big Show. The other wrestlers who've made it, the ones you're familiar with from TV, they work out and stay fit, and sometimes they learn new holds and new moves, but they don't bother much with actual training any more.

Once Cougar figured out that two of his heroes could often be found in the training room whenever they were home in Chicago, he managed to sneak into an adjoining room so that he could watch. For a while, Sam and the two wrestlers pretended not to notice. But Cougar's persistence finally paid off. At first he was invited to sit ringside so that he could pay closer attention. And then, at last, he got to train with Homosapien and M.

M and Cougar are roughly equivalent in size. Cougar has the edge in strength and weight, but M has the edge in agility and the old grey matter. The two of them have spent hours practicing athletic wrestling such as the head–over–heels moves and the tumble of holds and reverse holds that we saw in Homosapien's match with Blue. If Cougar has an ulterior motive for wanting to learn this with this particular sparring partner, he never lets it slip.

Soon the four of them – Sam is taking a more active role in these training bouts than usual – have a real act going on. As Cougar and M tumble diagonally across the ring from post to post, Sam and Homosapien are echoing them, tumbling along the other line of an X. As each bundle of bodies slams into the turnbuckles, they spring apart, and begin grappling, deadly serious, each pair still echoing the other's moves. Their timing has become perfect.

Today they are interrupted by sarcastically slow applause. The four of them break their holds, and look around to find their audience of one. It's Jack Dynes. He drops his hands and says, "You lot should be in the circus."

Cougar rediscovers his terror. Homosapien and M wait quietly for whatever Dynes wants to say. But Sam walks forward to lean on the ropes and address the boss directly. "What did I tell you?"

"Yuh, they're all looking good." Dynes considers them. "Here's an idea – Cougar and M can jerk the curtain in Boston."

Homosapien sees Cougar's confusion, and translates, "You've got the opening match."

M is beaming proudly. She's only ever fought woman wrestlers before now, and none of them have been a real challenge – Emma works out like a body–builder, while all the 'guest challengers' so far are obviously more concerned about maintaining their willowy feminine forms. Well, willowy except for the bits enhanced by silicone.

Cougar is bursting with triumph. It's all he can do not to jump in the air and yell, but he figures that decorum is called for in front of the boss.

"I want Lucifer to accompany M to the ring, though," Dynes continues. "We're not breaking that partnership. So, Homosapien can accompany Cougar."

Homosapien frowns. "Why me?"

"You can be his ringside manager."

The frown deepens. "Mr. Dynes," he says, frustration only held in check by the respect due this man, "you said I could have a title match against Porn ☆. When's that gonna happen?"

"Patience," Dynes advises him. Then he nods farewell to Sam, and heads out again. Jack Dynes always has a hundred other places to be.

M lets out a whoop and hugs Sam – the old man makes the most of the opportunity and hugs her right back.

Though Cougar is looking more hurt than triumphant by now. He turns sorrowing eyes on Homosapien. "You don't wanna be in my corner?"

"I'm not ready to be a manager, kid."

"Wrestlers usually only become managers when they retire," M explains. She comes over to put an arm around Homosapien's shoulders. "You know, Adam, maybe Mr. Dynes just realizes you've got brains as well as brawn. And beauty, of course! Maybe he figures you can be more than just a wrestler."

"Maybe."

The two of them turn to Sam for his opinion, but the trainer is all business. "Right, we've got less than a week to prepare. Little Johnny," he says to Cougar with a severe stab of his finger, "don't you go thinking that you've earned this. Don't you go getting above yourself, boy. If I had my way, it'd be another year before you made it to the Big Show – if you ever made it at all."

Cougar, having had the fear of God returned to him, manages to settle back down into training mode, along with M. Homosapien calls it a day, though. He has a lot on his mind right now and it ain't all good.

Virtual reality

David winces as Homosapien gets pounded every which way by Caesar. We are watching tapes behind the bookstore counter once more. *My* tapes, because David still refuses to watch the wrestling on TV like any regular fan – he just expects me to tape everything for him, and then complains if I don't bring it in the next day. I am expecting to be repaid with details of all the gories when you–know–what finally happens.

Another wince from David. Homosapien is really taking a beating. The close–ups show his beautiful face in agony. For a while, Homosapien seems to turn the tide – but then as they both ricochet off the ropes, Caesar fells Homosapien with a Clothesline and lands on him to make the pin. They are chest to chest, with Caesar's forearms holding down Homosapien's biceps. If you ever wondered why I like watching pro wrestling, then you don't need to look any further than this.

The referee drops down beside them to make the count. One …

Homosapien shakes his head as if clearing the cobwebs. Two …

Caesar's face is so close to Homosapien's – our hero lifts up just far enough to plant a kiss on the tip of Caesar's nose. And Caesar breaks his own pin! It's unheard of! Before the referee can finish giving him the three count, Caesar springs away, full of disgust, even though it was only the chaste kind of kiss you might give your least favorite aunt. Some of the crowd are laughing, some are jeering, most are yelling with anger or encouragement or both. The commentators can't seem to get a coherent sentence out about this new wrestling maneuver.

Homosapien is lying there with a little smile, kind of chuckling. Caesar is keeping his distance, face screwed up as if he's half outraged and half trying not to puke. But when Homosapien starts trying to get up off the mat, Caesar decides to go with the outrage. He strides in and starts laying into our man. Kicking him with a viciousness that shocks even me. Stomach, kidneys, head, groin – kicking Homosapien like the faggot he's just proved himself to be.

David is gaping at the screen, speechless, horrified.

The bell is sounding continuously, calling an end to the match, but Caesar ignores it. If there was any fight left in Homosapien, it's long gone. Finally Caesar decides he's had enough and he leaves the ring, strides up the ramp, oblivious to whether the crowd is yelling their approval or their hatred.

Homosapien is left alone, a battered wreck lying curled up in the middle of the ring. After the longest moment, he stirs. Drags himself to the edge of the ring. Tumbles off and lands hard on the mat–covered concrete floor. Another long moment, but this time he doesn't stir. The crowd are still lifting the roof off with their racket.

Finally the security guys accompany a couple of paramedics out there with a stretcher. And we go to a commercial break while Homosapien is being carefully lifted from the floor. I turn off the tape.

Silence. I look up at David. He is pale. Shocked. Finally David stutters, "Where was that? When – last night? Have you heard if he's all right? Can we call the hospital?"

I shake my head. "He's all right."

Though I don't sound too sure of myself, David clutches at hope. "How d'you know?"

"Because …"

David stares at me, begging me to continue. But when I don't explain, he starts adding it up for himself. Looking from me back to the blank TV screen, then staring thoughtfully at the floor. He crosses his arms and huddles into himself, as if he's cold.

Eventually he says in a hushed kind of voice, "It's not real, is it?"

With her usual impeccable timing, Candy (the drag queen who runs the beauty salon up the road) sways past the counter. "Professional wrestling? It's as real as I am, Davey darling."

"Thank you," David politely replies. Which proves in itself how rocked he is.

I remind David, "You used to think he wasn't even gay. You never figured that was real."

"That's different."

"How so?"

David throws both hands in the air in frustration. "It seemed like just a role. It still does. What he does on TV is just stereotypical stuff." He almost groans. "Patrick, tell me that match wasn't for real."

"I've seen guys take a worse beating than that," I slowly say, "and come back for a grudge match the following night, none the worse for wear."

David looks doubtful.

"Well, think of all the punishment Homosapien has taken over all these weeks – months – you've been watching. Has he ever been seriously injured? Have you ever even seen him *bruised?*"

"No. I guess not."

"Whenever you ask him if he's OK, what does he say?"

David frowns. "Not much, actually."

"But he always tells you he's all right."

"Yeah, he's very reassuring. Then he changes the subject."

I give him my best *Duh!* expression. "There's probably a clause in his contract that says he can't talk about this stuff. It's *meant* to be real. It's meant to be a real sport. Most fans swear that it is."

"They do?" David puzzles over this for a moment. And then he turns a very sharp stare on me. "So, how come you know different?"

Shrugging. "I'm not your regular redneck fan."

He says, only half sarcastic, "Patrick, I've never known you to think so much."

"Well, I'm still not gonna let you Pile Drive me – you'd break my neck."

David sits down on the stool behind the counter and hauls his laptop closer. He scratches his head, and makes one last comment. "Of course, anything that makes *you* think *that* much can't be *all* bad."

Come together

It's here at last. Saturday. *The* Saturday. David is all tensed up, waiting on Him, but tense in a good way. I think that my old curmudgeon of a boss is halfway to being in love. Or maybe it's just the spring sunshine having an effect. Whatever.

Anyway – finally, just after I've thrown out the lunch that David is too wound up to eat, Homosapien makes his appearance.

He walks into the bookstore, and immediately sees David rearranging (for the hundredth time that day) the New Releases. David straightens up, runs his hands nervously down his thighs.

Nothing is said. They just stand there for a moment, looking at each other. Oblivious to me or anyone else. And then they turn and walk out of the bookstore together. They head off down Whitman, in the direction of David's apartment. Leaving me to mind David's precious bookstore.

And that's it! I'd been hoping for a kiss at least. Actually, I'd been hoping that Homosapien would sweep David up into his arms and carry him out, just like Richard Gere or (more to the point) Lou Diamond Phillips. Oh, well. No doubt this was exactly perfect for them. If Homosapien had tried to do the sweeping thing, David probably would have slapped him.

There are three customers in the store, two of them strangers. I head down the back to fetch the bottle of champers we keep in the fridge. (David keeps his fine red wines in the darkest cupboard and I keep my cheap bubbly in the fridge.) I pop the cork, gather four mismatched glasses, and issue an invitation.

With no further ado, we settle down into the sofas in the reading nook, and we celebrate. The others chat amongst themselves, I'm not sure what about. I am too busy staring up at a certain poster, happily day–dreaming about a beautiful guy with a muscly physique and what he might currently be doing to my boss who hasn't gotten laid in *way* too long but who'd made Homosapien wait twelve weeks for this …

Intense doesn't even begin to describe it.

Later that afternoon

Two hours later, David shows up at the bookstore, looking kind of embarrassed.

I gape at him. Doesn't he have better things to be doing right now?

David shrugs. "He had to get to the Garden. Get ready for the show."

"And you didn't go with him … ? He *did* invite you, right?"

"Yeah." He looks even more embarrassed.

"Well, are you seeing him again tonight?"

"Yeah."

Thank heavens for that. "So," I say, a wicked grin spreading across my face. "Tell me all the gories!"

David looks somewhere else. But he can't help smiling. Even his *eyes* are smiling. Boy, did he get laid and then some! "Uh," David says, "I'm off to Apollo's. Hazelnut latté, right?"

I'm dumbfounded. "Dollop of foam, to go."

And he's halfway up the street before I can even draw breath. The lengths some people will go to just to avoid meeting their side of a deal! But I admit it – I was smiling too. Adam and David. There was something real nice about it.

Jerking the curtain

You know how when the wrestling starts on the TV, the crowd is already going wild? Well, that's partly because there's already been a warm–up match that's never televised. Also, the ring announcer gets everyone revved up, and when the cameras are ready to roll he counts them all down to show time. And they go wild.

So, the opening match is a difficult one for the wrestlers. The crowd is cold. The commentators haven't appeared yet – and even though the stadium audience never actually hears the commentators (in the WWW, the commentary is only for the TV audience), the fact they're not there yet means it's just not quite The Real Thing.

announcer   This is a special match tonight, booked just for *you*, our fans in Boston. I know you all love M as much as we do. So tonight you get to see her take her rightful place in the Big Show!

The crowd are definitely interested. There are wolf whistles amidst the applause.

announcer   This match is scheduled for one fall only.
Weighing in at 169 pounds, from Buffalo, New York, and accompanied by Lucifer, please welcome *M!*

They make their entrance to Lucifer's music. M is proud and happy, lifting her arms for the crowd's welcome, while Lucifer glares around at all and sundry. No doubt he is not pleased to be reduced to the role of M's valet.

As the two of them reach the ring, Lucifer's music ends, and a country piece begins. Sounds like a steel guitar skirmishing with a sawn–off violin. It sort of works.

announcer   And the contender, in his first match for the WWW, born and raised in the Badlands, South Dakota, at a weight of 200 pounds, accompanied by Homosapien – I'm pleased to introduce you to *Cougar!*

Cougar walks in, and for a moment he falters. The Boston Garden seats 16,000 people, which can be pretty daunting when they're all focused on you. But then Homosapien is at Cougar's shoulder, standing tall, and the crowd are making some noise, and Cougar takes heart. He strides down the ramp towards the ring.

The audience have all brought their signs, of course, and some are directed at our hero. *There's no kissing in wrestling!* presumably refers to Homosapien's match with Caesar – and I guess it makes sense that people are curious, following his rather unusual tactics. *It's cool to be queer* speaks for itself, though that sign is pretty much a lone voice in the redneck wilderness. Most signs are vicious variations on *Homo, go home.* Such as *Die Homo Die!* (One day they're gonna kill us all off with their sharp wit.)

But the point is that Homosapien is drawing some heat, some interest from the crowd. Jack Dynes doesn't care whether the crowd love him or hate him, as long as they react to him. It's, like, a death–knell for a wrestler if the audience is just indifferent.

I figure that's partly why Lucifer decides to take it further. Usually with an opening match, they just get into it, and there's little or no talking. But Lucifer decides he has something to say. Michael never liked Adam, and Lucifer's jealous that Homosapien is drawing heat. Lucifer's pissed off at being a valet. Plus, of course, it's an ideal opportunity to insult the crowd, which any heel should do as often as possible. He grabs a mike, and turns a fierce glare on the audience.

Lucifer   Shut up! Just shut the hell up! What the hell are you cheering this faggot for?

The cheers turn to boos, either because they don't appreciate the term or because they weren't cheering Homosapien in the first place.

Lucifer   Well, at least when Homo comes to town, you don't need to lock up your daughters or your sisters … You'd better lock up your sons and your brothers, though!

More noise – booing, laughter, catcalls. By this time, Homosapien has grabbed a mike too.

Homosapien   Hey, Lucy! Their sons and brothers are safe. Almost every guy here is safe from me. Why would I want to look any further than you?

Lucifer   Shut up, faggot!

Homosapien   You know what my favorite show is? *I Love Lucy* …

Lucifer   Hey, who's the new guy? Your bimbo? Your valet? Your boyfriend?

Homosapien   Don't be jealous, Lucy, he's not my boyfriend. Cougar's a wrestler – and he came here to wrestle.

Lucifer   Well, let's get that bell rung! This should be fun. Hell, even my *woman* can take this pussy!

Her best friend Homosapien can see that M isn't impressed by this remark, though she doesn't let it faze her. She retreats to her corner as the referee signals for the bell to sound.

But Cougar is just a tad too eager to get into the fight. He doesn't see that M isn't expecting him. They hadn't agreed to start this way. Homosapien yells "Emma!" but Cougar is already slamming into her, his weight forcing her into the corner post. Those posts and turnbuckles have so much padding that they're about the softest part of the whole ring, but M has the breath knocked out of her.

Despite which, she does her damnedest to make the match work, and to put Cougar over to the crowd, to make him look good. They slip into the routine they practiced, and the crowd get into it. They are cheering M – but all Cougar understands is that they're cheering. When the time comes for him to let M pin him, Cougar lifts his shoulder after the count of two. He doesn't wanna quit.

From there it's back to being unscripted. M copes as best she can, which is OK because she's pretty familiar with Cougar's moves by now, what with all the training they've been doing. Lucifer gets mad, real mad, as well he should – and next time Cougar is in swinging distance, Lucifer takes him out with a genuine blow. The referee pretends not to notice the interference. M pins Cougar. Homosapien gets close, yelling at his young protégé – the crowd might assume he's telling Cougar to break the pin and get up, but actually he's strongly advising the opposite. Cougar finally regains some sense, and stays down for the three count.

The bell rings, the referee lifts M's arm in victory, and the announcer states the obvious. M is smiling, proud and happy, soaking up the applause. It's a popular win.

Homosapien grabs Cougar by the scruff of the neck, and drags him up the ramp and behind the curtain. Maybe the crowd think he's helping Cougar along. Or maybe some of them know better.

Backstage

Everyone is, of course, furious.

Cougar is sitting there in Homosapien and M's inadequate dressing room, feeling at his jaw and looking very sorry for himself. Homosapien is pacing back and forth. He hasn't said anything. Yet. He knows enough trouble is on the way that he doesn't need to add to it.

Speak of the devil … Lucifer storms in with M at his heels. "What the *hell* do you think you're doing, boy?"

At the tone, Cougar bristles. "You hit me! You actually *hit* me!"

Homosapien makes sure he remains somewhere between Cougar and Lucifer.

"You fucking moron! Emma could have gotten hurt!"

M says, "I'm not hurt, OK? Michael? There's no harm done."

"You said he was ready," Lucifer accuses Homosapien. "You said the boy was ready for this."

"I said so too," M reminds him. Weary, she sits down at her makeshift table. "Michael, there's no point in blaming anyone. We'll tell Sam, we'll take all this back to training. We'll sort it out."

Lucifer is glaring at Homosapien. He takes a step closer, stabs a finger at him. "I hold *you* responsible, faggot. Anything happens to Emma on your watch – or any other damned time for that matter – I come looking for you. I'm tired of her making excuses for you."

Homosapien holds his gaze, not reacting.

At last Lucifer turns away. But just as he's about to open the door, M says, "Michael. There's one other thing."

"What?"

She's brave enough or determined enough to continue despite the biting tone. "I didn't appreciate that comment you made. About even your woman being able to take this guy. You could have put me over way better than that."

"Emma, you know I didn't mean it."

"You *did* mean it, Michael. We all show our true colors when we're not working to a script. But that's not even the point – the point is that you were out of character. Lucifer doesn't think that way about M."

"OK. OK, yeah. You're right." The big guy is chastened in ways that would have seemed impossible only two minutes previously. In fact, it's excruciating. The other guys hardly know where to look.

But Emma takes pity on Michael and gets up to pat him on the shoulder. "It's just that we've worked so hard to strike the right note together, and I don't want to throw that away." She smiles forgivingly. "At least you didn't call me your girl."

Lucifer gazes at her, smitten all over again. "D'you wanna have a drink after?"

Emma glances at Homosapien. Lucifer's face tightens again with jealous anger. But Homosapien saves the date. "I got plans already," he says. "You two go have some fun."

"I'd love to, Michael." Another friendly pat on the shoulder and Lucifer is out of there. Emma sits at the table again and buries her face in her hands. A muffled groan sounds.

Homosapien asks, "Emma? You really all right?"

"Yeah, thanks, Adam."

And Homosapien finally turns to Cougar. "What did you do wrong tonight, kid?"

Cougar just looks at him, still gingerly feeling his jaw.

Homosapien sighs. "You've gotta do the job, kid. You pay your dues, or you don't get anywhere in this business. You pay your dues even once you get somewhere. *You do the job.* Ask Sam what that means. Start praying that Mr. Dynes doesn't send you on home before you get the chance to learn."

"Yes, sir," Cougar mumbles.

"And the other thing. You haven't apologized to the lady yet."

Cougar manages to stumble through a few words, which Emma graciously accepts. After a moment, Homosapien just tells him, "OK, get out of here." And when he's gone, Homosapien adds his own simple apology. He's nothing if not a gentleman.

Later that night

I was eventually told some of the gories.

Homosapien takes a cab to David's place after the show. He's kind of quiet and tired, which isn't exactly what David was expecting based on his performance that afternoon. "Uh," says Homosapien. "Can we just, uh …"

"Sure," David replies. He fetches two beers from the fridge, and joins Homosapien on the sofa. "Are you OK? Did something go wrong tonight?"

"Yeah."

"Which?"

Homosapien smiles a weary smile at him. "Both."

"What?" (He's not usually that clueless. Honest.)

"Something went wrong, but I'm OK."

"Ah." David nods. They drink their beer, each contemplating the situation. Eventually David says very tentatively, "But it's not real, is it? I mean …"

A level stare and a direct tone. "It's *very* real."

"But Patrick says –"

"Maybe Patrick's a cynic."

David glances away, frowning. "He says you're not even allowed to talk about it."

"Well, everyone in professional sports has a clause in their contract that says they can't talk about stuff."

"Behind the scenes stuff," David clarifies.

"Yeah. Football, baseball, amateur wrestling, pro wrestling, everyone."

David looks at the man, belatedly aware of the irritated edge to his voice. Now is obviously not the time. "I'm sorry," David offers. "You've had a hard day's night already and my curiosity can go take a hike. But when even *Patrick* gets analytical …"

(Thanks, boss.)

Homosapien smiles a little. All is forgiven. He finishes his beer while David's barely halfway through his.

"Do you want another?"

"No." Homosapien looks at him. "Uh, can I stay the night, David? But I don't really wanna – I'd just appreciate the company."

"Sure," says David. He puts down his beer and stands up. "Come on, we could both do with some sleep."

Homosapien follows him through to the bedroom, looking absurdly grateful. The next morning, or so I hear, he more than made up for the missed opportunity.

Working out

The WWW has an arrangement with a gym in each town, so that the wrestlers have a place to work out while they're on the road – which is where Homosapien and M agreed to meet the following morning. Homosapien is running late, but he makes up for it by bringing two fresh juices with him.

When he hands one over, M takes the opportunity to press a friendly kiss to his cheek.

Homosapien smiles. "What's that for?"

"Just for being you." She echoes his smile for a moment before she gets serious again. "There's something I should have said before. I never make excuses for you, Adam. I never even try to *explain* you to Michael. He shouldn't have said that."

"I know you don't," he replies in the easiest of tones. Homosapien steps up onto a treadmill, M takes the next one along, and they match each other stride for stride.

Eventually, with our two heroes already halfway through their routines on the weight machines, Cougar shows up. "Yeah," he says, "I'm late. You can bust my chops for that as well, if you want." His blond mop is looking particularly dejected this morning.

"Nah," Homosapien cheerfully replies. "I was late too. I was getting lucky – what's your excuse?"

M almost squeals in delight. "Adam, you sly old fox – you met someone? Why didn't you tell me?"

A shrug, and an irrepressible smile. "Didn't know if it'd work out."

"You met someone and it's working out … ???"

"Yeah. I knew it was time to get me a life. There are bonuses in having a life."

"My God, this sounds serious. Who is he? What's his name?"

Cougar almost chokes. "Uh, it's a *guy?*"

Homosapien just casts him the coolest of glances and says to M, "Next time we come through here, maybe I'll introduce you …"

"Wow! This is great!"

"… on the condition that you don't ask me about him every day for the next six weeks."

M pouts a little. On her it looks good. "Every other day?" she offers.

Cougar has gotten up on a treadmill – the one furthest away from the weight machines – and is frowning his way through a warm up.

"Hey, kid," Homosapien says. "I've been thinking. What kind of wrestler do you wanna be?"

Cougar glares at him. "You know, everyone says you two are seeing each other." He doesn't get a response. "Everyone thinks you're straight. But everyone's expecting Lucifer to cut in. They're figuring there'll be trouble."

"Everyone's not always right," says M.

"What kind of wrestler, kid?"

For a moment Cougar's glare gets sullen. Then he offers, "I wanna be like Lucifer or Brute. I wanna be someone who really gets noticed. Makes a difference. Has an impact."

Homosapien nods thoughtfully. "Well, that's fine, but you're never gonna be that kind of size. Lucifer is 6 foot 7 tall, and you don't get that way by muscle–building."

"You saying I got no chance?"

"I'm saying you're cruiser–weight. You should concentrate on technique. Brute can knock anyone down, but that doesn't make him the best wrestler in the world."

"Well, maybe I don't agree with that."

M quietly says, "You don't have to agree, John, but you should at least listen."

Homosapien continues, "Agility counts for more than strength in wrestling. That's why Emma deserves to be in the Big Show. She's got the technique to cope with the likes of you and me." Between machines, he pauses for a moment to grab a drink of water. "You could try to learn something from the Mexicans, the *lucha libre* wrestlers. They really know how to put on a show."

"They let us train with them sometimes," M puts in. "Maybe you could come along too."

Cougar seems massively unimpressed by this idea. "Yeah, maybe," he eventually replies, before turning back to his work out.

M shrugs at Homosapien. They tried, at least, and even Jack Dynes couldn't ask for more.

Title match

At last Homosapien is given his title shot against Porn ☆.

announcer   This match is scheduled for one fall only. And the championship belt is on the line – the winner of this match will be declared the WWW champion!

The crowd pops! They're all revved up, ready for a serious match. Though I figure the redneck contingent will never take our hero to their hearts if he wins. *When* he wins. Surely he's gonna win? David is beside me, behind the counter at the store the following morning, with his fingers and toes and eyes crossed for luck, at least metaphorically.

And the match starts off seriously enough. Porn ☆ doesn't have half of Blue's technical ability, but he can put on a show – and, anyway, when two hunky guys are throwing each other round the ring, who needs anything else? They grunt and grapple, hold and release, for all the world as if they're filming one of Porn ☆'s old movies. Well, like David once said, porn is in the eye of the beholder. And this beholder is sure beholding. To the extent that, when Porn ☆ pins Homosapien, and the referee goes down for the count, I murmur, "I hope this ain't the cum shot already."

David just mutters, "Shut up."

But Homosapien performs his new maneuver. He plants a kiss on the nearest available part of Porn ☆, which happens to be his shoulder. Porn ☆ springs away in disgust. Homosapien pushes it – he smiles seductively, gets smoothly to his feet, starts stalking towards Porn ☆ – who backs away, a look of real loathing on his face.

And David's looking disgusted too. Especially when the match degenerates into complete and utter farce – our hero ends up chasing the other man round and round the ring, arms reaching for him, like a woefully bad silent movie. You almost expect to hear frenetic chase music on a piano, but instead there is just the cheers and jeers of the crowd, and the referee calling for the bell to end this spectacle. (And, of course, because the match ends with a disqualification, the belt can't change hands no matter what. So much for the title shot.)

Oblivious to all but his pursuit, Homosapien doesn't give up. It's just as well Porn ☆ can run faster than him. Ridiculous.

Which is when a posse of Bad Guys run out to interfere, led by Lucifer. Now that he has back–up, Porn ☆ quits running. Instead, he drops our guy with a vicious Clothesline – Homosapien takes the initial impact across his shoulders, but ends up with an arm slamming into his throat. And Porn ☆

sticks the boot in while he's down. Lucifer's there now, and two other guys, kicking and punching. It's vicious. It's gay–bashing. Literally. It's corporate–sponsored gay–bashing.

David is watching with his mouth hanging open, his arms wrapped round his own gut as if in protection. Yet again I'm thinking that this is the most horrible thing I've ever seen on TV. (I mean, I keep thinking that, and then sure enough it gets even worse the following week.) There's a final shot of Homosapien lying broken and alone in the ring and they go to a commercial break. David turns to me, pale with shock.

I ask, "He didn't warn you about that?"

A shake of the head. No.

"He should have warned you about that."

"Maybe he's … Maybe he's not all right."

"He's all right," I say as firmly as I can. Though I have to admit I'm kind of shaky about the whole thing.

After a long moment, David picks up the phone and starts dialing. Homosapien recently got himself a cell phone, and I like to assume that was so A Certain Person can easily stay in touch with him while the show's on the road.

Three rings later, Homosapien picks up. "Yeah?" He sounds weary.

"Are you OK?"

"Yeah, I'm fine, David. How are you?"

David scrunches his whole face up. "Don't change the subject."

"What … ?" Actually Homosapien sounds a bit out of it. "What subject?"

"Are you *on* something?"

"I need coffee. Can I call you back when I got coffee? Sorry. You woke me."

"Fine," David snaps. And he hangs up.

I take a good long look at my boss. He's fuming. It must be the new land speed record – worried to angry in ten seconds flat. "Uh, David?"

"What?"

"You wanna go easy on him? He doesn't know you well enough yet to make allowances."

I get a full level glare for my trouble. "Coffee," David barks. "Go get me a doppio."

"No way! I'm not missing out on this! I wanna know what happened!"

"Coffee!"

I actually growl in frustration – but then I dash out the door. Apollo's know our order by now, so as soon as one of them glimpses me in the street, I wave frantically and they start grinding and espressing. I am back at the bookstore within 5 minutes. Which thoroughly thwarts David's dastardly plan, because the phone rings just as I dash back in.

Just as well it's not a customer, because David snaps "Yes!" into the phone.

"David, it's me. Sorry, I –"

"What the *hell* was that?"

"What?"

"Last night. Your so–called title shot. What was that about?"

"Uh … Well, I had a job to do. I did it."

"I didn't think pro wrestling could get any more ludicrous than it was – *but it just did!*"

There's a long silence. Finally Homosapien sighs. "I knew you'd hate it. I knew it. But I didn't have any choice. OK? That's all I can say."

"And you're sorry," David prompts.

"I'm sorry that you hated it," Homosapien replies with much sincerity. But he gently adds, "I'm not sorry about doing the job. That's what he pays me for."

"Who?"

"Jack Dynes."

David kind of grunts. It seems the argument has run its course, and neither of them are satisfied, but that's life. 'OK. OK, look, I'll call you.'

"Yeah?"

"I gotta think about this. Then I'll call you."

There's another silence. Homosapien isn't even breathing. I'm guessing that he's too scared to ask whether 'this' is the wrestling or their rather tentative relationship. "OK," he finally says, "I'll be waiting." And he hangs up.

A few minutes later, David retreats to the storeroom so that he can do some work on his own. I quietly hit redial. When Homosapien answers, I whisper, "It's Patrick. You all right?"

"Is *David* all right?"

"Yeah. He's mad as a cut snake, but he'll get over it."

"Good. I'm fine, Patrick. Thanks."

We commune in silence for a moment. Then I ask, "What on earth do you see in my old curmudgeon of a boss, anyway?"

"Well, *you* like him."

"Don't tell him that!" I chuckle under my breath.

Homosapien seems to be thinking about it. But I figure he's known all along, even if he's never put it into words before. "He's righteous," the wrestler finally says. "David is a righteous man."

"Yeah."

We hang up without saying anything more. Yeah, Homosapien knows what's what. David is one righteous dude. That kind of thing can really get up your nose. And under your skin.

After much further thought, I finally get it. I finally get a clue about what Adam and David see in each other. It's an attraction of opposites all right, but it's not just about brawn and beauty on one side and brains on the other. It's about David knowing exactly who he is, and knowing what it is to live as a gay man – and Adam wanting to learn. And it's about Adam getting a life, exploring what life can offer beyond ambition – and David wanting to learn.

Well, at least it makes perfect sense to me.

Doing the job

Homosapien is 10 minutes early for the meeting he scheduled with Jack Dynes, but he waits in the corridor outside Dynes' hotel room. Homosapien is capable of being so patient and still that it's eerie, as if he's a statue. No, as if he's a bear hibernating, and you really don't want to risk waking him.

Finally his watch reads 11:30:00 and Homosapien quietly knocks on the door with one knuckle. He is surprised when Sam the trainer opens the door and invites him in, but sees no harm in Sam being there while he talks with the boss.

Dynes doesn't get up from his chair, but he does reach out to shake Homosapien's hand. "Adam. What can I do for you this fine morning?"

"Uh, Mr. Dynes, sir. I was wondering if … I mean, I was hoping that I could have another title shot."

"Not right away," the man says, dismissive, half his attention on the paperwork he's skimming through.

"Not the championship belt. I know there's no point in replaying that just yet. But I've been working hard, sir, and – Well, I mean the tag team title."

That gets the man's attention. "Who's your partner?"

"Cougar."

"Yuh?" Dynes is skeptical, and Sam is shaking his head. "After that fiasco of a match with Emma?"

"Yes, sir. I figure – Well, can I ask, sir, why you contracted Cougar in the first place?"

Dynes puts the paperwork down and stands, turns to stare out the window, hands deep in his pockets. "The kid has something – something beyond the usual starry–eyed wannabe. He's either going to be really good or really bad."

Sam speaks for the first time. "He's not ready, either way."

"Too late," Dynes replies. "*Make* him ready. Give him enough rope and see if he hangs himself."

Homosapien can't quite repress a grin. "Does that mean we have the shot?"

Dynes nods, expression thoughtful. Then he says with mock severity, "That's all the favors you're receiving today, Adam O'Connor. Go on – get out of here."

Homosapien gets while the getting is good.

Interview 1

Homosapien and the mostly–serious commentator Terry are sitting over polystyrene coffee in a stadium canteen. From the camera angle, it looks like the cameraman has perched his rear on the next table along. Otherwise, the canteen is pretty much empty, and Terry is looking a bit wary.

Terry   Homosapien, what's going on? You have all the right stuff, you could become a truly excellent wrestler, but lately your tactics have become a little … perhaps the best word to use is *unorthodox*.

Homosapien You know what they say, Terry – if you can't stand the heat, stay out of my bedroom.

Terry Is *that* what they say?

Homosapien But I'm not here to talk about my personal life. I'm here to demand another chance. I've earned it – you said yourself that I've earned a title shot.

Terry I really can't see Mr. Dynes or Porn ☆ agreeing to another match with you. At least, not this millennium.

Homosapien Cougar's my partner, and we want –

Terry is looking a bit challenged by this. He interrupts with a question: "Your *partner?* Do you mean that he's your … ?"

Homosapien rolls his eyes in exasperation. "My *tag team* partner."

Terry Oh.

Homosapien Yeah. And we want the tag team title.

As he says this, Rumbler (the big fat less–than–serious color commentator) passes by with a tray full of food. He is totally unimpressed by Homosapien's ambitions. "Oh, puh–*lease*. The day that a queer wears a WWW belt, is the day that pigs fly and hell freezes over."

Homosapien glares up at him.

Totally undaunted, Rumbler rumbles on. "I'd tell you to pack your bags and go on home, but your mama won't have you back, will she? You broke that poor old lady's heart. She's probably sitting at home now, all alone, wondering where she went wrong with you."

That does it. No one mentions a wrestler's mother and lives. Before anyone else can move, Homosapien has launched himself off the chair and into Rumbler – kind of a Spear Tackle without the run–up. The tray and the food go flying. Rumbler lands on his back on the tiled floor and Homosapien lands on top of him, fists flying, knees jerking. Terry is remonstrating from a safe distance. Two security guys run over and try to stop Homosapien from pummeling fat old Rumbler to death, but they're no match for an incensed wrestler. All is chaos. Which is just how Jack Dynes likes it.

Cue a commercial break.

Interview 2

Microphone in hand, Terry is chasing Jack Dynes down a stadium corridor, with the cameraman jogging along behind them. "Mr. Dynes? If you have time for a few quick questions?"

"I'm busy, Terry."

"I can see that, Mr. Dynes, but there are things the fans want to know."

"Like what?" Dynes asks over his shoulder, not breaking his stride. Wrestlers and backstage people shrink up against the corridor walls to let the little convoy pass.

"We're getting cards and letters and e–mails –"

"So, ask me a question, Terry!"

"Well, just how long can Porn ☆ retain the championship belt? How long before he defends it against a *serious* contender?"

Just then Terry runs smack right into the boss – Dynes has come to a sudden stop beside Homosapien – our hero, who is apparently just leaving for the night, because he's in street clothes and is carrying a sports bag. "Here's a serious contender," Dynes announces.

"Thank you, sir," says Homosapien, looking a bit surprised and a bit happy.

"But," says Terry, "you can hardly call his match against Porn ☆ a *serious* challenge …"

Ignoring Terry, Dynes says to our hero, "Tell you what – if you can find yourself a partner, I might let you work your way up to challenging Caesar and Brute for the tag team belts."

"Thank you, sir!" Now he's looking a lot happy.

"But …" says Terry, still objecting.

Dynes strides on down the corridor, leaving Terry and the cameraman and Homosapien behind.

Homosapien is so jubilant at this turn of events that he just has to express it. "Yahoo!" he hollers, punching both fists high in the air. That's still not enough, though. He looks around. He sees Terry – and he grabs Terry up in a big bear–hug, and plants a big bear–kiss on his cheek.

We hold on a shot of Terry looking rather queasy and uncooperative while Homosapien hugs him and dances around with him, before cutting to a commercial break …

Working out

When Homosapien arrives at the gym the next morning, he finds Cougar alone there, in the throes of a heavy duty work out. "You're in early," Homosapien comments while getting his towel out of his bag.

Cougar grunts.

"You OK?"

"Couldn't sleep."

Homosapien wanders over to where Cougar is on the bench press – and notices that the kid's lifting a hell of a lot more weight than usual. Which is damn dangerous. "You shouldn't be doing this alone, John."

"I don't need you mothering me!" Cougar's voice is strained with anger as well as effort.

"Then I'll spot you instead," Homosapien calmly replies. He keeps his hands ready to support the weights, just in case. After a moment he says, "We have our first tag team match scheduled."

Cougar just grunts again, apparently uninterested. His face is red and dripping with sweat, and he stares somewhere in the region of Homosapien's torso rather than meet his eyes.

"Against the Bizarro brothers in two weeks, at Baltimore." Homosapien is puzzled by the lack of response. "I thought you'd be happy. This is your chance to really get a foothold in the Big Show."

"Well," Cougar blurts, "I just wish I didn't owe that chance to a faggot."

Homosapien lifts an eyebrow. Until now Cougar has been far more star-struck than nasty.

"In fact, the more I think about it," the kid continues, "the more I hate it. You taking an interest. Me being partnered with you. It ain't right!"

"You've been hanging around Lucifer too much."

"And why the hell shouldn't I?"

"Look, there are a hundred kids working out in gyms all round the country right now, a hundred kids – or even a thousand – for every *one* kid who'll get to wrestle in the Big Show. Don't ruin your chance."

"People will think I'm –"

Homosapien lifts his eyes to heaven for patience. "Well, even if they do, we won't be partners for ever. Once you're established, you can move on."

With a bit of help, Cougar lifts the weights one last time and shifts them back into the stirrups. He lies there, absently shaking his arms out, stretching the muscles, but mostly just staring up at Homosapien – his torso, his biceps, his hips. His groin.

"If you like," Homosapien offers, "we can talk to Mr. Dynes about a storyline. We can have a falling out, you can get a woman as your new manager, an *obvious* woman, that kind of thing."

Cougar remains silent, stays lying there, still staring.

Eventually Homosapien realizes that Cougar is sporting a hard–on. Ah, so *that's* the problem … Homosapien smiles a little, gently. "It doesn't have to become an issue," he says. "Anyway, I'm seeing someone, and –"

"You fucking queer!" Cougar springs up, so furious that he's balling his fists and bouncing around on his feet like he's in a boxing ring. "Don't you fucking well think about me like that. *I* ain't no faggot!"

Cocking an eyebrow again, Homosapien glances pointedly at what appears to be evidence to the contrary.

"You think that's for you?! That ain't for you!"

Which is when M happens to walk in. Cougar immediately zones in on her. He wants her so badly that his aching is visible – and I don't mean just in *that* way. He doesn't move, but of course M picks up on the tension. "Morning, boys," she says. "What's up?"

A long fraught moment. Then Cougar stalks out, rather than let his urges get the better of him.

"So, what's with Johnny?" M asks.

Homosapien shrugs. "Too much caffeine … Not enough of the other."

They step onto adjacent treadmills, and begin striding along, matching each other pace for pace. "Three day break coming up," M reminds her friend. "D'you have plans?"

"Well, I was gonna train with Cougar for the tag team match." Another shrug. "Maybe I'll head for Boston instead."

M's smile indicates that she knows what kind of mischief Homosapien will be getting up to in Boston. "Sounds like fun. Hey, just let John cool off – he'll be OK by the time you get back."

"Yeah," Homosapien replies, though he sounds unconvinced.

They stride on in sync.

Boston

So, Homosapien flew into Boston, caught a taxi to the bookstore, and then I didn't catch sight of either him or David for the following 24 hours. Well, what is a couple to do with all this fine spring weather other than disappear behind closed doors and curtained windows?

When they finally show up again, the old curmudgeon is looking so darned content that I don't have the heart to hassle him. And for some reason he doesn't bother hassling me, either – strange tales but true! – despite the fact he's never happy with the results of leaving me in charge of his precious store.

While David's sorting through the cash register and stuff (which of course is in perfect order), I take Homosapien by the hand and lead him down the back to our little reading nook. He sprawls happily on the sofa underneath his poster while I fetch him a beer from the fridge.

Then I perch on the arm of his sofa so that I can quiz him with at least the illusion of confidentiality. "So … has David been hassling you about what happened in the title match?"

"No."

"No?!"

The smile gets broader. "Guess I kept him too busy to talk much at all."

I laugh. "David too distracted to argue … *There's* a notion."

"It won't last," Homosapien says, proving he's both wry–funny and people–smart.

"It can't last. But you like him anyway, right?"

"Yeah, I like him anyway." He echoes me from our sneaky little phone call: "But don't tell him that!"

This is a nice guy. I wonder yet again what he's doing with David. But then I dismiss such sidetracks – there are more important topics for my interrogation. "So … what did you mean when you told David you were just doing the job that you're paid for … ?"

Homosapien smiles the most beautiful smile at me, gentle and regretful. "I can't talk about that, Patrick."

"What *can* you talk about? Come on – I'm a fan! I wanna know something! Anything!"

He considers. "Well, I could tell you about Emma. She's the best thing in the WWW."

"M? Cool! Tell me about her and Lucifer."

And Homosapien starts talking. It's obvious he's leaving some stuff out, but then I kind of pick up some stuff that I probably shouldn't, so I figure we're pretty much even.

And, as you've guessed, this is where I learned some of The Story So Far. I just found it all *too* fascinating.

Interlude

The next day, I come to work with a black eye, and a few less obvious aches 'n' pains. I try to make light of it – I'd gotten all tarted up in black leather and chains (kind of a faux–and–I–know–it Hellfire rig) so that the bruising looked like I was just accessorizing – but David and Homosapien take it all too seriously. Nice to have these righteous Knights In Shining Armor on my side, but seeing as I won't tell them what happened, there isn't much they can do about it other than yell at me (David) or do his patented Big Beautiful Butch and Silently Sympathetic thing (Homosapien).

Because, you see, David still doesn't know about Mr. TDI.

Coming out

"Excellent!" is my first reaction. I pore over all the details of the photo and the caption. But then it belatedly occurs to me that David's reaction won't be as happy. Though maybe he need never know – he skips the *Kinsey 6* gossip pages, after all, and heads straight for the serious stuff. But, no, somcone will be sure to tell him. I figure it better be me.

See, what happened was this – on Homosapien's second night in Boston, David took him back to Chez Lui. Once David could drag his date away from all the wrestling fans, the two of them indulged in a bit of slow–dancing and hot–necking. Now, Chez Lui keep a big glass bowl of those disposable instant cameras on the bar, because of course there are a hundred Kodak Moments a night in a gay club. So, someone took a photo of my boss and our hero in each other's arms. And it ended up in *Kinsey 6* …

> *Our favorite WWW wrestler Homosapien graces Boston nightclub Chez Lui and Q4 bookstore owner David Vigil with his presence.*

I take a deep breath, and then (magazine in hand) wander on down to the front counter where David is moodily tapping away at his laptop.

"David. Have you seen this?"

He glances at the photo – does a double take and goes back for another look – "Oh, *fuck!*" He grabs the magazine and stares at it some more. "The fucking moronic *fuck*–wits!"

As I predicted – not as happy.

Use the Farce, Adam …

Homosapien's new tactic takes an interesting turn.

He's in the middle of a long, involved match with Blue, digging deep for the best of his technique and the bulk of his strength. They've both worked hard, and are taking a break. Well, actually, Homosapien is lying spread–eagled on his back in the middle of the ring, apparently unconscious, and Blue is propped up in one corner, chest heaving, trying to catch his breath. He's too wrung out to realize he could get the pin and the three count just by falling on Homosapien, even if he's not capable of anything else … The referee is looking from one man to the other, wondering how this is going to resolve. If *both* wrestlers were unconscious, the ref could give them a ten count and declare the match over, but that's not the case. Surrounding them, the crowd are noisy, impressed, restless. They've gotten off on the match so far, and they want more.

Finally Homosapien starts shaking his head and picking himself up, while Blue hauls himself up taller, though he still needs the support of the corner post. When Homosapien looks up and around to find his opponent, he's met with an interesting sight … Blue is now leaning back on the top ropes, and his passivity has turned from weary to flirtatious. Honest to God, Blue is giving Homosapien the come–on. It's there in his beautiful eyes and the welcoming curve of his body and his sweet knowing little smile.

Homosapien stares for a long moment, staggers to his feet. You can tell he doesn't trust this – it's just too good to be true, for a start! – but he's drawing closer. As if mesmerized. And who wouldn't be? Blue just keeps on gazing right at him, inviting, as if it's just the two of them alone, and the referee and the crowd and the TV audience have all disappeared. Homosapien gets closer, more and more unguarded, judgment obviously impaired by his recent lack of consciousness …

Because, of course, as soon as Homosapien is close enough, within less than an arm's length, Blue belts him one hard. And another. And another.

Homosapien staggers back under the onslaught. Soon Blue has the pin, and the referee is going down for the three count …

One!

Two!

Homosapien comes to his senses long enough to try the New Tactic. He plants a kiss on Blue's temple, which is conveniently close –

– but this time the Tactic doesn't work!

Until now, the victim, the kissee has sprung away in horror, breaking the pin. This time, Blue glares, obviously unimpressed, but he just takes it.

Three!

Blue has won the match! He's not above a little retribution, though. He cuffs Homosapien one on the jaw to make a point. And then he gets back up to his feet, lifting his arms to claim the victory and acknowledge the crowd. They're wild for him.

Homosapien manages to scramble up and head off backstage, head lowered in shame. His own strategies used against him, and how! Oh, it's tragic.

Tragic? Well, actually, I think it's kinda funny. Poetic justice always deserves a laugh, in my not–so–humble opinion. But I'm not gonna admit that to David. He never thought this tactic was cool anyway, and as far as he's concerned it's just all gone completely to hell now. He's standing there glowering at the TV. So I glower too. Because I value my cojones and I like them just where they are.

In contrast to Blue taking advantage and making it funny, Lucifer gets more and more contemptuous. He's brutal in the most straightforward ways, which makes a mockery of Homosapien's playful tactics. And the rednecks in the crowd love it. I guess that's inevitable – if the queer is going to rub their faces in his queerness, then they're gonna love seeing him get his comeuppance. Despite which, Homosapien maintains his composure and good humor, on screen at least. I guess that's all part of what Adam meant about Doing The Job.

Teamwork

Baltimore, and the first tag team match for Our Hero and Cougar.

Homosapien gets ready in the makeshift dressing room he shares with M. Then he waits for a few minutes, hoping that Cougar will show up for a last talk about strategy in relative privacy. But no such luck – so he goes to find the kid in the faces' dressing room.

The other wrestlers ignore him as he wanders in and looks around. They are milling about, changing out of their street clothes, some of them talking, some of them silent, some of them using weights to pump up their biceps. Blue is sitting there alone with his eyes closed, deep in prayer or meditation, or maybe just snoozing.

Homosapien walks through into the communal bathroom, where he finds Cougar peering anxiously into the long mirror over the sinks. For a long moment our guy just watches, and (unaware of his tag team partner) Cougar turns his head this way and that, all the while examining his face and his hair. Finally he fumbles around in his bag, and produces … a bottle of liquid foundation! … with which he proceeds to cover up a small outbreak of pimples.

A chuckle alerts Cougar to the fact he has company. Homosapien says, "You look beautiful, kid."

"I do not!"

"Sure you do. You've got all those old hags out there beaten by a country mile. Well, except for Blue, of course." Then Homosapien winks at Cougar, and says, "We make a good team that way, eh?"

Cougar pales, then goes bright red. They've been talking to each other's reflections in the mirror, but now Cougar turns to face his partner. "You can just stop that," he blusters. "I'm not playing along with this queer stuff you do. Like, kissing your opponent – for God's sake! I'm just not gonna do that."

Homosapien asks thoughtfully, "Even if Mr. Jack Dynes tells you to?"

"God! No way!" Then a scary idea occurs to Cougar … "He didn't, did he? I mean, he didn't tell you I had to do that?"

"No," Homosapien reassures him. "Don't sweat it, kid. That's my storyline, not yours."

After a moment, Cougar relaxes a bit. "OK, then, that's all right." He turns back to the mirror, trying to work out whether the pimples are disguised or not.

"You played football in college, right?" Homosapien asks.

"Yeah. So?"

"What did you like about it?"

"Uh." Cougar takes a moment to consider this. "I don't know. Uh, I guess it was great when the crowd got behind you. Home games were the best. Away games were a bit hard."

"So, what got you through the hard games?"

"Uh, I don't know. What's that got to do with anything? It was something I was good at. I just wanted to make it big."

Homosapien frowns, puzzled. "So, why didn't you stick with it?"

Cougar shrugs. "Didn't do real great in class, got some bad grades. Dropped out."

"Well, the point is that football is a team sport. I was on the amateur wrestling team in college – same thing. The team is more important than the individuals."

"No, it isn't."

Homosapien opens his mouth to retort, "Yes, it is," but then he thinks better of it. What's the use?

In any case, the stage manager appears in the doorway to announce, "Homosapien, Cougar – five minutes." They have a match to be ready for.

A match that, despite their best efforts, they lose.

"Good match tonight," Jack Dynes says, startling Homosapien out of his musings. As usual, the boss has just burst into Homosapien and M's dressing room without knocking.

"Thanks," says Homosapien. M smiles at him, happy for her friend being praised.

"You can work your way up to a title shot."

"With Cougar?"

Dynes nods. "But watch him. His contract is only as good as the next match right now."

"OK. Thanks." Homosapien isn't going to say any more, but M elbows him in the ribs. Just before his boss disappears out the door again, Homosapien says, "Mr. Dynes?"

"Yuh?"

"I, uh … I miss the days you promoted me as a serious wrestler despite the fact that Homosapien is gay."

"Adam, you're drawing a lot of heat with these antics."

"Yes, sir."

"You provoke the crowd, and you know very well that's the business we're in."

"Yes, sir, but –"

Dynes interrupts him. "Keep this in mind, if it bothers you – some of them love you for it." And with a conspiratorial wink, the boss rushes off again.

Homosapien sighs. M gets up to give him a hug. "Let's go get a drink," she suggests. "In fact, let's go back to my room, raid the mini bar, make a lot of noise, and let everyone *really* wonder what's going on."

Another sigh. But then Homosapien manages to smile up at his best friend. "Best offer I've had all day."

Coming out nationwide

I'm innocently flipping through the latest issue of my favorite wrestling rag when A Certain Photo catches my eye … The accompanying article reads:

Like, Oh My God … ! David is famous! Not that he'll think it's a good thing. *Au contraire …* Oh God!

Déjà vu. I wander on down to the front counter where David is reading one of the new arrivals, and I hand over the magazine without saying anything.

He glances at the photo. But this time he's very sober and serious. He reads the little article, re–reads it. And sighs. As I predicted – *au contraire.*

The phone rings, and David absently picks it up. "Q4 bookstore."

"It's me. Have you seen *Sharpshooter*?"

"Yeah, Patrick just showed it to me."

"You OK?"

"I'm fine, Adam. What about you? How's it going down with the boss?"

Homosapien sighs. "I don't know. I called, I asked to see him, but they just said for me to wait."

"Working out what he's gonna do," David speculates.

I butt in, I can't help myself. "Why's he have to do *anything* … ?"

David gives me a withering look as if he didn't realize I was *that* naïve.

Homosapien says, "Is that Patrick? Tell him it'll be all right."

"Yeah, he knows, he's listening in. As Usual." Another glare at me, before David returns his attention to Homosapien. "You got family or anything?"

"No, not any more. You?"

"Not any more. So, uh, don't worry about me. Just do what you have to do. OK? You love your job, I know that. So, take care of yourself."

But before David can extract any kind of promise, Homosapien is called away to Jack Dynes' room. David sighs and hangs up the phone. He looks so worried that I actually put my arm round his shoulders and give him a semi–hug. He's so worried that he actually takes some comfort from this.

Coming out to the boss

Homosapien knocks at the door of Jack Dynes' hotel room. As before, Sam opens the door and beckons him in. The boss is sitting at the little table, a copy of *Sharpshooter* in his hand, folded back open to The Page.

"Well, well, well," says Mr. Dynes while musing over The Photo. "Adam O'Connor. Did we know that you're gay?"

"I just assumed, sir …"

"We all just assumed, didn't we? And made asses of ourselves." Dynes gives Homosapien a severe look. "You and Emma … ?"

"Friends, sir."

"Really."

There's a silence, which Homosapien manages not to fill.

Finally Dynes comments, "There's a certain wrestler who'll be glad to know that …"

"All due respect, sir, but that's up to the lady."

Dynes considers this for a moment, then nods. "All right. But we're talking about *you*, Adam O'Connor. About you being gay."

"I didn't set out to mislead people, sir. It's just … It's smart to keep a low profile."

"Well, you *stay smart*, son. If you have to react to this, you only react *in character*, all right?"

"Yes, sir."

Dynes glances down at the photo again, and then tosses the magazine aside with more than a hint of exasperation. "I don't know what the hell do to with this … Who's the so–called *gentleman in question?*"

"Someone I met, sir."

"Someone you'll be seeing again?"

"Yes, sir." Then he insists, "*Yes,* sir."

(Aaaawww … Ain't that sweet?)

"OK. All right. But *low profile,* remember? That's all I can figure for now."

"Yes, sir!" And he's about to be dismissed, so Adam quickly gets in first – "Uh, Mr. Dynes. Is this going to affect my bookings, my storylines?"

Dynes sighs, and exchanges glances with Sam. "No. But that's on a match to match basis too. Now, get out of here."

"Thank you, sir." And, once again, Adam got.

Caught out

Another day, another town.

Homosapien goes looking for Cougar in the stadium dressing rooms, and finds him alone in the bathroom popping pills. Well, green and white capsules, to be precise. It suddenly all adds up together. All the symptoms, all the clues, all the hints.

Steroids.

Homosapien walks further into the room, lets the door swing closed behind him. Cougar stares at him through the mirror, half scared and half defiant.

"God," says Homosapien. "I don't even know where to begin. Are they legit? Or did you get them black market, and you don't have the first clue what you're actually taking?"

"Don't start –"

"Are you on a proper cycle? Do you have off periods? Is someone monitoring your blood pressure who knows what he's doing? Taking urine tests?"

"Adam –"

"Do you realize you can get a *year* in jail just for *possession?*"

Cougar's eyes are sparking fire by now. "Enough with the lecture!"

"*Why?*"

"Cause I'm just doing what I gotta do."

Homosapien folds his arms, settles a hip against the bench. "Why?"

"Because!" Cougar almost snarls in frustration. "I wanna have an impact. Remember? I wanna be a big guy, like Lucifer. You said it yourself – I'm not gonna get that way by muscle–building."

"You're not gonna get that way, *period*. Give it up, kid. Go with your strengths. You *do* have strengths."

Cougar's angrily throwing all his gear back into his bag. "Leave me alone!" Zipping it up, slinging it over his shoulder. "I never asked to be your partner!"

Homosapien quietly says, "Did you talk to Sam yet? About what *doing the job* means?"

"I said leave me alone!" Cougar's striding by Homosapien now, fists clenched, shaking with fury. He pauses just long enough to spit out, *"I never asked for your help, faggot!"* And then he's out the door. And Homosapien is alone again. Nothing new there.

Consolation

"I think I did more harm than good," Homosapien says. He swallows the rest of his beer, crushes the empty can in one hand and then tosses it at the bin. It falls short by almost two feet.

M, whose hotel room this is, just sits beside him staring at the crushed can on the plush carpet, thinking vaguely about getting up and tidying it away. Headlines loom about wrestlers trashing hotel rooms. She's too comfortable where she is, though. She takes a mouthful directly from a bottle of red wine, having misplaced the room's only uncracked water glass some while ago.

The pair of them are sitting on the floor, leaning back against the foot of her bed. Raiding another mini bar. The irony has not escaped them.

"I *said*," Homosapien tries again, "I did him more harm than good."

"No. Adam, no. You tried to help him. He didn't wanna be helped."

"That's not enough."

"It's all we've got."

Homosapien considers this through his beer buzz for a long moment. "OK. Go on, then."

"Go on, what … ?"

"Give me the rest."

"Uh," she manages, playing for time. "OK. You tried to help him. He didn't want to be helped. He doesn't have the discipline to be in professional wrestling. That's all there is to it."

"Discipline, yeah." Homosapien mulls this over for a while. Reaches for another can of beer. "I tell you he dropped out of college? Wanted to play football, but failed some classes. Gave up."

"See what I mean? That's Johnny Cougar – always takes the easy route." M sighs. "You gonna tell Sam? Bout the roids?"

"Nah. Dynes said give him enough rope. He's hanging himself. End of story."

M sighs again, and sinks across to snuggle into her best friend's side. "Happier topics. Tell me about this guy you met. The one in the photo, right? What's his name?"

Homosapien smiles for the first time in a while. "David. Wait for Boston – eight days – you can meet him. We'll go to that club. It'll be fun."

"The gay nightclub?"

"Sure," Homosapien says, sounding ultra–satisfied. "They'll love you even more than me. Promise."

At which point he falls into a doze, so M doesn't have the chance to ask what he was promising, or what he was asking her to promise. She smiles a little, cuddles in closer, and takes another mouthful of wine.

Chez Lui

It's a lovely warm Friday night, and the joint is jumping, and this time it *is* because they're expecting a celebrity to drop by – two, in fact. With Homosapien's agreement, I'd alerted the manager and the DJ and the trendsetters. So, when Homosapien and M appear in the doorway (arms around each other's waist and both looking gorgeous even though they're ultra–casual in jeans and t–shirts), the DJ immediately switches to the rocked–up *Homosapien* and the crowd's attention focuses in on our wrestlers as if there's nothing else in the world more fascinating. Other people would find that a bit unnerving, but these guys are used to being the centre of attention of 20,000 screaming wrestling fans, so a few hundred gays ain't much chop.

Anyway, while David and I wait discreetly in the background, Homosapien and M slowly work their way through, obliging with autographs and handshakes and hugs and chaste kisses, smiling all the while as if they're loving it – which I suppose they are. Chez Lui's supply of disposable instant cameras is selling fast, and the camera flashes are like strobe lighting as everyone takes their turn posing for photos with the wrestlers.

Suddenly, though, I see Homosapien's face darken with anger. He extracts himself from the latest fannish embrace, grabs the shirt of one of the photographers, and hefts him to the balls of his feet. M looks on with real concern. As David and I start pushing our way towards them, I see it's actually a real photographer, with a real camera – one of those expensive, serious things with so many accessories that the guy has a big black bag slung over his shoulder. I assume it must be a reporter.

Whoever it is, Homosapien is not impressed. We pick up the conversation midway. "Why?" Homosapien is demanding, right in the other guy's face. "What could he possibly want them for?"

"Publicity," the guy stammers. He's about half Homosapien's size, and is obviously feeling thoroughly intimidated. "Any publicity is good publicity, right?"

"He didn't like the *Sharpshooter* thing."

The photographer shrugs as well as he's able. "Maybe it grew on him. He even said we might film a promo here." Homosapien glowers, with M backing him up, and the photographer weakly adds, "Maybe."

The people packed round them are silent in the middle of the loud nightclub, gaping at the confrontation. Once we get through, David says, "Hey, Adam. What's the problem?"

Homosapien looks at him, and lets the guy go. "Photographer from the WWW. Jack Dynes sent him."

"Huh," says David, a bit taken aback. "What's his angle?"

"I don't know. It's all news to me." Homosapien turns back to the photographer and gets in his face again, though this time he doesn't grab him by the shirt. "There are people here who value their privacy. You get their permission, all right? You get releases for anything you wanna use."

The photographer shrugs again. "Well, all right."

Then Homosapien really makes his point. He takes the guy's camera, and he coolly opens it up, and he rips the film out. It's useless now, of course. The photographer sags. "You start over," Homosapien advises him, "and you get releases."

He turns away. The people around us let out a cheer and the party spirit returns. David is so impressed or in love or horny or something that he winds his arms around Homosapien's shoulders and kisses him like the world's gonna end. Homosapien grabs him round the waist and holds him so close it's a wonder either of them can breathe. More celebrating from everyone, including M. I'm so happy I give her a hug, which she's kind enough to return.

The photographer is madly loading a new roll of film. It's obvious he could do this in the dark or with his eyes closed. He's quick, but he fumbles a bit, like he's shaken. And just as he gets the camera ready and aimed, David and Homosapien break their embrace, and the guy misses the shot. Hah! Got him back, and how!

That next week, the wrestling rag *Sharpshooter* calls David at the bookstore, asking for an interview. He laughs, like he doesn't really mind too much, but he pretty much says only the one thing to them, over and over.

"No comment. Come on, guys, give me a break. No comment!"

Tag team title match

announcer	This match is scheduled for the best of three falls – and the winners of this match will leave the ring tonight wearing the WWW championship belts!
	First let me introduce to you the reigning tag team champions … Weighing in at 282 pounds, from Juneau, Alaska, please welcome *Jay Caesar!*
	And Caesar's partner, all the way from Thunder Bay, Ontario, weighing in at 306 pounds, let's welcome *Brute!*

The heaviest of heavy metal music accompanies them to the ring. And then, thank heavens, the metal fades and the rocked–up *Homosapien* begins.

     And now the contenders … From San Francisco, California, at a weight of 243 pounds, put your hands together for *Homosapien!*

Our Hero appears, gorgeous in his purple leggings and boots, happily dancing away, showing off all his considerable assets. *Dee*–licious. He's singing along – "Homo superior / In my interior / But from the skin out / I'm Homosapien too." You go, girl!

The crowd are outright booing him by now, though. Jeering and sneering. I spot one sign bearing The Photo along with the message *There's no slow–dancing in wrestling!* which might indicate there's still some wrestling fans out there with a sense of humor about all this. But most signs are bigoted or dumb or just plain mean.

Meanwhile, Caesar and Brute are prowling round the ring, staring up at Our Hero with the most furious expressions, hands itching to wipe that smile off his face. Homosapien ignores all of this, not letting anything get to him through his happy mood.

Cougar's own deadly guitar / violin skirmish replaces Our Song.

     Born and raised in the Badlands, South Dakota, at a weight of 210 pounds, please welcome *Johnny Cougar!*

Homosapien has waited for him. Cougar walks in, and lifts his arms in anticipation of applause – which is, unfortunately for him, rather half–hearted. A moment later, Homosapien leads the way, striding down the ramp towards the ring.

Caesar and Brute are still prowling, but our guys just calmly walk around the ring to their corner, and climb up onto the apron. The referee nervously hovers somewhere between the two teams, ready to risk life and limb to assert his authority. Homosapien hi–5s Cougar, and gracefully steps through the ropes to get into the ring. The referee begins remonstrating with Caesar and Brute, apparently insisting that he won't start the match until one of them is out of the ring and waiting in their corner.

Finally Caesar retreats, launching himself over the top rope in a careless display of athleticism. The referee lifts a hand, shakes it to signal for the bell to sound, and the match is on …

Brute and Homosapien circle each other for a long moment. And then they lock up, hands grabbing each other's shoulders, heads tucked in next together, each shifting their weight to and fro in an effort to gain the advantage. Their tag team partners are yelling abuse and encouragement.

And then Brute, definitely the weightier man, forces Homosapien back so far that he loses his balance. Still locked together, Brute follows him down to the mat. Their momentum carries them ass–over, and Brute forces another tumble so that he ends up on top – and then he bodily holds Our Hero down, and just starts pounding into him with his fists. No finesse to it, not at all! The crowd are loving it. There's nothing much Homosapien can do, but he struggles as much as he can.

Cougar is making a lot of noise, protesting to the ref, and stretching his hand out to his partner, trying to make the tag even though Homosapien is way out of reach.

Apparently deciding to vary his method of humiliating his opponent, Brute gets up, dragging a rather limp Homosapien up with him. Our Hero is thrown into the heels' corner, ending up with his back to the post, his arms draped along the ropes, his head hanging half–conscious. Caesar takes the opportunity to put him in a Sleeper Hold – leaning over the ropes to wrap his arm round Homosapien's throat, thereby cutting off the supply of oxygen to his brain.

The referee protests, because Brute is the legal man – he's the only one who should be hurting Our Hero. Caesar holds on for another defiant moment or two, and then lets go. A quarter–conscious Homosapien slides down the ropes until he's sitting on the mat, held upright only by the corner post.

Suddenly Cougar is there too, on the apron next to Caesar. He's yelling, obviously angry with Caesar for interfering. Caesar just looks down at Cougar as if at a pesky little mosquito buzzing around.

Ignoring the distraction, Brute grabs Homosapien by one wrist, and drags him out into the ring, obviously planning to continue what he started and maybe not finish it for a very long time. It's a massacre.

Cougar is still yelling, outraged, and Caesar is still looking at him disdainfully. Finally Caesar just knocks him aside, and returns his attention to what Brute's doing.

It's a gentle kind of cuff, knocking Cougar off the apron and back onto the floor. It's the most harmless move of the whole match. And the floor around the ring is thickly padded just for moments like these. But it doesn't take an expert to see that Cougar's fallen all wrong.

Cougar is just lying sprawled there, his head at an odd angle, not moving.

The crowd behind the barricade is still jumping up and down, making as much noise as ever, completely unconcerned. But Caesar glances back after a moment, obviously wondering why the mosquito hasn't started buzzing again – and he does a bit of a double take. A reaction that looks pretty genuine to me, which only confirms my fears for Cougar.

Caesar leans into the ring, saying something to the referee – who comes over, takes one look at Cougar and signals for the bell to sound and the match to end. The commentators are calling for the paramedics. The referee and the wrestlers all gather around their fallen comrade. It's serious.

It's so serious that they go to a commercial break rather than keep filming.

Hospital

"I'm OK!" Cougar declares, lying there half cheerful and half high on whatever the nurses pumped into him.

Standing together beside the hospital bed, Homosapien and M wear matching dubious expressions.

"See?" Cougar scrunches up his face with effort, and manages to wiggle a toe or two. "I'm fine!"

"That's good," M soothingly replies. "I'm glad."

"You couldn't move …" Homosapien says, voice unexpectedly hoarse.

"That didn't last long. I was getting the feeling back by the time they were carrying me out. I was getting the feeling back, and God it *hurt*."

Homosapien stares at the white sheets, the chrome bed, the white floor, everything glaring up at him under the harsh fluorescent lights. Something is roiling away inside of him, and he's really not sure if it's worry or anger. "Why did you …" Abruptly it's anger. Fury. "Why the hell did you do that?" he spits out, keeping his voice low which only makes it more venomous. "You weren't meant to be over there in the first place! You better not try blaming this on Caesar."

M lays a hand on his arm. Now is not the time, this is not the place.

Cougar says, "I was thinking –"

"You fucking well were not!"

"Adam," M murmurs. "Stop it."

"I was thinking," Cougar doggedly continues. "Wrestling really ain't for me. Football ain't for me, I figured that out already. But wrestling ain't, either."

M says, "I thought you loved pro wrestling." And she's right about that.

But – "Nah," Cougar replies, still half cheerful and half high. "You know, I thought it was for real when I went for my first lesson. I really did. So, I might try boxing or something. I figure that's what's right for me."

Homosapien turns away for a moment, rolling his eyes in exasperation. But he's not one to give up easily. "Kid, it's not about professional wrestling being wrong for you. It's about you needing a bit more discipline. It's about you and your attitude."

Cougar sniffs at this, turning his nose up, obviously offended. "I figure boxing will suit me just fine."

"Not if you don't do something about the discipline and the attitude."

There's a silence.

Eventually Cougar sulkily says, "I'm not even meant to have visitors yet. Not for more than a few minutes."

"We'll come back to see you tomorrow," M says. "You take care of yourself, John. You let them take good care of you."

"There's no need," Cougar replies. "To come back tomorrow, I mean." He's not even looking at them now.

Homosapien bows his head in defeat. "See you, kid," he says. "Have a good life." And he walks out.

A moment later, M joins him in the corridor. They watch Jack Dynes talking with the doctor, obviously concerned. When he's done, Dynes comes over to Our Heroes. "Not as bad as we feared, eh? How's he coping?"

"Not great. But he'll be OK," M says.

"He wants out," Homosapien adds, flat as a tack. "We can make that easy for him, right?"

"Yuh." Dynes looks at Homosapien very thoughtfully for a long moment. "Yuh, we can. Once we get him through rehab and all." No point in asking to be sued.

Homosapien nods and walks off down the corridor.

It's left to M to be polite to The Boss. "Thank you," she says, shaking his hand. "Just let us know if there's anything we can do."

Dynes nods sincere agreement, grasps her hand in both of his for a moment, and then disappears into Cougar's room. M jogs down to the exit to catch up to her friend.

Tag team match

M and the WWW's Ultimate Bad Guy make their appearance to the wall of red and gold fireworks and the wonderfully edgy chords of *Kashmir*. The crowd love these two. There's no love–to–hate about it – they just love Lucifer *period*, because he's so baaad, and they absolutely adore M. Tonight she's dressed in a few strips of black leather and not much else, and the sight is almost enough to straighten me out …

Nah, not really.

But she's gorgeous.

announcer   This tag team match is scheduled for one fall only. Weighing in at 300 pounds, from Hell's Kitchen, New York City, and accompanied by the delightful M, please welcome *Lucifer!*

The two of them walk down to the ring, and climb in. Lucifer can't stop moving, prowling around, eager to begin.

A big band version of *The Stripper* strikes up, and Porn ☆ makes his appearance, gyrating those hips like there's no tomorrow. For some reason, though, this guy ain't never done it for me. He's cute enough, and he's built, but I suppose he's too much the ladies' man.

announcer   Lucifer's partner for this match only, from Hollywood, California, weighing in at 230 pounds, let's welcome *Porn ☆!*

Porn ☆ joins Lucifer in the ring, but he's much more laid–back than his partner – Porn ☆ just props himself in their corner, and starts chatting with the delectable M.

Our Song begins …

announcer   The first of our contenders, from San Francisco, California, at a weight of 243 pounds, heeerrre's *Homosapien!*

Our Hero appears on the stage at the top of the ramp, happily dancing and singing along as usual. And it's over to the commentators …

Terry   Well, OK, so Homosapien is obviously ready for the match – but who's going to be his tag team partner? As we all know, Johnny Cougar took a fall during his and Homosapien's title match challenge, and he was hospitalized. He's going to be all right, folks, I'm sure you'll all be as glad to hear that as we were, but I can assure you he's in no condition to wrestle tonight.

Rumbler   And who the hell else is gonna wanna partner with this Homo guy? He's disgusting! I wouldn't get in the ring with him if you paid me!

Terry   Luckily for us, no one's going to be doing that. But, folks, I'd just like to send a Get Well message to Johnny Cougar on behalf of everyone here at the WWW. I understand that he's home now, and that his Mom is taking real good care of him.

Rumbler   For God's sake – will you get a grip … ??? At this rate, they'll be broadcasting us on the Hallmark channel!!!

Terry   Yeah, right … Hold on – I think the mystery is about to be solved.

Homosapien is still on the stage. But the music has been cut, and he has a microphone in his hand. He's waiting for the crowd to quiet down enough for him to speak. This takes a short while, because of course a whole lot of them don't wanna listen.

Homosapien Thank you. It's good to be back in Chicago, home of the WWW, home of our biggest fans.

This raises some loyal cheers, despite the fact they hate the guy.

Homosapien Well, we have a tag team match scheduled here tonight, and you're probably wondering who my partner is gonna be. And, well, I wanna tell you that the partner I want is already ringside.

Rumbler   What … ??? Lucifer? Porn ☆? He's gotta be kidding!

Terry   Maybe he means you, Rumbler …

Rumbler   No way – not if you paid me a million bucks.

Homosapien M –

The crowd is shocked. And then they're delighted. There's a lot of gaping, but there's a real buzz of excitement too.

Homosapien   M, in years to come, do you wanna say 'I coulda been a contender'? Or do you want to *be* a contender?

M is standing there on the ring apron by Lucifer's corner, as rocked by this as everyone else. In fact, she's speechless. She stares up at Homosapien for a long moment, and then looks around her, kind of dazed.

Lucifer, of course, is furious. If looks could kill, Our Hero would be a little pile of smoking ash by now. Lucifer grabs a microphone to see if words can kill too.

Lucifer   You fucking runt faggot! You get back down that slimy hole you crawled out of, you don't come round here again messing with me and my people. *You hear me?*

Homosapien just completely ignores him. He's only got eyes for his best friend.

Homosapien   M … ? D'you wanna do this? You and me?

Lucifer   Hey, faggot! You know what M stands for … ? *Mine.*

Homosapien   What does it really stand for, M?

She looks around again. She takes a microphone, and then she gracefully climbs into the ring. Lucifer gives way before her, so that she's centre stage. The whole stadium is hushed, waiting on her reply. And when she finally speaks, she only says one word. She renames herself.

M   Millennium.

The crowd go wild. That's a yes!

Lucifer is stunned. He just stands there, watching her walk out of his life and into Homosapien's corner. Homosapien runs down the ramp, slides into the ring, and begins laying into Lucifer.

The referee belatedly signals for the bell to sound. Millennium and Porn ☆ are waiting in opposite corners – ready, willing and able to wrestle – calling advice and encouragement to their partners. Surrounded by 20,000 roaring voices.

Whoever thought this one up – well, they sure as hell know what makes good wrestling!

So, Homosapien is taking advantage of Lucifer's state of shock, and is laying into him like there'll never be a better chance. Lucifer staggers back against the ropes, and Homosapien follows him all the way. Then, just as

Homosapien is about to knock him right out of the ring, Lucifer shakes himself all over and wakes himself up.

And Lucifer starts laying into Homosapien, tit for tat, driving him back across the ring. Those blows all look too damned *real*. Like they're really connecting. Which I suppose ain't so surprising, because Homosapien just stole Lucifer's girl and Homosapien ain't even straight!

The match becomes a real rough 'n' tumble slugfest. Both men are reeling, half unconscious. They slam each other down to the mat, but it's having such an effect that the slams are getting weaker and weaker.

About the same time, it occurs to each of them to go tag in their partners, and let them take over for a while. Homosapien staggers over to Millennium and tags her in, just as Lucifer struggles to Porn ☆ and does the same.

Millennium and Porn ☆ both rush into the centre of the ring – and drop each other with a Clothesline!

After a moment of lying there, Millennium is the first to recover – she quickly spins around and pins Porn ☆ – but he pushes her over, reversing the pin. They struggle back and forth for a while, very athletic, very proficient, very evenly matched. The crowd are loving it.

And then they each tag their partners in again, and Homosapien and Lucifer immediately return to their slugfest … The difference between the two halves of the match is amazing – one's all skill and respect, while the other's all brute force and anger. Once Homosapien and Lucifer have punished each other to the limit again, they tag their partners in and so it goes on, back and forth, for maybe 15 or 20 minutes.

Until one bout between Homosapien and Lucifer ends with them each slowly crawling back to their corners, looking for the tag. It seems like neither man is more than a quarter conscious, they've each taken such a beating. Millennium and Porn ☆ are leaning into the ring, stretching a hand out to their partners, encouraging them for all they're worth. In his enthusiasm, Porn ☆ edges closer to where Lucifer is dazedly crawling, and the referee reprimands him – he has to stay within an arm's length of the corner post. Porn ☆ argues, but eventually retreats the required distance.

The crowd's attention has been focused on this little drama – a roar goes up when they realize that Homosapien is just about to make the tag! His hand brushes Millennium's – and she flies into the ring as if she's been waiting for this moment all her life.

Lucifer, on his hands and knees, is *this close* to making a tag with Porn ☆ when Millennium catches up with him. She gets a firm hold on him round his shoulders, braces herself for leverage, her thighs ready to do the work – and she somehow manages to flip him over so that he's lying on his back, legs in the air. Before anyone can even blink, she has Lucifer in a pin – a real technical pin that doesn't rely on brute strength – and she holds him there.

The trouble being that the referee has his back turned, still arguing with Porn ☆ even though the man has retreated. Seeing the situation over the ref's shoulder, though, Porn ☆ renews his side of the argument, coming out of the corner again, keeping the ref's attention fixed on him.

Lucifer is returning to full consciousness, and he's beginning to struggle. No matter how clever Millennium's pin is, you gotta wonder how long she can maintain it, given that she's strong but only half Lucifer's size.

The crowd are on their feet, roaring at the referee. Homosapien is yelling at the ref for all he's worth. Eventually Our Hero even leaves his corner, though that's illegal, drops to the floor and runs around towards the other side of the ring – and that finally gets the ref's attention.

The referee is about to start in on Homosapien, but Homosapien just points vehemently to the ring – where Millennium is still managing to hold Lucifer, but only just. Lucifer is struggling for real by now, trying to lift a shoulder off the mat, trying to dislodge his pesky opponent.

Dropping to the mat, the referee begins the three count. A fairly quick three count, perhaps acknowledging that he's been tardy.

One.

Two!

Three!

The bell sounds and the crowd erupts! They've been making a whole lotta noise, really getting behind this match, but they *adore* the fact that Millennium has won. They love it so much that – for now at least – they don't even care who her partner is.

Millennium lets her opponent go, tries to straighten up, but she's obviously feeling the effects of a long and intense match. Homosapien gets back into the ring, obviously also feeling the effects, but determinedly heading for his partner to congratulate her. Despite the punishment he's taken, he's quietly smiling, real satisfied and proud. Porn ☆ drops his head to the padded ring post, thoroughly deflated by this defeat at the hands of a woman and a queer.

Lucifer's not deflated, though. He's furious. He gets to his feet, murderously glaring at Millennium. She has her back to him, hands on her knees, still stretching out against all the kinks and bruises.

The referee and Homosapien notice what's about to happen at the same time. They each start to move just as Lucifer launches himself at his former companion. Homosapien heads for Millennium – he goes in low, and tackles her to the mat so that Lucifer is now throwing himself at thin air. Except that the referee has launched himself with the noble intention of getting in between Lucifer and his prey. And the ref is squashed like a bug under the full force of Lucifer's fury.

Porn ☆ belatedly steps in. He drags Lucifer off the unconscious referee, hauls him out of the ring and up the ramp. Lucifer is in trouble, he's done the unthinkable in hurting the ref, and for the moment all his partner can do is get him out of there. They disappear backstage.

Victory forgotten, Homosapien and Millennium crawl over to the poor referee, trying to figure out if there's anything they can do to help him. But already the medics are on their way, running down the ramp with a stretcher and a neck brace.

And, on a shot of the two beautiful, concerned faces of Our Heroes, we go to a commercial break.

As for me, I figure to hell with the referee. I'm still cheering!

Boston

Homosapien has three days off, and comes to Boston again. It's wonderful to see him – he's still looking triumphant, patently pleased with the turn his career has taken. And so he should be – that was a good solid match he and Millennium put on. The fans' on–line chat has been enthusiastic and the *Sharpshooter* coverage was so positive that it left the reporter's objectivity lying in the dust somewhere, looking very sorry for itself.

On top of which, David seems in an equivalently bright mood. I used to think the old curmudgeon was half in love with this man, but it's pretty obvious by now that he's fallen the rest of the way.

Despite all this, when Homosapien comes to the bookstore, the two of them *don't* just head off back to David's apartment without a word. Tall tales but true! (Lord, at this rate they might even take advantage of the summer weather and go do the tourist thing. As if they *don't* have better things to be doing. Like each other.) Homosapien just strides in, grabs David up in his arms and they kiss even more passionately than they did at Chez Lui. Then David asks him if he'd like a drink. When Homosapien says yes, David heads down to the kitchenette.

"Hey, Patrick," Homosapien says to me.

"Hey, sunshine," I say right back. He's smiling like he couldn't be happier. Irresistible!

To my everlasting surprise, David calls out, "Patrick! Beer or wine?"

"Uh," I manage. "Whatever you're having!"

The two of them sprawl comfortably in one of the sofas in the reading nook, not holding hands or anything, but arranged carefully enough that they're pressed together at shoulder and hip and thigh. I settle opposite them, smiling almost as broadly as they are. We all sip at our beers. We chat about something inconsequential, I forget what now.

I even forget how the topic came up. I think I must have drifted off into my own thoughts for a time, but David catches my attention when he says, "So, I'm this scrawny guy who's barely fit enough to walk the ten blocks back home. What do you see in me?" And I'm gaping, because David's actually secure enough with this guy now to not only ask this, but to ask it in front of witnesses!

Homosapien chuckles under his breath. "You think wrestlers turn me on? Bodybuilders?"

"They don't?"

Another chuckle. "I couldn't do my job if they did. If you wanna know why, you can ask Patrick."

David looks across at me, and I smirk. "Could make a match *real* interesting to watch," I comment. "Purple lycra don't hide much."

"Oh!" Obviously David hadn't considered this. But he refuses to be deflected. "So, what *does* turn you on?"

Homosapien swallows another mouthful of beer. He's not embarrassed by this. If anything he seems to be wallowing in it. Maybe they've never hinted at any of this to each other before. Maybe they've hardly even spoken. Eventually, Homosapien murmurs, "Your eyes. Your mind."

"My *mind* turns you on?" David scoffs. "No one says that anymore."

"I guess I do."

David's just looking at him, fascinated.

Homosapien rests his head back against the sofa, face turned to David like there's nothing else for him in the whole wide world. "So, what do you like about me?" he softly asks.

"Uh …" David clears his throat, shifts uncomfortably. It's obvious that he's bluffing when he replies, "Well, of course it's just a physical thing. Have you looked in a mirror lately?"

Our Hero isn't fooled for a moment. He's still sitting there, head back and totally relaxed as if he's bathing in contentment. And he sings, quietly, barely above a whisper. He sings a line from his song.

And I think of your eyes in the dark and I see the star …

David surrenders. The moment holds. They are so caught up in each other that even I'm breathless.

Then Homosapien smiles, loosening his grip on the moment, but making it more real too. "David?"

"Yeah?" There's no response, at least not in words, so David just smiles back at him. "See, *that's* what I like about you. Sometimes you enjoy life so much that you just burst into song."

The smile becomes a grin. "You know, I could carry you those ten blocks back home."

David almost snorts with laughter. "Oh, I think I can manage." He stands up, grabbing Homosapien's hand and bringing him up to his feet as well. "If the reward's gonna be worth the effort."

"Yeah, it will be. I promise." And Homosapien winks at me with the most delicious of grins, as the two of them head off out the store.

Working out

Homosapien has a new move he's thought up – working title The Homo Superior – because, let's face it, the old Chinlock is *not* the most impressive finishing move. He's working through it with Sam (the trainer). For a while now, they've been grappling back and forth on the mats in silence, while Homosapien tries to make the move work. But every time they get to it, Sam pins him instead and Homosapien can't seem to find the leverage to reverse it the way he intends.

They grind to a halt once more, with the old guy easily in control of the hefty young creature. "You know the only thing that's gonna get you out of this?" Sam asks.

"What?"

"A kiss." But Sam springs away from the hold with a laugh. "Don't go trying that on me, though! You can practice that on the *gentleman in question*, eh?"

"Um …" Homosapien slowly gets to his feet. "Yeah, well, I've been meaning to talk to Mr. Dynes about that."

Sam heads for his bag, collects the bottled sports drink he's brought, and lifts his chin to indicate he's listening.

"I don't think we should do that anymore."

"What – you and the gentleman … ?" Sam is genuinely confused.

"No – I mean the *antics*, as Mr. Dynes calls them. That's just not necessary any more. We've got other things working for us now."

Sam just looks at him for a long moment. "You and Emma?"

"Yeah, I think we can really build on that. The fans love her. And pairing her with me makes it even more interesting."

"Well, you *do* work well together …"

"Though she deserves more than being partnered with the laughing stock of da Dub Dub Dub."

A shrewd look is turned on Our Hero. "And what about Lucifer?"

Homosapien shrugs. "It adds to the storyline, doesn't it?"

Sam is silent for long moments, considering all of this.

Eventually Homosapien says, "What do you think? Should I go talk to Mr. Dynes?"

"No," Sam slowly replies. "No. I'll talk to him." He nods at Homosapien. "I think you might be onto something."

Homosapien smiles. Feeling mischievous, he says, "*Now* I could kiss you!"

"Dream on, boy." Sam considers him for a moment, getting back to serious business. "All right – getting out of that hold. That Superior move you wanna try – it all depends on your opponent's centre of gravity, right?"

"Right."

"Then I've got an idea that don't involve kissing …"

Interview

Homosapien and Terry (the commentator) are sitting in armchairs, in what looks like a stadium's hospitality suite, all prepped for an interview. Terry seems pretty impressed with Our Hero, though he starts with a tough question.

Terry	Homosapien, there's been talk in the past about you not taking wrestling seriously enough. Is that still an issue? Because you've chosen the most unorthodox of partners …
Homosapien	Millennium is as good a wrestler as any of the guys in the WWW, Terry. If I'm the only one who's smart enough to see it, then it's no wonder I'm the one who's gonna benefit by it.
Terry	So, you still have the tag team title in your sights?
Homosapien	Yes, sir! There's no reason why Millennium and I can't be wearing those title belts within six months. No reason at all.
Terry	I have to ask, though –
Lucifer	Homosapien – you **beep**ing whore! *You beeping son of a beep!*

And the WWW's Ultimate Bad Guy comes crashing in, landing on Homosapien, pummeling all the way down – even while the chair is falling backwards onto the floor. For a long moment all we see is two pairs of denim–clad legs sticking up in the air from behind the chair, and all we hear is thuds and grunts and dialogue that's mostly beeped out.

Finally the cameraman turns back to Terry, though, who's still sitting in his chair in a state of shock. Security guards belatedly run in past him.

Reality

Every night that there's a wrestling show, there's violence between Lucifer and Homosapien. Every time he's near a microphone, Lucifer insists long and hard on getting legitimate matches booked with Our Hero. If he doesn't get one, though, that doesn't stop him – he tracks Homosapien down wherever he might be and beats him up anyway. He interrupts Homosapien's other matches, he jumps him in corridors, he jumps him during interviews.

If Millennium is nearby, she does what she can to prevent it. Pleading with Lucifer, yelling at him, getting in the way and tussling with him. He cast her aside once, slammed her into a wall and she slid down it, half unconscious, blood on her lips. That scared Lucifer enough that he walked away.

The next time, however, he lays Homosapien out with just one heavy duty punch – and Millennium gets in the way again, lying over her new partner where he's sprawled on the floor. Lucifer roars in fury, but she holds her ground, looking up at him half scared but all determined.

It's getting serious. It's getting real serious. Homosapien is walking around with a black eye. A real one. And I know it's real cause the WWW's make–up department ain't *that* good.

David watches anxiously, fast–forwarding through the tape, looking for Homosapien's match. "Come on! God, where is he? I can't bear this."

"Turn it off, then."

He just glares at me, returns to the screen. Glares some more. "*Look* at these guys! None of them attack each other the way that bastard attacks Adam!"

Of course he's right. The tape's showing a match between the Bizarro brothers, who recently became mortal enemies. And, as we all know, there's nobody like kinfolk to tip love over into hatred. Even so, with all that angry betrayal simmering in the air, the match is a walk in the park compared to one of Lucifer's slugfests with Homosapien.

I carefully consider the action as one of the Bizarros head–butts the other in the nuts. "That's gotta hurt," I say, perfectly in time with the commentator.

"You're kidding!" David protests. "If that was real, then how come he's already on his feet again? No man would be standing upright, let alone fighting back."

"So, now you're saying it's *not* real?" I murmur, risking life and limb.

"I don't get how anyone could possibly think otherwise. It's ridiculous! God, even *you* figured it out!"

"I guess most people wanna think it's real."

David shudders, folds his arms across himself as if he's cold. "Then I bet they're really enjoying these matches with Lucifer," he says, voice hard and even, "because I figure *real* is exactly what they're getting." He shudders again, hurting. "Fucking Godforsaken bastards."

Phone call

Homosapien   Yeah?

David   It's me.

    Pause.

Homosapien   How are you, David? How's Patrick doing?

David   Oh, please – don't tell me – you can't talk about it.

Homosapien   I'm sorry, David.

David   Christ! You'll apologize without any provocation whatsoever, *but you can't talk about it … ?* Things must be real bad.

    Pause. Pause. Pause.

David   Adam, he's really hurting you, isn't he?

Homosapien   I'm just doing the job, David.

David   For God's sake, they let him gay–bash you every damn night. They pay him to do it. They pay *you* to take it! What the hell kind of job is that?

    Silence.

David   Can't they keep him on a leash?

    More silence. But eventually Homosapien sighs and replies.

Homosapien   David, the audience is loving it.
David   So … ?
Homosapien   So, they're not gonna put a leash on him, are they?
David   For God's sake …

My curmudgeonly boss sounds weak now, like he's gonna be ill.

David   For God's sake, Adam …

And the crowd goes wild …

Lucifer is already in the ring, pacing back and forth, when Homosapien makes his entrance. The crowd are on their feet, roaring for blood. Our Anthem plays as loud as ever, but Homosapien ain't dancing no more. He walks out to the stage at the top of the ramp, serious. Well, not serious exactly. More like … solemn.

"Cut the music!" Lucifer yells into a microphone before Homosapien can get any further. "Cut that damned faggot music!"

Homosapien looks around in annoyance, hands on hips, as the sound technicians cut his theme song before he's even reached the ring.

Lucifer leaves a long silence. It's obvious he wants to say something. The crowd's roar gets louder and louder as they wait on him. Finally – "I got something to say to you."

Homosapien is waiting, brow raised, like, *Yeah, what?*

And Lucifer announces, savoring every word, "I ain't gonna lie down for you no more, faggot."

For the briefest of moments, I see surprise flicker across Homosapien's face. Maybe no one else is watching him closely enough to notice. Anyway, the crowd are right behind Lucifer and they are loving his belligerence.

Homosapien lets them have their joyous reaction and then he beckons for a mike. He hefts it in one hand for a moment, considering his opponent. Then he says, "As if you ever lay down for me anyway, Lucy." Another long moment, before he adds, "As if I ever wanted you to."

Everyone's hollering and catcalling and dying for Lucifer's response.

Lucifer lifts his mike again. And all he says is … "Faggot."

Homosapien stares down at him, eyebrow raised, unimpressed. "Excuse me?"

Lucifer gestures to the crowd, encouraging them to join in. "Faggot!"

And they oblige him, they start chanting … "Fag–got. Fag–got. Fag–got." There's a singsong sound to it. Which contrasts strangely with the sheer nastiness.

Smiling, Lucifer shuts up and just relaxes back in his corner of the ring, watching Homosapien standing there, having to take it. Verbally abused by 20,000 chanting rednecks. And of course he's not going to answer back – Homosapien is a Good Guy in all but sexuality, remember, so he never abuses the fans. Lucifer thinks it's hilarious.

Finally Homosapien drops his mike and strides down to the ring. Lucifer steps forward to meet him and they grapple.

The match is different to any I've seen before. It's a slugfest, sure – but there's a desperation to it. It's a wrestling match with all the familiar holds and moves – except that half of those moves just aren't working. Homosapien gets Lucifer all set up for a throw, and then finds he can't budge the man. Homosapien gets the guy pinned, but can't even hold it for a one count. Lucifer just isn't going to cooperate. The match drags on, brutal and draining for both of them, except that Lucifer seems sustained by his own nasty righteousness and by the vicious cheers of the crowd.

I can't tell you how it ended. Beyond a certain point, I just couldn't watch any more.

Phone call

David	Q4 bookstore.
Homosapien	Hey, David.
David	Oh God …

My boss sounds as distraught as I've ever heard him. There's a moment's silence, and then Homosapien replies with the most incredible gentleness.

Homosapien	I know it bothers you. And I know why, OK? David, I don't want you to watch any more.
David	I'm not gonna pretend it's not happening!
Homosapien	David, please …
David	If you're not gonna do something about it, then I will.
Homosapien	There's nothing you can do.

David   Don't be so sure about that.
  Pause.
Homosapien David, this is my *career*.
David   Yeah, pretty strange, huh?
Homosapien I don't tell you how to run your store.
David   You would if you thought I was getting hurt by it.

  Pause. Pause.

And then, sounding infinitely worried, Homosapien asks, "What are you gonna do?"

David seems almost cheerful as he comments, "Probably best you don't know, right?"

"Right," Homosapien weakly replies. "Right."

Sharpshooter

"Your magazine," David says over the phone to *Sharpshooter*'s editor: "you buy into the whole illusion. You write it up as if it's real."

"Pro wrestling *is* real," the editor replies. He sounds distant, lazy, as if he's bored or he just doesn't care.

"What kind of journalism is that, for God's sake? What happened to the Fearless Exposure Of The Truth?"

"Current statistics prove ..." Paper is shuffled ... "that 84% of the population believe that pro wrestling is real."

"Then you owe them the truth!"

"As for the readers of our magazine," the editor flatly continues as if David hadn't spoken, "for the wrestling fans, it's closer to 90%."

"What? That's ridiculous!"

"Thank you for your interest, Mr. ... uh ..."

"Vigil, you jerk! David Vigil."

"Thanks." And then the dial tone. Who'd have thought that one word could carry so little gratitude?

David is staring at the phone, too befuddled to remember he's furious. "What the ... ?"

I say slowly, figuring it out: "It's their business too. I guess."

He just looks at me. Looks at me as if he really wants to know something, and I might have the answer. Stranger things have happened, but not often.

"They're in the pro wrestling business, as much as the WWW is, right? So, if it's in Jack Dynes' interests to keep the illusion going, then it's in *Sharpshooter*'s interests too."

After a moment David nods, and then he frowns. "OK. We go to Plan B."

"What's Plan B?"

"I don't know yet." He screws up his face in that way he does when he's trying so hard to think that he doesn't give a shit how stupid he looks. "Get me a coffee, Patrick. Get yourself one, double strength. All right?"

He doesn't need to ask twice.

I said use the Farce!

Homosapien is walking down the backstage corridors, still sweating hard and breathing hard from his match with one of the lesser Good Guys, a Goth creature called Louis du Lac. Jack Dynes cuts Adam off before he can reach the shoddy sanctuary of Millennium's dressing room.

Dynes	What was that?
Homosapien	Sir?
Dynes	Don't play dumb with me. You know how that match should have ended.
Homosapien	I lost, sir. I was meant to lose.

Long pause … Adam tries not to shuffle his feet. He knows what Dynes is asking about.

Homosapien	I thought Sam was going to talk to you. We've been working on this new move, the Homo Superior, and if I could use it as my finishing move next time I'm due a win –
Dynes	You'd better remember who you're talking to!
Homosapien	Yes, sir. Sorry, sir.
Dynes	You were meant to get out of that hold with a kiss, not with this Superior thing. Which didn't even work anyway.

Adam takes a deep breath. Maybe it's time to lay it on the line.

Homosapien Sir. You say I don't want it enough. You say I'm not serious enough. I guess you mean my motivation. But these antics and things – they're not gonna make me want it any more than I already do.

Another breath. Time to lay it *all* on the line.

Homosapien In fact, maybe they make me want it less.

His boss looks at him for a moment, kind of thoughtful. Then he says just one thing before walking away …

Dynes I know that, Adam O'Connor. I know.

Adam looks after him, trouble not only gathering on his brow, but settling in for the long haul.

Phone call

David answers the phone. At first he looks puzzled and then he turns surprised. "Your boss wasn't interested." He glances at me, like he knows at least *I'll* be interested.

I can't hear the other end of the conversation, so I sidle up and whisper, "Who is it?"

"Then, why call me?" David listens for a moment, then puts his hand over the mouthpiece and says, "The *Sharpshooter* journalist. John Gurrie. The one who wanted a story about me and Adam."

Getting closer, I catch Gurrie in mid sentence – "really is *The* Story in pro wrestling, but my editor won't believe me about that, and more fool him."

"So what can you do?"

"Nothing. But you can take it elsewhere. I hate to let it pass me by, hate it with a vengeance, but you can take it to another magazine. At least I can do an in–depth insider's article once the story's broken."

David is frowning. "But who else would be interested? It's not as if wrestling has a broad appeal."

"That's where you're wrong. It's a big industry, and the audience is enormous. OK, they're mostly young men – white, working class, lower middle class – but that's a demographic spread all through the country. All through the world. There's a lot of people out there who are wrestling fans and a whole hell of a lot who are related to those fans, family or friends. Plus a whole lot of people who depend on it for their livelihood. It's a big story, and it's just waiting to blow."

"All right." David's frown has deepened. "All right. Let me think about it."

"Just let me know, OK? Just give me the word when it's all set."

"All right," David says again, distracted. He hangs up, and sits there for a long while, deep in thought.

Another dramatic reconstruction

They are tense, pacing to and fro, considering The Great Questions Of Our Time. Finally Sam has the nerve to state it baldly.

Sam	If Lucifer's thing with Homosapien gets any more real, it'll show up the regular matches for what they are –
Dynes	Staged.
Sam	Choreographed.
Dynes	Fixed.
Sam	– and maybe it has already. There must be some who've twigged. And we'll lose them. They won't care anymore. The audience want it to be real.

The owner grows thoughtful. Tense, pacing and thoughtful.

Dynes	Or do they … ?
Sam	If they knew the truth, pro wrestling would die.

Dynes is still thoughtful. Sam tries to pre–empt any quibbling.

Sam	Everything is at stake here, Jack. *Everything*.
Dynes	I've been thinking about the movies, Sam. The willing suspension of disbelief. Maybe that's relevant, maybe that has something to do with what we do.
Sam	But movies are entertainment. This is sport!
Dynes	People want to get lost in the reality of the movie. But they still know it's not real. They still know that in two hours the credits will roll and the lights will go up.

Sam just stares at him for a long moment.

| *Sam* | Mr. Dynes – Mr. Dynes, you're the boss, and no doubt you're onto something I just can't get a grip on. But there's an issue with Lucifer. That's what I was wanting to talk about. |

Dynes comes back from his intellectual vacation.

Dynes	You want me to tell him to take it back a notch?
Sam	Two notches. He'd have done some serious harm if Adam wasn't so good.
Dynes	One notch. Adam O'Connor still needs a few obstacles in his path.
Sam	Well, one notch or two, Michael won't like it.
Dynes	He doesn't have to like it. As you say – I'm the boss.

Vanity's Progress

David is selling his story as hard as he can, and getting nowhere fast. "An exposé," he says to yet another editor. "Big business founded on a lie. Audiences being hoodwinked, and paying through the nose for the privilege."

The *Vanity's Progress* guy is having none of it. "Hardly our cup of tea, is it? I wonder you even thought to call us."

"It's *exactly* your cuppa. If anyone's into the Fearless Exposure Of The Truth, it's you. I read every word of your stories, every month, so I know what I'm talking about."

"I'm flattered, truly I am. But professional wrestling? It's a bit beneath the notice of most of our readers, don't you think?"

"OK, yes, I admit it – I used to think it beneath my notice. But not anymore. Apart from the big business angle, lives are at stake."

The editor sighs. "Undermines your whole argument, really, doesn't it? You're coming to me with a story about professional wrestling not being real, though your motivation is that it's all too real for your anonymous source."

"*He's getting hurt!*"

"Exactly, my dear."

David takes a moment to choke the fury back down, then says through gritted teeth, "Your writers can cope with that kind of complexity."

"But can the wrestling fans, hhhmmm … ?" And on that note, the editor of *Vanity's Progress* quietly hangs up the phone.

Tag team match

Homosapien and Millennium have a tag team match with the Bizarro brother who went bad and Fixx, a lesser heel. It's a good match – strong on the technical side of things and pretty evenly balanced. The crowd enjoy it and I kind of suspect they lengthen the match because of that. I haven't worked out how they do it yet, but I think the wrestlers or the ref or the commentators pay attention to how the crowd react, and lengthen or shorten a match to suit. Which is beside the point right now.

It's a good match, and only ends when Fixx disqualifies himself and his partner by getting into a knockdown argument with the referee. Moron. Still, that's Bad Guys for you! (There are actually morals in pro wrestling. Like, that kind of behavior is self–defeating. Who'd have thought?)

Lucifer doesn't interfere for once. But as Our Heroes are walking back up the ramp, his image appears on the big screen overhead. He's in a dressing room, beer in hand, glowering at a TV monitor showing Homosapien and Millennium. To describe him as resentful would be an ironically exaggerated understatement. Lucifer slugs down the last of the beer and reaches for another. Which is when he finally realizes that he's on camera.

The glare is turned on the cameraman instead. "Get that **beep**ing thing out of my face!" He stands, shoves, and the picture is suddenly lopsided.

Lucifer storms off out of sight. It's not attractive. It's not even fun anymore. It's just all too real.

Interlude

Mr. Tall, Dark & Intense calls. I tell him I'm busy. He says, With what? I say, There's all kinds of stuff going on, and I have to be with a friend right now. He says, Who, David? I say, very firmly, Yes.

He laughs. Not a nice laugh. "David Vigil is *not* your friend."

I actually have to swallow over a lump in my throat before I reply, and it doesn't go away. What is all this coming to? Our man Patrick – our narrator, our guide, our hero – does not ever get Deeply Involved. Not Ever. Certainly never enough to get a lump in my throat! Finally I manage to say, "It takes one to know one." And then I hang up.

It takes someone who is not my friend to recognize someone else who is not my friend. I wonder if he managed to figure out that's what I meant. But whether he did or not, I know it won't hold off Mr. TDI for long.

Friends

It's mid summer, and da Dub Dub Dub arrives in town again, and Homosapien comes right over to the Q4 bookstore. He and David are kind of quiet this time round. Subdued. Not like the last visit, only three weeks ago, when they fell even more in love right here on this very sofa. I guess everything's more difficult now.

Homosapien sleeps at David's apartment. Sleeps with David, I assume. My curmudgeonly boss certainly looks well shagged. But otherwise it's just as if they're friends, not lovers. Otherwise it's as if they're avoiding being alone together.

The two of them hang around the store and hang around me. Which is good, in a way. I mean – you've guessed this already – I want a piece of Homosapien too. Not the same piece as David, but I want to hang out with him, pretend he's a friend. So I'm happy for him doing that this visit. Mostly, though, I just keep thinking about how this isn't the point of them being together. Not really.

And they don't talk about The Issue. Well, Homosapien says, "You haven't done anything? Have you? I haven't heard about anything." And David says, "Nothing yet. Not for want of trying." And as far as I can tell, that's it. Except that a few times David and I catch each other watching Homosapien walk around, and he's obviously a bit stiff and sore which is so different to his previous easy strength – and my boss and I exchange grimaces.

They're friends for each other, that much is obvious. David and Adam. Who'd have thought? They are such different kinds of people. And being friends is good. But it's kind of sad they're not really lovers too.

The light bulb switches on

"I've got it!" David loudly, proudly declares a few days later.

"The Meaning Of Life?" A nearby customer, full of hope.

"Ricky Martin's cell phone number?" Another, even more so.

"Penicillin should clear it up, darling," Candy confidentially suggests.

"No no no," David says, half amused and all exasperated. "Patrick? Where'd you get to?"

I break my 'dramatically cast away' pose, get up from the sofa, and make my appearance.

"*Kinsey 6*," he says.

"What?" I ask.

David beckons me closer, and then whispers in my ear: "If pro wrestling needs outing, then they're the rag to do it. Right?"

The brilliance of this idea crashes into me. "Right!" I echo, still stunned.

And – wouldn't you know it? – when David calls the *Kinsey 6* editor, she's intrigued.

Kinsey 6

So, here's a few bits from the article they published just over a week later, mostly written by one David Vigil …

> *Better Out Than In*
>
> *In much the same way as a closeted homosexual, the sport of professional wrestling is pretending to be something it's not. It pretends to be a competitive sport; it is in fact a staged entertainment.*
>
> *As most of us know, the benefits are in coming out, not staying closeted – those benefits being in the recognition of our own true selves, in validating our shared identity, in exploring all the layers of identity available.*

Professional wrestling already plays with notions of identity. In terms of roles, Homosapien is a character played by Adam O'Connor in the WWW's ongoing saga, and Lucifer is a role played by Michael Rosen. It even seems that the WWW federation owner Jack Dynes, as occasionally seen by the audience, is a character played by a man who happens to bear the same name and job description. In terms of the traits that differentiate the Good Guys in wrestling from the Bad Guys, while Blue is the quintessential Good Guy, Homosapien is a Good Guy in all but sexuality. While Jay Caesar and Brute do not deviate from their allotted Bad Guy personae, Lucifer is a Bad Guy who is now being cheered as a hero – though this approval is for expressing the fans' homophobia.

And that's where the closet or the false mask can cause such harm: in perpetuating fixed, narrow, judgmental notions of identity that are simply not true. In reducing both the characters and the spectators to less than they can be.

Let's challenge those homophobic fans, this still–homophobic society. Let's withdraw Rosen's corporate–perk license to assault a man he feels confronted by, withdraw his ability to break the law with impunity. Let's take away the lie that allows one of Dynes' employees to gay–bash on company time and pretend it's just a game.

Let's remember that the Silence of the closet equals Death.

Out of the closet ...

Jack Dynes' response for the next few days is, well, silence. Which is both rather appropriate and very threatening.

Adam keeps to himself as the WWW continues its regular tour. He watches everyone around him at the hotels and the gyms and the stadiums. They are all reading the article, of course: the wrestlers and managers, the trainers and bimbo valets, the cameramen and technicians passing the magazine around from one to the other. Those who wouldn't be caught dead with a gay rag in their hands read a photocopy of the article instead. And they stare at Adam. Whispering. Hostile. Worried – for their own sakes, not his. Is the whole federation gonna come crashing down? Does the 'big business founded on a lie' thing mean it's all over?

Silence, silence and more deadly silence from Jack Dynes. The tension rises like a storm about to break. The kind of storm that might end the world. No one knows what will happen next, except they're running a book on whether Adam will be sacked or not. Emma reports that the odds aren't in his favor.

"Life sure was simpler when they thought I was your girl," she says.

He sighs. "Yeah."

But they both know better than to try to resuscitate that old lie.

At least David warned him. Sent him a copy of the article before the issue hit the newsstands. Adam read it through time and again, though it made even less sense to him than to me. David has the gift of the gab, sure, but sometimes it's a bit of an intellectual gab. Emma said she thought she grasped the ideas, but she just wasn't across the whole queer theory thing and she wondered if the argument wasn't a bit circular.

The day before the rag was released, Adam passed the warning on to Jack Dynes by faxing the article to him, with a cover sheet giving his name but no explanation. What could he say? Silence was the only reply.

For the first time, Adam feels badly towards his lover. He tells me later how much he resents David's assumption that coming out is the good and wise thing to do. The *only* thing to do. "It's easier for some than others," he grumbles, and quite rightly so. Not that either of us confront David about this. (Maybe we should have. You'd think I'd feel safe putting in my two cents worth when a big beefy wrestler is standing firm beside me … But I don't.)

Plus, Adam finds it excruciatingly embarrassing to have Homosapien and Lucifer used as the main examples throughout the article. And if *he* finds it embarrassing, then Michael's reaction … Well, let's just say that it gives

Michael all the motivation he needs for Lucifer *not* taking it down a notch or two. Adam is not looking forward to the next few matches, not at all.

Meanwhile, Jack Dynes' silence continues.

... and into the fire

"I don't have the *time* to deal with *you* right now."

Finally Adam has run into Jack Dynes in an anonymous corridor in yet another stadium. Dynes is in a hurry. Homosapien has a match to get to. There are people around them, listening surreptitiously, dying of curiosity. Wondering if this is it, if Adam O'Connor will be packing his bags.

"You and your damned *gentleman in question*. You should think less of him and more of your contractual obligations!"

"Yes, sir," Adam says. He is quailing a bit on the inside, despite his best intentions.

Dynes is glaring daggers. "So it's only a *special interest* magazine." Those two words are dripping with sarcasm. "No one else has picked up on it. Yet. So there's no fallout. Yet. And he didn't use anything he couldn't have got from just watching."

"No, sir."

"And what do gays care anyway? Who's gonna read it? All those big words."

Adam clears his throat. "Maybe we shouldn't underestimate the audience, sir."

But Dynes is still on the attack. "Did *you* understand it?"

"No, sir."

A long pause, accompanied by another daggery glare. "Don't you have a match to go to?"

Adam becomes aware once more of the crowd above them getting impatiently noisy. "Yes, sir."

"Well … ?"

"Yes, sir. Thank you, sir!" And Homosapien sets off for the curtain at a jog. Apparently still employed. For now, at least. The others turn back to their work, not knowing whether to be disappointed or not. (Depends on whether they lost money on a bet, I guess.) For the first time in a long while, Homosapien is booked to win.

Ponders …

Dynes	You know, maybe this guy is onto something.
Sam	Such as … ?
Dynes	He doesn't understand us any better than we understand him, but maybe there's something there.
Sam	I don't see it, Jack.
Dynes	I've been thinking about the movies. Nothing's just black and white any more. Everything's shades of grey. Everything's complicated.
Sam	Well, *complications* I agree with.
Dynes	Everything's complicated …

Phone call

Adam and David haven't spoken since the article appeared. I don't think it was because they were mad at each other; I think it was just because they were both waiting to see what Jack Dynes' reaction would be.

So, finally Adam calls, and I answer the phone. "Hey, gorgeous," I say, subdued.

He laughs a bit, and I know it's mostly all right. "Hey, Patrick."

"Still got a job?"

"Yeah, he didn't sack me. Yet."

"It's tough, ain't it?" I say with fellow-feeling. Then I pass the phone over to David.

And *then*, while they're talking, guess who walks in the door? Mr. TDI. I go kind of cold. I'd been loitering around the counter to listen in to the phone call, though I'd been about to make myself scarce and leave them to it, but I quickly change my mind.

He wanders the shelves, picks out a book or two and flicks through them then puts them back. He's not paying attention to anything but me, though. I watch him, wondering what on earth he might do. What he's capable of.

Eventually he just leaves, throwing a pointed stare at me on his way past the counter.

"Who was that?" asks David afterwards.

"I don't really know," I reply. And the scary part is that's true.

Tad Scott Foster

I am walking to work one morning, thinking of nothing much other than whether I should take a detour to Apollo's before we open, when Candy *yoo–hoo*s me from unlocking the front door of her beauty salon. "Paddy love!" She's the only person in the world I let call me Paddy. (Anyone who likes can call me love.) "Paddy love, did you see *Tad Alive* last night?"

"Great Scott!" I respond with the show's used–and–abused catchphrase. "No, haven't seen it for weeks." It's not exactly something I go out of my way to watch, but I know Candy's a fan. Never figured out why.

Candy is digging through her enormous carry–bag, and I stand there mesmerized by the bright, glossy pink daisies all over it. At last she surfaces with a videotape. "I didn't catch the first bit, but you and your darling Davey better watch this." She winks at me, nicely roguish. "The ripples are widening."

And with this mysterious remark, Candy slips inside.

"Huh," I say with great intelligence. Then I decide I really better go fetch our usual doses of caffeine before we face whatever this is.

A half hour later, David presses the play button and we see a grainy image of talk show host Tad Scott Foster standing in front of his set. As the picture clears he's looking around, craftily, judging the audience's reaction. They're kind of quiet, only letting out a couple of hoots and a few jeers.

"Yes, it's about time I came out …" Tad says, obviously continuing on from an announcement.

Another long teasing pause. The audience are getting restless, wanting the punch line and wanting it now. They're not sure if they like this.

"Great Scott …" murmurs the band leader, shaking his head.

Tad turns away for a moment, turns back again with a magazine. And it's *Kinsey 6!* It's *The* Issue! Just in case the audience don't recognize it as a gay rag, Tad flips through it, letting the camera catch glimpses of the beefcake photos.

Then he holds the magazine closed again, close to his chest. "I'm coming out … I'm coming out *as a pro wrestling fan!*"

The audience pops! They love it. And maybe they even love pro wrestling too.

"Great Scott!" exclaims the band leader in a state of shock.

Tad flips through the magazine again, this time looking for something in particular. David's article. In a pondering kind of voice, Tad reads out the opening lines:

> *In much the same way as a closeted homosexual, the sport of professional wrestling is pretending to be something it's not. It pretends to be a competitive sport; it is in fact a staged entertainment.*

"Well, well," he muses. "Who'd have figured?"

The band leader is back to shaking his head. "Who'd have thought?" he echoes.

Tad looks up at the audience. "So, who here thinks that the wrestling is real … ?"

There is a loud cheer from the audience and much stamping of feet. It doesn't sound like all of them, but it is definitely a vocal majority.

"Yeah. Yeah, me too." Tad casts a look across the audience, cocks an eyebrow at the band leader. "Maybe we should invite this guy on the show. The guy who wrote this …" He looks for the name. "David Vigil. Whaddaya think?"

This time there is some booing mixed in with the cheering.

My heart is in my mouth. I look at David – and he's looking kind of fierce. Like this is what he wanted. A soapbox to stand on. I wonder if it's the right kind of soapbox, though.

"All right. That's what we'll do." Tad tosses the rag back on his desk, and they move onto other things.

I just stand there for a long moment, until David hits the stop/eject button. "Wow," I say.

"Yeah," he replies, obviously planning strategies already.

"Are you sure this is the way to go?"

"Yeah," he says. Though he also shrugs.

"What about Adam?"

David glances at me, irritated. "He's big enough to look after himself."

"It helps to have friends, though," I say. "Friends who'll look after you too."

But David stalks off down the back of the store without replying. And I decide that if *he* doesn't warn Adam about this next step, then I will.

Tad one / David nil

David   It's a parody – of sport, of theatre.

Only two days later, and David is flown to LA to appear on *Tad Alive*. For now he's talking uninterrupted – being given enough rope to hang himself and taking every opportunity to do so.

David   It's a parody of *real* sport. But it's cathartic, you know?
                 I didn't think much of it at first. In fact, I thought it was
                 ridiculous. But it gets you in. Part of it is, it hooks you like
                 a soap opera – nothing's ever finished. You gotta know what
                 happens next. You are *compelled* to tune in next week to see
                 how the cliffhanger ending resolves. Except that it doesn't
                 – it carries on to the following week, and the week after that,
                 and so on. But it also gets you in because it's cathartic.
                 Everyday life – it's frustrating. You feel like you wanna hit
                 something. The boss gives you a hard time, a customer
                 won't quit while they're ahead, a distributor won't talk a
                 deal, you feel like going home and kicking the cat, picking
                 an argument with your loved ones. Instead you can watch
                 the wrestling and work through all that vicariously. Work
                 through it *safely*, because it's not real. It's not as if someone
                 is suffering as a result of your aggression. I never could
                 watch a boxing match – because it *is* real. Pro wrestling is
                 cathartic because it's safe.

Tad   And yet you're saying that it *is* real.

David	In this one instance, yeah. The theatre of it, well, it's a mask this guy is hiding behind. Michael Rosen – he's Lucifer, he plays that character – he's just using the pretence of reality to actually *be* real. He's hurting this guy for real. My friend, Adam O'Connor. He's actually being assaulted on national television and no one's doing anything about it.
Tad	I'm confused.
David	Yeah, it's confusing. I think – what I think is that professional wrestling should be honest about what it is and what it's not –
Tad	It should come out of the closet.
David	Yeah – and then Michael Rosen and his kind won't have anywhere left to hide.
Tad	You're claiming that these two wrestlers in da Dub Dub Dub – that Lucifer is actually beating up Homosapien. Actually hurting him.
David	Yes. I think they call it a shooting match.
Tad	What?
David	They call it a shooting match when the violence becomes real.
Tad	So … now you're saying sometimes it *is* real. They even have a name for it.
David	Well, yeah, but –

You can see in his face that David knows he's just lost serious ground.

Tad	What does Homosapien think of this? Why isn't he telling us all about it? Why isn't he pressing charges for assault, if you're right?
David	Well, he won't talk about it. I guess it's in his contract. He has to maintain the illusion.
Tad	Huh.

The talk show host looks around, at the audience, at the band leader.

Tad	I think we'd better hear from him. What say we invite Homosapien on the show?

There is loud approval from the audience. I wonder if it isn't just for the idea of having a celebrity guest, rather than for Homosapien himself.

Tad	Maybe he can explain this a little clearer.

David   Look, no offence, but I don't think that's gonna work. If
                 you want the inside story, you should try for the owner, Jack
                 Dynes. He's the one who calls the shots.
Tad   Thank you, David Vigil …

He's trying to wind this up – and David's had his allotted five minutes
and then some, but he ain't near done yet.

David   The truth is more complex than the black–and–white of
                 lies. If they came out –
Tad   That's all we have time for.
David   – they could get away from these homophobic, racist, sexist,
                 fascist storylines and –

David doesn't know it, but all we see now is a close–up of Tad Scott
Foster shrugging off this loser. And then we go to a commercial break.

That could have gone better.

A tabloid asks the question

One of the national tabloids picks up on the story post–Tad, but it's only a
short piece, and obviously not intensively researched.

> ### *A FAKED SPORT?*
>
> *Professional wrestling – a sport unacknowledged by critics but always
> taking gold, silver or bronze in the ratings wars and worth millions
> annually in advertising and merchandising revenue – might be fake.*
>
> *Talk show host Tad Scott Foster's interviewee David Vigil last night
> claimed that pro wrestling was nothing more than a cathartic 'parody of
> real sport'. Jack Dynes, owner of and booker for the major federation World
> Wide Wrestling, was unavailable for comment. A WWW representative
> observed, 'With all due respect to Mr. Vigil, the man knows nothing about
> professional sport.'*

But this drop in the hard news ocean barely causes a ripple, and it seems
like the story is then dropped. Which no doubt means that the WWW
started breathing easier again.

Tad two / Adam nil

When Homosapien appears on the show a couple of nights later, everything seems fine. He's welcomed by an enthusiastic round of applause and cheering, Tad shakes his hand and pretends Homosapien's grip is crippling him, everyone's laughing good–naturedly. Homosapien looks happy, despite the black eye and split lip. Tad looks like he's Homosapien's new best friend.

That's when I should have smelt the rat.

They're sitting down now and the applause at last dies away. Tad is leaning forward, like he wants to talk about something confidential, but also like he's loving every minute of this. "Now, Homosapien – a friend of yours, David Vigil, he told us that you're forbidden to talk about pro wrestling."

Homosapien is totally unfazed. "As you'd know, Tad, there's some things that belong behind the scenes in professional sports. So, everyone involved has a clause in their contract that says they can't talk about those things."

"All right. But we invited you here tonight – in fact, we thought it was only fair to give you a right of reply. David Vigil was saying some things the other night that you might take exception to."

The smile never falters. "David is a good man, a clever man, and he *is* a friend of mine, but he has his opinions. He's entitled to his own opinions."

Tad nods sagely, acknowledging this. No doubt Adam was coached by Dynes, but so far it's working well. Even the crowd give a spontaneous burst of applause to show their approval.

Then the host casually comments, "You've got one hell of a shiner there!"

"Yes, I do."

"Where did you get that?"

"Wrestling is a physical sport, Tad. It's definitely a contact sport, no two ways about that!"

People laugh, but Tad follows up: "Was it a match with Lucifer?"

For the first time, Homosapien looks careful. Physically he's still at ease, but his face is wary. "It might have been. I have so many matches and I'm working out and training every day – sometimes it's hard to keep track."

"I would have noticed if someone did that to me!"

"Yeah, *you'd* notice, Tad," Homosapien replies with a forced laugh. "You're not fighting for a living."

"I don't know, it can get a little rough around here …"

The band leader and the band and the audience all crack up, like the lackeys they are. I wonder what the hell Candy sees in this guy, always trying to score off his guests, always trying to come out on top. Homosapien is enough of a gentleman – or maybe that's *enough of a professional wrestler* – to cooperate.

To everyone's hilarity, the two of them – Tad and Homosapien – get up now and do a mock shadow–boxing thing that looks completely unscripted. I can tell when Adam is making the talk show host look good, but he does it so naturally that you have to be looking hard.

They finish to roars of approval from the audience. Homosapien is truly wonderful – he lifts Tad's arm in victory. Like he knows exactly how all this works and how to play along. Then Tad stands there with his arm around Homosapien's shoulders. After a while he gestures for quiet, and then asks, "So, when can you come back?"

Homosapien smiles. "When do you want me?"

"Tomorrow night."

"I'll have to check with the boss, but I'd be happy to."

And the crowd roars again as we cut to a commercial break.

Phone call

"That went well," David says cautiously when Adam calls the next day.

"Yeah. Yeah, I think it did." He sounds a bit surprised about that.

Which is maybe why David says, "Um, Patrick says he's been thinking about it, and he's smelling a rat."

"Like what?"

David glances at me, and I shrug. But I am feeling a lot more suspicious now than I was during the actual broadcast. "He doesn't know."

"Well, I'm on again tonight. Mr. Dynes postponed a match for me."

"So, he's supporting this?"

"Yeah …"

We're all three silent for a long moment. Nothing's quite working out the way any of us figured it would.

"Watch it, all right?" Adam says. As if we wouldn't. "Emma's on with me this time."

"Cool," I say.

"Yeah," he says, a lot more certain now. "She's still the coolest thing in the federation."

Aw … best friends … They're so sweet.

Tad three / Adam nil

That night, Adam and Emma are sitting there next together on Tad Scott Foster's guest sofa, and everything seems to be going well. The audience appreciate Emma even more than they did Adam on the previous show. The conversation between host and guests is hardly the most profound thing you ever heard, but it's friendly and fun.

Then Tad says, "Homosapien – we put together some clips of your matches, and we wanna play them now."

Adam nods, pleased. "Sure."

"Why don't we all take a look at this?"

A monitor lowers into the space in front of the sofa, and its blue light flickers over Adam and Emma's faces. Then we cut to what they're seeing …

The first clip is of a match between Homosapien and Porn ☆. But we don't get to see the match. We don't get to see the wrestling. The clip just shows what happened afterwards, when Homosapien chased Porn ☆ round and round the ring. And the leer on his face makes it obvious the chase is about lust, not about wrestling.

Then they show the time when Caesar was pinning Homosapien, and our hero forced Caesar to break the pin by planting a kiss on him. Then another chase. Another kiss. A bit of unprovoked and unwanted flirtation.

You get the idea. It's well edited, I'll give them that, and set to just the sort of silent movie piano music I'd always heard in my own head for those chase scenes. But it's horrible. It's about making Adam look as foolish as they possibly can. Once David gets over his shock, he's gonna be furious.

The last clip is of an interview that Terry did with both Homosapien and Porn ☆. The outraged Porn ☆ is threatening to file a sexual harassment suit. Terry, stuck in between the two wrestlers, is trying not to squirm in distaste.

Porn ☆	It's illegal! There are laws against what this fairy does!
Homosapien	Not in this State, honey. Not in the privacy of my own bedroom.
Porn ☆	Sexual harassment! In the workplace!

Homosapien gives him a long long look, and then says very very suggestively. "Did you know that the ancient Greeks wrestled naked … ?"

Porn ☆ looks like he's just been hit by a train.

Homosapien	Terry? Perhaps we should have a traditional match. Return to our roots. I think I'm gonna suggest that to Mr. Dynes.

And on Terry's sickened face, the clips end and we're back on the set of *Tad Alive*.

The audience are going nuts – hooting and hollering and stamping their feet. Tad Scott Foster is looking very pleased with himself. Obnoxiously smug. Emma is shocked and trying to hide it. As for Adam – well, he's bright bright red and looking even more nauseous than Terry had. Emma slips her hand into Adam's, trying to be supportive, and he crushes it.

Once the audience quietens a bit, Tad asks, "What do you have to say for yourself, Adam O'Connor?"

For a long moment, Adam can't get any words out. But then he bursts.

Homosapien	You're distorting everything!
Tad	And you guys aren't … ?
Homosapien	You know – you know – that's not how I court someone in real life.
Tad	So professional wrestling isn't real life … ?
Homosapien	I never said that! You can't ever say I said that! Unless you manage to distort that too.

The host tries to speak, but Adam cuts him off with the angriest of gestures.

Homosapien	It's about putting your opponent off his game. It's like sledging in football, it's like talking shit before a boxing match. You annoy them, then they're not thinking about the match any more. They're not performing at their best.
Tad	So, everything we just saw … that was Homosapien? That's got nothing to do with Adam O'Connor? *Your* life? *Your* sexuality?

Adam grimaces. He is too angry and too humiliated to think straight. Maybe he's even a bit scared – of the reactions. Of what Jack Dynes will do to him. Given the topic that Adam himself just raised, maybe he should have taken a deep breath and backed off. But, instead, he did indeed think straight. Quite literally.

He stands up. Still holding her hand, he brings Emma up with him. Twirls her around and into his arms, then bends over her like he's Clark Gable in an old black–and–white. And he kisses her. A big, beautiful, romantic kiss. Except that it's a complete and utter lie.

She cooperates. Trusting him, going with him. But when they break apart afterwards, even though she's smiling at him, she looks troubled and she's too surprised to really hide it.

"Great Scott …" says the band leader. Enviously.

The audience are cat–calling. They all want to kiss Millennium too. I am gaping. David is – well, he's all of the above. Horrified, sickened, angry, humiliated, scared, troubled.

Tad Scott Foster – the bastard who managed to provoke all this – is looking even smugger than ever. We go to a close–up of him, and he just says, "We'll be back. Don't anyone go anywhere!"

Intrusion of the interlude

I am late to work. Not my usual late, but ninety minutes late. I put on my Nonchalant Face and walk smoothly in, saying, "Sorry! Sorry!"

David is on the phone and there are no prizes for guessing who he's talking to. He's looking troubled. Also kind of unsure, which is not something I'm used to seeing on his face. "Of *course* I wasn't jealous," he's saying in that tone he usually reserves for imbeciles. "Just – well, there goes your credibility. What were you thinking? *Were* you thinking?"

I wince. What stuff to say! So much for trying to meet poor Adam halfway. Anyway, at first David just gives me a generic frown, not wanting to be interrupted – but then he looks at me properly. Moments later, he's wound up the brewing argument, hung up the phone, and come chasing me down the back of the store.

"What happened to you?"

"Sorry I was late. Couldn't be helped. Just dock my pay, OK?"

"Your *arm*," David says.

I look down at my left arm as if I have no idea what he's talking about. It's in a plaster cast and a sling, and the white–washed–so–often–it's–grey sling just does *not* go with my outfit. Not that my outfit is very coordinated anyway. "Uh," I say intelligently.

"What happened?" He's fierce. I'm guessing he's angry about me being careless as well as late.

"I was at the hospital. There were twenty people ahead of me in ER."

*"How did you break your fucking **arm**, Patrick?"*

"There's this –" I am *not* going to cry. "There's this guy –" I am *NOT* going to cry. "You know?"

"Tell me."

"He makes me laugh!" I'm tearing up, God damn it to hell.

David is looking at me, very dubious.

"You'd think that was a good thing!" I manage to force out.

And then I'm wailing. It's all very embarrassing. Sobbing in this loud, hoarse, broken way. Making a spectacle of myself.

Enough said.

A while later, I come back from visiting that little hell–on–earth, and there I am curled up on the sofa, with David holding me. I mean *really* holding me. Wrapped around me. Just being very patient and very comforting. I am as flabbergasted at that as much as anything.

"It's OK," I say, trying to shift away. "I'm OK now."

"No, you're not," he says, arguing with me but in a quiet, friendly way. And he keeps hanging onto me.

Well, I didn't really want to move in the first place, so I stay there.

After a few minutes, he strokes my hair. Then he says, very gently, "You'd better tell me, Patrick. From the beginning."

"I don't know …"

"You should have told me before. When you had that black eye. I should have figured something was going on." David sighs. "You should have called me this morning. I'd have taken you to the hospital."

"No, it was six in the morning," I mumble. "Six in the morning, and there were already twenty people there."

David tightens his arms round me for a moment – and even though he whispers, he's just as fierce as when he was yelling. *"You don't have to do that stuff **alone**, Patrick."*

OK, that was when I started crying again. Well, weeping anyway. And then I told him. I'll save you the details and all the sniffy bits. It's about Mr. Tall, Dark & Intense. Of course.

See, just about every time he touched me, well, he tickled me. Not his intention. There we'd be, in the middle of doing the wild thing, and a caress or even just him moving against me would set me off giggling. The kind of giggling that would not stop. And he did not take kindly to that. He did not like the notion that I was laughing at *him*. Not that I was, but – but I guess he was a bit sensitive in the old Ego Department. I guess he tended to take things personally. I guess he could do with an anger management course or two. Or three.

When I was finally done, David was quiet for a while. Then he said, "You should press charges."

"For what?"

"Assault. He broke your *arm*."

I sigh. "No one else gets to know all that. No one!"

Another moment passes. Then David says, "Next time Adam's in town …"

"What? You'll send the boys around?"

"Yeah. Hell, we'll send the girl! Emma could kick his ass to LA and back. Teach this jerk a lesson or two."

"David …"

"Well, we gotta make sure he knows it's over!"

"He knows," I say grimly.

"How?"

"Give me *some* credit! I told him. For once I really told him. And I think he believed me. Hey, I *know* he believed me. It was the blood that did it. You gotta believe someone who's dripping blood on your carpet, don't you? Someone who won't go get himself fixed up until you *listen*, right?"

"Right," David said. And then he just held me some more.

Who said he's not my friend … ? When I finally got my act together, I even discovered he'd got one of the customers to turn the 'open' sign to 'closed' on her way out.

Least likely to …

Homosapien calls. David doesn't have much to say, so there's more silence than talking. Which, given how caustic David can get when he's angry, maybe isn't a bad thing. Eventually:

Homosapien You give Patrick a hard time?

David What?

Homosapien That day he was late. You sounded real mad. Figured you were gonna fire him.

David Oh. No. No, he had his reasons.

More silence, in which David does not explain what they are.

Homosapien Uh, David?

David Yeah?

Homosapien I wish – I wish that … uh …

David sighs.

David Yeah, I know. But we were never gonna get voted Most Likely To Succeed, were we?

There's an even longer silence. I wonder if Adam knew that was coming. *I* didn't. When Adam finally replies, it's in a very small voice.

Homosapien I guess not.

David I'm sorry.

Homosapien OK. I mean, no, it's *not* OK, but let's not … Look, can I call you from LA? We can still talk, right?

David Yeah, I guess.

And they both sigh.

Going to the fair

There is a charity event in Los Angeles for kids with cancer, which is run like a country fair. The kids wander round in the sunshine eating candy floss, and there are rides to go on and events to watch. The WWW is participating. Homosapien and Millennium are there along with a few other stars, the two of them wandering around arm in arm, signing autographs and posing for pictures with the kids. And then Homosapien has a match against Blue, who of course the kids tend to adore. He's a *super*hero.

They keep it fairly short and sweet. More a display of technique than aggression. The kids enjoy it, but what they really enjoy is when one of the wandering clowns stops by and begins heckling our wrestlers. "Go on!" he calls to Homosapien. "Get him! Ah, come *on* – my *mother* can fight better than you."

Homosapien and Blue try to ignore him, but you can tell by their glares that the clown's getting to them. The kids giggle, lapping it up.

"You're like kittens playing with a ball of string! Just one of you hit the other and get it over with!"

After their usual back–and–forth tumble, Blue ends up pinning Homosapien. The ref gives him the three count and Blue springs up, lifting his arms in victory. Homosapien retires to his corner and leans on the ropes, panting.

The clown blows a loud raspberry and turns away.

"Hey!" Blue cries out. "Hey, you with the attitude!"

The kids all know who he means; they look up at the clown, who freezes as if suddenly scared. As the kids back away from him, the clown turns around.

"You think you can do better?"

"Yeah." Though he doesn't sound so sure of himself now. "I guess."

"Come on, then!" And Blue beckons to him.

The kids aren't so sure about this either. They watch in silence as the clown warily climbs into the ring. The clown and Blue circle around, sizing each other up. Homosapien watches eagerly, calling support and advice to his former opponent.

Finally Blue gets frustrated enough to swing a punch at the clown's big red nose. The kids gasp. But as the punch lands, the nose makes a honking sound. The clown staggers back a step. Blue frowns, follows him, and tries again. Honk! A few of the kids laugh.

Blue punches the clown in the gut, causing a reverberating rusty spring sound. Another punch, with sound effects worthy of Wile E. Coyote. The kids are giggling again. The clown folds in half, barely even able to defend himself, let alone fight.

Dragging him upright, Blue grasps the clown round the throat, and lifts him up until he's dangling there at arm's length. The clown's feet are paddling around as if he's trying to walk on air, his long pointy shoes brushing the floor of the ring. Blue holds him there for a long moment. And then tosses the clown down onto his back in a classic Chokeslam. There's a trampoline noise, and sure enough the clown bounces up a few inches before landing again, bounces and settles. He lies there spread-eagled. Defeated.

Homosapien comes over to shake Blue's hand in congratulation and then lifts his arm for the approval of the crowd. The kids laugh and cheer. They're having a ball. Blue, Homosapien and Millennium sign some more autographs, pose for some more pictures with their fans. The sun shines in a perfect blue sky. It's easy to forget that some of these kids won't see the year out.

"You entertain these poor children by beating up a *clown*?!" David is gaping. Adam has called him during a break.

"He was heckling us!" Adam protests.

"Those kids are gonna be traumatized! It's like beating up Santa Claus!"

"Nah. Santa Claus is always a Good Guy, but clowns are heels as often as faces."

"I can't believe you beat up some clown," David mutters.

Adam clears his throat. "It was just Fixx in a clown suit."

"Oh." David thinks about this. "Oh! OK, I get it. A plant. It's like the shows they put on at carnivals, back in the late 1800s."

"Carnivals?"

"Yeah, back when wrestling first came to America. They'd put on Athletic Shows where the wrestlers challenged the locals for $25 a match. Except the carneys would rig it so that the wrestlers always won. The local might be a plant. Or if he was for real, and if he was any good, they'd just hit him on the head with a two-by-four."

"Uh," was Adam's only response.

"You don't know all this stuff?"

"You *do?*"

David laughs, though not as if he finds it very funny. "They should teach you guys The History Of Wrestling 101. But it's not all bad. Abraham Lincoln was a wrestler. George Washington was the champion of Virginia."

"Yeah? Amateur wrestling, though."

"Oh. Yeah, I guess."

Adam takes a moment before saying, "I've got to go, David. We've got another match."

"Another clown?"

"Nah. This time it's a reporter."

"A reporter?!"

"Fixx in a suit and tie. I'll tell you afterwards. Gotta go."

It's evening now. The young kids have gone home, and the fair is swarming with teenagers instead. Teens with cancer.

This time the wrestling match is between Homosapien and Lucifer. Homosapien figures that's because a match between him and Lucifer is about as real as it's gonna get. And the heckler is indeed Fixx in a business suit and a bad tie, complete with a Media Pass pinned to his lapel and a camera slung round his neck. "Oh, come *on!* This ain't real!"

The two wrestlers, slugging it out, shoot glares at him.

"We all know it's fake! Right?" he asks the crowd. The teenagers mostly shrug him off; they just wanna watch the match. "Fakers! Fakers! Fakers!"

As if to prove him wrong, Lucifer slips out of a hold and slams a fist into Homosapien, which he only just manages to deflect.

"Bunch of pussies!" the heckler continues. "My *mother* could take you on! My *grandmother* could!"

Eventually, following the agreed script, Homosapien takes the fall.

The crowd cheer as the referee lifts Lucifer's arm in victory. But Lucifer breaks away. Stepping up onto the bottom rope and leaning out over the top, he stabs a finger at the heckler. "Who you calling a pussy?"

The heckler backs up a little, but the crowd close in behind him. "Me? No, I, uh …"

"You so sure it's fake? You get on in here and I'll show you how fake it is!"

The heckler is quickly finished off with one serious Spear Tackle and no amusing sound effects.

Still more autographs. This time all the wrestlers are sitting along one side of a table while the fans file past them. Homosapien discovers that any time Lucifer is presented with a magazine or publicity shot that includes Homosapien, his image gets defaced with googly-eyed glasses or a goatee or even the word FAGGOT scrawled across his chest. He smiles for the fans and shrugs it off, as if this is just a joke and the natural result of Michael being in persona. It's not, of course. Even if Jack Dynes is happy about the matches being real, he wouldn't be happy with this. It's going way too far. But Adam just grins and bears it and signs yet another autograph.

Late that night Adam heads back to the team's hotel, alone. When he gets there, though, the rather startled receptionist informs him that his room was cancelled earlier that evening, and that the hotel is now full. Adam sighs. But if that was a prank of Michael Rosen's, then it backfires, because Adam sleeps in Emma's room instead. And over breakfast the following morning, they don't bother pretending that they didn't share a bed.

Phone calls

Adam has his usual three days off, but he doesn't come to Boston. He apologizes to both me and David and explains that he has stuff to take care of back home – which is indeed Tulsa, Oklahoma rather than San Francisco. But it's hard not to feel that this unexpected romance is pretty much over, even though Adam and David still talk on the phone every other day or so.

Perhaps they can be friends. Perhaps we can all still be friends. I've often thought that friends are the most important thing for gays. Families often don't survive the coming out process and boyfriends come and go, but friends are friends are friends. So maybe there's no harm in Adam and David being friends. It just seems a pity, is all.

Anyway, David has gathered a few heavy academic tomes about wrestling, though he says there isn't much out there. I just flip through them for the pictures, but he actually reads them and thinks about them – and then he talks to Adam about them, which is hardly gonna revive the romance.

David	Some academics link professional wrestling to the medieval morality plays.
Adam	You're kidding me. *Morality* plays?
David	Yeah, it's all about these larger–than–life battles between Good and Evil, Vice and Virtue, Justice and Injustice. Heels and Faces, right?
Adam	I figured it's about what it is to be a man. And what it isn't.
David	Absolutely. And you're challenging that. Like, being a masculine kind of man can include being gay.
Adam	You make it sound like pro wrestling is a *good* thing.
David	Um, well, actually I think maybe it is. Or it can be. Or something …
Adam	Most people – if they're not fans – most people think it's stupid.
David	But if they actually *watched* it and *thought* about it … Well, actually, a lot of what happens on the surface is still pretty stupid. As if they always have an eye on the lowest common denominator.
Adam	What? Now you're talking math … ?

Yeah, it's kind of dispiriting. But hey at least they're still talking.

Singles match

Heavy metal music blares from the speakers.

announcer	Born and raised in Thunder Bay, Ontario, and weighing in at 306 pounds, let's welcome the man known as Brute by name and brute by nature!

The crowd go wild. Brute is, of course, a heel, so he draws a lot of booing. But he's popular with the redneck contingent, so there's a lot of cheering as well. Which all basically adds up to a lot of noisy approval.

Then Our Song kicks in.

announcer	And now, at a weight of 243 pounds, a man who claims *your* home town of San Francisco as *his* home town – accompanied tonight by the one and only Millennium – heeerrre's *Homosapien!*

Our Hero gets the usual mixed reaction, although this time there's a determined amount of cheering which I figure must be a representative group from the SF gay community. It's nice that they've taken Homosapien to their hearts enough to brave the rednecks.

And to prove my point the camera zooms in on a group of guys all dressed in the same shade of purple as Our Man, holding up signs saying things like *Homosapien: Out and Proud* and *Lynch the Rednecks* and *You go, girl!*

Despite all of which, Homosapien still doesn't dance to his music like he used to. He just strides out with Millennium pacing at his shoulder and they both look pretty grim. The days of Homosapien being happy and up–beat no matter what the crowd threw at him are mostly gone. And I miss them.

What he does do, though, is leap the guard rails and go through the audience to his little fan club, where he shakes hands and even submits to a hug 'n' a kiss from one guy. Homosapien smiles for them, though it's the kind of stoically grateful smile you usually find at funerals.

Finally the match begins. And the match is just kind of dogged and grim too. It only lasts about five minutes, and it's more about thuggery than athleticism. Nevertheless, with his home town – well, with a portion of his home town behind him, Homosapien wins. He has beaten Brute down enough that once Homosapien puts the Chinlock on him, Brute just sags and then crumples and it's all over.

The referee lifts Homosapien's right hand in victory and Millennium comes into the ring to lift up his left hand too. Homosapien and Millennium are pleased, even though the crowd is mostly unresponsive. The cameras zoom in on Our Fan Club, who are ecstatically bouncing and cheering.

But one of them gapes at the ring, then his ecstasy turns into alarm. He grabs his friend's arm and points at what's happening.

Finally the cameras cut back to the ring. Lucifer and Caesar have run out. And Caesar is on the apron, holding Millennium back against the ropes. She twists and struggles and hollers, but can't get free. The beaten Brute drags himself over to prop himself at her feet and winds his arms around her legs, taking the opportunity to cop a feel. He gets a heel dug into his thigh for his trouble before he secures his grip.

As the camera pans across into the centre of the ring, I don't know whether I really want to see what else is happening. But, yeah, as you probably guessed, Lucifer is there laying into Homosapien. Having been caught unawares, Homosapien never had much of a chance. Under a rain of blows he falls to one knee, receives a vicious kick to his ribs, and he's down. There are catcalls and laughter from the rednecks and protests from the gays. Millennium screams in fury.

But then the *Blues Brothers* music thumps out, and the crowd pops. It's Blue!

Blue runs out, still calling back over his shoulder and beckoning as if marshalling a whole posse. And he crashes up into Caesar, felling him with one blow. Millennium is now free to deal with Brute – a swinging punch and a swift kick is all it takes. The two thugs retreat halfway up the ramp before Blue or Millennium can punish them any further.

Which leaves Lucifer still laying into Our Hero. Blue and Millennium loom up behind him. Everything goes very very quiet. Belatedly Lucifer realizes something is up and looks around. Does a double take to find himself alone with three foes. Which is when Blue and Millennium link arms and run at him, toppling Lucifer with a double Clothesline. He drags himself out of the ring and follows the other two bad guys up the ramp.

Homosapien struggles to his feet. Millennium gives him a hug and he leans on her, putting an arm round her shoulders just to stay upright. Then he holds out his right hand to Blue, offering to shake hands to say thanks.

Blue looks at him for a long moment. Looks out at the crowd, considering. This is momentous. He probably only ran out here for Millennium's sake, being a gentleman who hates seeing the odds stacked that high against a lady. But now he's being asked to align himself with the queer who's maybe blown pro wrestling's biggest secret.

Our Fan Club are going crazy, shouting their encouragement, jumping around, waving their signs. *It's cool to be queer* indeed. The rest of the crowd are either silent or supportive. Basically Blue is so popular with such a vast majority of the fans, that he'll be loved despite anything. The rednecks who are *too* rednecked to like him are just sitting back in their seats like they don't care.

After long long moments of anticipation, Blue steps forward, and shakes Homosapien by the hand. Which is met by cheering and applause. Homosapien smiles, and softens, and looks happier than he has for a long while. Blue walks beside them as Millennium helps Homosapien back up the ramp.

Blue, the WWW's Ultimate Good Guy, has chosen a side. And, best of all, it's *our* side.

The tabloid asks again

The tabloid that ran the short piece *A FAKED SPORT?* now prints a longer investigative story titled *Pro Wrestling: The Truth Is Somewhere Out There*. The reporter bypasses the WWW and concentrates on a smaller federation and training school run out of Georgia. Here's a couple of bits.

> *I am met with hostility. 'You call this fake?' one of the trainees asks me, showing me serious, colorful bruising across his back. 'You get in here and you try it.' I decline his invitation; no one's arguing that these men aren't strong athletes or that there aren't risks involved. Nevertheless, the training session I'm permitted to watch does seem to be about the wrestlers going through the motions of a fight, especially when compared with the boxing training session being conducted in the same gym. I wonder if the training session itself is staged for my benefit.*
>
> *When I ask the Georgian booker if the match results are fixed, he denies it, then refuses to talk to me any further and soon has me escorted off the premises.*

The journalist concludes:

> *Is professional wrestling fake? The jury, only recently alerted to the charge, is definitely still out. But it's a charge worth investigating – if for no other reason than millions of fans spending millions of dollars annually deserve to know the truth.*

I figure the question isn't going to go away now. David seems a bit ambivalent about his part in raising the question in the first place given that it seems to have done as much harm as good. And he still worries over Adam's matches with Michael Rosen. Of course we both do. But turning the spotlight onto pro wrestling doesn't seem to have changed any of that. If anything, it's made it all worse, because it's given the other wrestlers something else to resent Adam for.

The *Sharpshooter* reporter John Gurrie calls David, and says he's working on the in–depth insider's article he wants to run.

David   Your editor changed his mind?

Gurrie	No, but he'll have to sooner or later and I wanna be ready. Christ, I told him we should break this ourselves, but he wouldn't hear of it. Said it's too big a can of worms.
David	Yeah. Pandora's box.
Gurrie	So I was wondering if I can interview you, as part of the background about how the story broke.
David	Uh. I don't know.
Gurrie	You were *looking* for a chance to speak not so long ago.
David	I don't know that it won't just make things even worse.
Gurrie	For your friend Adam? But it's like you said, better out than in.
David	I used to believe that. Now I'm not so sure.
Gurrie	*I'm* sure. Look, you think about it and I'll call you again in a few days. I'll be writing about what you've said anyway. It's on the public record. You wanna add something, you let me interview you.

David sighs, ends the call, and sits there looking totally deflated. I remember Adam saying he loved David for being a righteous man, but I'm sure Adam would love him still even though they've both had the stuffing knocked out of them. Call me a romantic ("You're a romantic!") but I'm sure he would if he had the chance.

Working out

Adam is working out in the WWW's gym in Chicago; alone, because Emma is out of town with some family stuff. He hears the familiar sounds of training from the next room, though Sam seems a bit subdued and for once isn't yelling at his charges. Then Adam hears Jack Dynes' voice too, and not only becomes curious but decides to go thank his boss once more for the win in San Francisco.

As he nears the door to the training room, Adam catches an unknown (male) voice saying, "Yeah, I'm game. Lots of eyeliner, and one of those little black beauty spots, just *here* …"

"And if we ever win the tag team belts, sir, we should demand matching handbags. You know – handbags that match the belts."

"*Man*–bags." (Obviously a *Friends* fan.)

Jack Dynes says, "Yuh. That's clever."

"That was Karen's idea," says the second unknown (male) voice. "Karen's my girlfriend, sir."

Adam opens the door, but waits there about halfway in, not sure what he'll find or whether he's welcome. Sam looks at him unhappily. There are two young wrestlers in the ring, leaning on the ropes to talk to Dynes; they stand respectfully when they see who it is, but look to the boss to say something first.

"Well, well – Adam O'Connor," says Dynes, holding out his right hand.

Adam walks over to shake hands. "Morning, sir. Morning, Sam." Then he waits, looking at the new guys.

Dynes introduces him. "Adam, this is Nick and Clancy." The two of them reach down to shake hands. "We're calling them Butch and Sundance. They're going to be running with the gay antics angle."

"You really paved the way, man," Nick says reverently. "You can draw a lot of heat with that stuff."

Adam is too shocked to say anything. On the one hand, he never really liked the antics anyway. On the other hand – well, where does this leave him? He hadn't planned on being obsolete already.

"I know you've been wanting to get back to the more serious persona."

"Yes, sir," he manages to reply. And that's true, except … Adam's doubts are doubled by the fact that Sam is watching him with obvious misgivings. "Thank you, sir." And Adam manages to get out of there.

He calls Emma, and explains the situation. She's quiet for a long time before replying.

Emma   You've got everything going for you, Adam.

Adam   I'm being replaced! I'll be redundant!

Emma   You've got Blue on your side now, not just Millennium –

Adam   Hey, you are *so* over with the crowd, Emma.

(I should explain the wrestling–speak. Being *over* with the crowd doesn't mean you're done, you're finished – it means you've reached them and you're getting lots of heat in return.)

Adam   They love you, Emma. I don't need anyone else.

Emma You've got *Blue*, Adam – for God's sake! And the fans know you. A *lot* of them respect you; some of them adore you. How much courage did it take for those gay guys to show up in San Francisco? Given the usual crowd, they were taking one helluva risk.

Adam Yeah, I know. But I, uh – Well, what's your point?

Emma What's the one thing Jack Dynes always said you needed?

Another silence stretches.

Adam Yeah, all right. The passion.

Emma He said you've got to want it.

Adam I've done nothing but wrestle for *years*. How can he say I don't want it?

Emma But do you want it *badly enough*, Adam? Because it's all there for you if you do.

Adam I love you, Em, but I've gotta go.

Emma Love you too, Adam. I really do.

Adam says goodbye and hangs up. He sighs, and drops his head into his hands. That wasn't what he'd expected. But there's a little voice inside of him that knows it's what he needed.

Another intrusion

Mr. Tall, Dark & Intense strolls past the store one day while I'm at the front counter. He stares at me through the window. I freeze for a moment. The cast on my arm isn't due to come off for a while yet, but at least I'm not wearing the sling any more. My arm aches.

He lifts his hand as he gets to the door, as if he's about to push it open and come in. I pick up the phone, let my finger hover over the 9. Stare back at him, as if daring him, though I really don't have the chutzpah to dare him. He used to know that. Probably still does.

But whether it's the threat of a 911 call or the fact that David suddenly looms behind me (though with no intent other than serving a customer), Mr. TDI changes his mind, drops his hand, steps back. Throws me one last glare and then keeps on strolling down the sidewalk, shoulders at ease, as if he doesn't have anything to fear from us. Which he probably doesn't, let's face it.

I wonder how long this will go on for.

Butch and Sundance

David starts coming to my place to watch the wrestling, on the evenings when the store closes early (rather than his previous practice of insisting I just tape the shows for him to fast–forward through later). We sit on the sofa together, and have a glass or two of something. He's actually teaching me how to appreciate wine. The expensive sort that isn't just about the buzz or the fizz. There was this one time when he brought over some red wine, along with pears and cheese, which I thought was an odd kind of combination – but the flavors all together like that were a revelation.

Anyway, this isn't a story about wine, is it?

David and I are sipping on something sparkling and light and sweet, which makes me sad in a beautiful sort of way … Um, David and I are watching a show broadcast from Buffalo, New York (which means that the WWW – and, more to the point, Adam – will be back in Boston again soon, but we carefully avoid any mention of that). The show returns from an ad break to the inspiringly bouncy notes of Jimmy Somerville's *You Make Me Feel (Mighty Real)*. David and I both sit up. Actually, it's a wonder we don't stand up and start dancing – that's how inspirational this song usually is. But it's so totally unexpected to hear Jimmy Somerville in the midst of a pro wrestling show that we just sit there wondering.

A pair of wrestlers appear at the head of the ramp, a spring in their step and a swing in their hips. They look like they're planning on reforming the Village People.

announcer   Let's give a warm Buffalo welcome to the WWW's newest tag team, Butch and *Sun*–daaaaance! At a combined weight of 333 pounds, Butch and Sundance hail from Blythe, Cal–i–*forn*–i–a … !

David and I exchange glances. All the clues scream *camp*.

Patrick   He didn't tell you about this, right?

David   Not a word.

Butch is dressed – well, *barely* dressed – as a cowboy, with no shirt under his waistcoat and only snug–fitting, side–laced leather shorts under fringed chaps. He gyrates along with the music, and then suddenly pulls a long six–shooter out of nowhere, and caresses the barrel, blows imaginary smoke away from the tip. Hhhmmm … As for Sundance, he's obviously at least part Native American, and gorgeous with it. The soft leather loincloth and boots are a bit of a worry, though – they'd be quite acceptably traditional if they weren't dyed such a bright pink. His long dark hair mostly falls loose round his shoulders, with a few slim braids and three long pink feathers as adornment. His brown skin is decorated with paint in ways that cleverly emphasize the svelte, supple moves of his body. Whoever did *that* knew exactly what they were doing. A real professional. (Hey, *I* should be paid for such work …)

Once the pair reach the ring, we get a close–up of Butch's face, and it's immediately clear that Sundance isn't the only one wearing war–paint. Butch is daubed with mascara and about a ton of eyeliner, along with a beauty spot cunningly placed high on a cheekbone. Again, the way it's done, it looks good on him.

If the crowd weren't sure how to react before, they're totally clear by now. A round of booing and jeering breaks out. Butch grins, as if he's only been waiting for the heat. He grabs Sundance's hand and twirls him around as the music still bounces along; pulls Sundance into a close embrace, their arms around each other's waists. Then Butch dips him, just like the old dance move, and draws him up slowly … into a kiss …

The crowd hate it. Me, I'm watching with my jaw dropped down around my ankles. I'd like it if it wasn't for … "What about Homosapien?" I ask. I clear my throat, sit up straighter. "What about Homosapien!" I protest.

"I know," says David, quietly worried. "I know!"

The Gothic good guy Louis du Lac and the good Bizarro brother are announced as the challenging tag team, and they run out to the ring as if they really mean business. Which they do. The more that Butch and Sundance camp it up, the more determined their opponents become and the louder the crowd get. It's a good match if you judge it by the heat generated – the audience are on their feet for most of it, and they really *care* about the result. They want the queers to get beaten into the ground.

As for me, I admit I'd liked the look of Butch and Sundance at first, but they get more and more nelly as the match continues – as if the whole idea had been for them to really run with the gay antics that Adam complained about being saddled with. As the noise builds, Butch and Sundance's confidence builds with it. I'm not against a bit of nelliness in Real Life. (I mean, Candy's my third favorite Bostonian, though she must be up there among the five nelliest people on the planet.) But this can't be real. This must be satire. They're only doing it to provoke the worst in people.

"Patrick," David says, calling my attention back to the screen.

I look up in time to see our own Homosapien. A camera has found him watching the match on a monitor backstage and he's obviously thinking it all a bit incomprehensible and a lot distasteful.

Glancing at David, I see he's sort of shrunk back into the corner of the sofa. He literally seems smaller and he's gone quietly still. Regretful. Maybe even yearning. Thinking back, I can't remember the last time that Adam even called him. It must be almost a couple of weeks now. Even when I feared the romance was all over, Adam was still calling every other day. As if they could at least be friends. But I guess not any more.

Anyway, the camera stays on Homosapien for a few moments, as he stares – arms crossed and face wincing – at the monitor. But finally the match comes to an end and we are back ringside. The Good Guys win, of course, and the crowd goes wild at the result. Butch and Sundance limp off up the ramp, holding each other up. There isn't a shred of sympathy for them in the whole arena.

Even while du Lac and Bizarro are receiving their victory cheers, we cut back to the corridor where we found Homosapien. He was walking away from the monitor, but the roving interviewer has caught him before he gets very far.

interviewer	We've just seen Butch and Sundance's debut match – and, Homosapien, I noticed that *you* were watching with interest. Are they friends of yours?
Homosapien	No, sir.
interviewer	*More* than friends, then … ?
Homosapien	*No*, sir, they are *not*.

The camera suddenly pans away from Homosapien, and we see that Butch and Sundance are walking past, still limping along in each other's arms. They catch sight of Homosapien, and swerve closer. Smiling, as if certain of his approval.

Butch   Hey, man. Not too bad for our first match, right? We'll get them next time, yeah?

Homosapien is glowering at them.

Sundance   My people have a saying about winning –
Homosapien   It was a *farce!*
Butch   What?
Homosapien   You heard me – that match was a *farce*. Wrestling is the oldest sport in the world. And you disrespected it.

Butch and Sundance look up at him, wounded, woebegone. Their embrace tightens, as if they're consoling each other. Homosapien presses closer, furious.

Homosapien   Forget about gay pride! Forget about *any* kind of pride! You'd do *anything* for a paycheck, wouldn't you? Obviously, you'd sell your *dignity*.

Under this onslaught Butch, at least, starts to recover a scrap of defiance.

Butch   Well, yeah …
Homosapien   So, you took the oldest sport in the world … the oldest sport with a history that deserves our respect … and you made it look like *the second oldest profession!*

I guffaw at this. I can't help it – I let out a big old guffaw.

And – strange tales but true – David is smiling, though it's kind of wry and weary. "He got that line from me," David says. "The second oldest profession. He got that from me."

I grin at him and jump into my friend's arms. Cleverness never looked so sexy …

Boston

So, the WWW descend on Boston again, and – as if to make up for not visiting during his three days off – Adam arrives in town on the very first flight that morning and strolls into the bookstore looking hunkier than ever. It's still early–ish, so David sends me up to Apollo's for a round of coffee and tells Adam to go with me. Which is kind of cool. We talk, me and the pro wrestler – or, rather, I natter away, and he listens and smiles and nods and he laughs in exactly the right places. I hardly draw breath. When we get back to Q4, I hand over David's doppio, then Adam and I settle into the sofas down the back and just keep on talking.

"Why don't you two go out and grab some lunch?"

I look around. David is nearby, shelving the new books that came in yesterday. "Lunch?" I ask.

"Yeah." He glances at us over his shoulder. "Take Adam to Reverie. They do the best seafood." David turns to consider Adam. "You like seafood?"

"Uh … yeah." Adam seems about as thrown as I am. We both look at the clock, which does indeed say it's almost one. "What about you?"

"I'm good. Bring me back something. Spaghetti marinara, if it's on today."

"Yeah, OK." Adam stands up, glances at me. I get up too. So, we're going to Reverie for seafood. Just the two of us. I'm rather relieved when Adam deliberately goes over and plants a kiss on David's cheek before we head off.

Adam and I are quiet for a while as we stroll down Whitman in the last of the summer's warmth, and take the first turn. I am musing, trying to figure out what feels wrong. There's nothing wrong, surely. But something's sort of skewed.

"Hey, Patrick – if you see that guy around," says Adam, "you tell me."

When I look at him, he tips his head in the direction of my plaster cast (which is due to come off on Monday). I look down at it dully, suddenly realizing that I spent the morning telling Adam (among other things) all about Mr. TDI. He knows more than even David now. "Why?" I ask. "You gonna beat him up for me?"

"It would be my pleasure." There's a furious glint in his eye.

My insides turn to mush. Not at the thought of the violence, justified or not, but instead at the thought of having my very own Knight In Shining Armor.

As if he knows all about my mushy insides, Adam is suddenly right beside me with his arm around my waist. It's nice. So I slip mine around his too. And we keep on walking, in the easiest of rhythms, fitting together warm and snug.

We just keep talking for the rest of the day, at Reverie, then back at the bookstore. As you probably figured, Adam brought me up to speed on his side of The Story So Far. But finally he has to go get ready. "You two wanna come to the show tonight?"

"Really?!" I exclaim in glee. "The wrestling?!"

"Well, yeah," he says, rolling his eyes. "I ain't in the ballet."

I look at David. He has a sad kind of smile on his face. "You go," he says to me.

"No, we should *both* go."

"I can't get away till closing time – that's eight on a Saturday," he explains to Adam. "Patrick, you should go. You know you want to."

But I am full of doubts. I can't even quite say why. "Nah. Maybe next time." I look around the store, suddenly realizing that I haven't done an ounce of work that day. "I should be shelving those books for you."

"I'm almost done. It's been quiet today, if you hadn't noticed."

I sigh, and look up at Adam. "So, yeah, maybe next time."

"Sure." He gives me a quick hug, friendly like. I return it, then back off, feeling confused. Adam and David exchange a farewell kiss – just cheek to cheek, though – and then he's gone.

I start helping with the books; together David and I work along the last section of shelves in silence.

When the phone rings, David goes to answer it. "Q4 bookstore." He glances at me. "Yeah," he says to the caller. "Did you forget something?" It must be Adam. "Oh, OK. Yeah. Not till ten. Yeah, OK, sure. See you then." He hangs up.

"What?" I ask.

"Breakfast tomorrow. He wants us to meet him and Emma at their hotel."

"Yeah?"

"So I'll pick you up at seven–thirty."

"OK. Yeah." I sigh again. I don't even protest at the uncivilized hour I'll have to get out of bed on a Sunday morning. Something's going wrong.

I watch the wrestling – a delayed telecast – by myself that night. It isn't as much fun watching it alone as watching it with the old curmudgeon, not any more.

So, when we get to the hotel, Adam and Emma are already in the restaurant drinking coffee. Hugs and kisses all round, then an urgent request for more coffee. A sweet young waiter sashays in with the coffee pot, and seems to be cruising Adam even while pouring. Obviously multi–skilled.

David starts talking with Emma about really mundane stuff, though she seems happy enough, which leaves me to resume yesterday's conversation with Adam. Which is nice.

After a much–needed coffee, we all manage to tear ourselves away long enough to visit the all–you–can–eat buffet. David and I are back at the table *way* before the two wrestlers, who come back with plate–loads of sausages, bacon, eggs, hash–browns, toast, you name it.

Emma glances at David's small bowl of muesli and yoghurt. "I'll be working out later," she says, a bit defensive.

"I won't!" he cheerfully responds.

The waiter returns with the coffee pot. He is definitely cruising Adam. And who can blame him? The man is delicious even at eight in the morning. I glance at David, but he seems oblivious. And he probably wouldn't mind anyway; he's never been the insecure type who can't cope with a bit of flirting. And of course he and Adam aren't exactly the Big Romance any more. Though they should be, in my not–so–humble opinion.

In ones and twos the other WWW wrestlers start appearing, some of them more awake than others, some of them louder than others. The other breakfasting guests, young and old and in–between, stare with confusion or worship or fear at these imposing men and their assorted companions. The wrestlers pointedly ignore our two friends, and gather round a long table that's obviously been reserved for them. The kitchen staff step it up a notch or two, bringing out pan after pan of sausages and eggs. Our waiter is faithful to Adam and doesn't cruise anyone else. Probably because he values his life.

For a while I keep my eye on the other wrestlers, hoping that Butch and Sundance will turn up, even though they weren't in the show last night. But they don't. (Oh, and luckily Michael Rosen isn't there either. I'm sure David wouldn't be able to resist confronting him.) Anyway, I belatedly wonder why

I didn't ask Adam about Butch and Sundance the day before. I guess we spent the whole day talking about ourselves! So I ask him now.

Adam exchanges a look with Emma. "I don't know," he says. "I guess I made it clear I didn't want to do the farcical stuff. I didn't know they'd bring in two new guys who *would*."

"So, where does that leave you?" David asks.

"Like I said, I don't know." Adam is obviously really uncomfortable with this. No wonder he didn't mention it yesterday, even though he brought me up to date otherwise. He sighs. "More like you, maybe," Adam says, looking at David. "More serious, more righteous. More about –" he lowers his voice, there being kids nearby – "more about gay rights, and stuff."

David looks completely taken aback. "Oh." I guess he never thought of himself as a model for a wrestling character before. "But won't that, uh …" He trails off. Suddenly looks troubled. Embarrassed, even. "Well, what do I know? If you think that'll work …"

"I could get a tattoo," Adam muses. "The rainbow flag, the gay pride thing; on my chest, like I'm wearing a pin."

Both David and Adam are frowning now. There's something here that neither is happy about.

Emma takes the cue and changes the subject; tells us about the latest scrape her young niece and nephew got into. It's a funny story, and we're all laughing by the end of it. (The waiter winks at Adam as he whisks round with more coffee, God bless him.)

"You know the kids have been dying to meet you," Emma says to Adam. "Next time we're in Portland, I'll take you there for the afternoon. If we're lucky, Peter will put on one of his world famous barbecues."

Adam is amazed. "But your brother doesn't approve of pro wrestling."

"Yeah, they *didn't* approve. But the kids got to pestering them so much, he and Sherry actually sat down and watched a show – remember that match we had in Kansas City against Fixx and Porn ☆? It was pretty funny. Athletic too. They decided that what Big Sis does for a living isn't so evil after all."

"That's great. Yeah, of course – I'd be happy to meet them."

With excellent timing, the little girl from the family at the next table finally gets game enough to come ask Emma for an autograph. "Sure," Emma responds with a smile. She reaches into her handbag (as if it's a hip version of Mary Poppins' carpetbag) and brings out a WWW trading card featuring Millennium. "What's your name, honey?" And when she's done, she pulls out a copy of her best friend's trading card. "I bet you'd like Homosapien's autograph too, huh?" The girl nods and happily takes the card round to Adam for him to sign.

This is, of course, the drop that starts the flood. (The flake that starts the avalanche? Nah. Neither of those is quite the right expression, but you know what I mean.) Half the breakfasting guests descend on the wrestlers, clamoring for autographs. The wrestlers respond with more or less grace, depending on how well caffeinated they are.

"You know," I say once the frenzy dies down again, "I noticed some kids in the audience last night. There were families there. Young kids. Not many, but it used to be all rednecks. Guys in their teens and twenties. So, since when did pro wrestling become a family outing?"

Adam and Emma nod; David frowns; they all muse over this for a moment or two. Finally David says, "I don't mean to disrespect the oldest sport in the world …" The rest of us grin. "But I'm not so sure that's a good thing."

"I think it's good," Emma responds. "Well, maybe I'm just talking about one particular situation, but I always thought that Peter and Sherry were *too* protective. The kids knew about pro wrestling anyway, through their friends and all – so why not have them learn about it at home, where the parents can explain whatever they need to? They can't block the world out forever."

I don't know if any of us had anything else useful to say about the topic, because next thing we knew, we were totally interrupted. The cruising waiter had been discreetly pouring more coffee and had just turned away from Adam towards Emma, when one of the other waiters trips over his own feet, carefully managing in the process to push our guy right into Adam's lap.

Most of us freeze in shock, but Adam deftly catches the cruiser before he can topple further backwards and do himself an injury. The coffee pot goes flying across the carpet.

Adam pushes his chair back and stands cradling the cruiser in his arms; and then he gently sets the guy upright again. "Sorry," the cruiser breathes, absolutely mortified. But Adam is the perfect gentleman; he holds out his right hand as if to shake on it, but then lifts the guy's hand for a kiss before releasing him.

The manager strides over, and offers his apologies. Once it's obvious he's laid the blame in the right place (the other guy is set to work mopping up the spilt coffee, though alas the cruiser gets a glower too), the four of us decide to get out of there. And, anyway, David and I have to go open the bookstore.

Now, that's just wrong

It's a quiet Sunday afternoon, so David and I are sprawled on the sofas down the back of the store with a glass of wine each. After a while I finally remember to ask, "What did you think about Homosapien becoming more like you?"

But David immediately looks all troubled and embarrassed again. "Well, uh …" It seems he would prefer to talk about almost anything else. I don't relent, though, so he makes the effort necessary to get the words out. "Well, uh, my first thought was how boring that would be in pro wrestling."

"Yeah?"

He swallows. Hard. Checks for customers, but none are in earshot. "And then I thought … well, it's boring in real life too, isn't it? I finally got how boring I am."

I sit up, horrified. "You are *not* boring!"

"That's crap, Patrick. Don't lie to me."

"A bit serious, maybe. Sometimes. But not boring."

He isn't convinced. "Anyway, uh … Look, Patrick – you're more his type than I am. I don't know what I was thinking, to tell you the truth. So, uh – you just go for it, all right? I know you like him."

I gape. David is … Unbelievable. David is not only giving up on Adam, but thinking he can pass him on to me … ? No way! Eventually I find my voice. "You have *got* to be kidding."

David shakes his head. If I didn't know better, I'd say there was even a tear in his eye.

It's outrageous! I mean, I've always liked Homosapien, and Adam himself is even better, and of course he is absolutely drop–dead gorgeous. But he isn't mine and never will be. I try reasoning with David. "It's not even that opposites attract. Because you're not opposites. More like two halves of one whole. And each of you – Well, he values the way you're brainy and serious; he loves that you're righteous. And you quit dismissing him ages ago, and you like how he's figuring out how to live the best he can. You're so good together."

But David just shakes his head again. It seems like it's all over.

David doesn't argue when I ask to leave work early that day.

Senior Citz

Soon it isn't just kids appearing in the audience, it's their grandparents too. Pro wrestling really is becoming something that the whole family can enjoy.

Except for maybe while Butch and Sundance are doing their thing. We cut to some audience reaction shots. The rednecks are jeering and hooting, the grandparents are frowning or screwing up their faces in disgust. One takes his young charges in hand and walks them back up the aisle. (I hope they're just going for more ice cream.) There's a lot of people, though, just sitting back and shaking their heads, and sometimes their mouths are curling as if they can't help but be amused. And I'm smiling, I admit it. But how could I *not* smile, watching the supple Sundance … ?

There were a couple of shows where Jack Dynes kept promising us a wonderful surprise. Then finally, in the opening moments of a show in Atlanta, he said that *this* is the night. It seems like every five minutes throughout the show, someone – one of the wrestlers, or a commentator, or a bimbo valet, or the roving interviewer – asks him what the surprise is, and he grins with excitement and nods conspiratorially and replies, "Something Wonderful."

Anyway, Blue is announced for the last match. The crowd give him their usual enthusiastic welcome. And then the stadium goes dark. Usually it's quite light during a show, so you can see the audience and read their signs. But now everything goes dark. The audience are restless. A 20,000–strong murmur builds, pierced by an occasional catcall.

Then the opening notes of a piece of music creep out, slithering. I don't recognize the tune, but it's chilling. It would be right at home in the soundtrack for that antique black–and–white *Nosferatu* movie.

A spotlight hovers, circles, finds the top of the ramp.

And a senior citizen strides out! OK, this isn't what I expected. He's dressed in old–fashioned trunks and boots, and there's a little old lady with him in a snug spangled corset; both are adorned by sequined capes. They glare around at the audience, some of whom are gasping and cheering and applauding like they recognize this pair. I'm gaping. Honestly, this guy is ancient enough to be my granddad. My *great*–granddad. Yet he's here to challenge Blue??!!

A second spotlight hits the ring, and I see that Jack Dynes is there, taking the microphone from the announcer. He thunders over the music: *"Hey! Atlanta! Didn't I promise you Something Wonderful?"*

More and more of the crowd are getting it. Hardly anyone is left seated. A reaction shot shows one of the sweeter gramps waving his hands above his head and hollering fit to bust. Reliving his youth, obviously.

Dynes   Put your hands together for one of Atlanta's favorite sons, one of the golden greats of this wonderful sport of ours … He's honoring the World Wide Wrestling federation by coming out of a retirement richly deserved … Please give the warmest possible welcome to … *Matthew Malign!*

By this time the crowd are more than ready, willing and able to go wild. So they do.

Dynes   And – even better than that, Atlanta! – Matthew Malign is accompanied tonight by his *beaut*iful, his *faith*ful, his *splen*did companion … *Poison Ivy!*

The old lady lifts her arms in triumph. The crowd love it. Malign and Ivy make their way down the ramp to an over–the–top ovation as the creepy slithery music continues. The house lights are back on, though they seem dim compared to the two intense spotlights. There are a few signs held aloft in the audience saying things like *Malign by name, Malign by nature* and *Poison Ivy makes me itch* and *Matt Malign the once and future comeback king.* Blue is stalking back and forth, flexing and stretching and occasionally twitching, as if totally hyped for this match. Malign reaches the ring, and stands there like he is indeed royalty while Ivy slips the cape off his shoulders.

Dynes signals for the bell to sound and finally the match is on.

While he's wary, as if remembering (all too well) Malign's historical wins, Blue takes it easy on the old guy for a long while. But after suffering his third beating, Blue gets wise, and starts giving as good as he's getting. Finally he starts making some ground. I'll hand you over to the commentators …

Terry   And Blue drops Malign with *another* Clothesline. Malign immediately starts getting back to his feet *again*, though. The resilience of this man is magnificent – though it must be twenty years since his last professional match.

Rumbler   He's probably been practicing on the nurses at the retirement home …

Terry   Would you stop that snickering? I can only hope I'm *half* that fit at his age!

Rumbler   You're only half that fit now.

Terry   Well, thank you, though I know you don't mean it as a compliment. Blue puts Malign on his back with a Chokeslam, and goes for the pin. That's one … That's two … But Malign manages to lift a shoulder! I don't believe this man! The crowd are loving it – and who can blame them? As you'd know, Rumbler, Matthew Malign was born and bred right here in Atlanta.

Rumbler   Oh, he's an embarrassment. Look at him! He can barely stand upright. I think he's suffering from senile dementia.

Terry   Dementia, indeed … Huh.

Rumbler   I hope Mr. Dynes has an ambulance standing by. We'll be lucky if Malign doesn't suffer a heart attack.

Terry   Oh, but look at that! Would you look at that! Blue's flat on his face! Malign is turning him over, going for the pin … And he's won! Matthew Malign has won his first match for the WWW! What a wonderful way to return to his old profession.

And so on, and so on. What Terry didn't mention is that Blue was only flat on his face because Ivy managed to trip him up without the referee seeing.

I muse on all of this while getting ready for bed. My first constructive thought is to wonder whether Jack Dynes brought Malign and Ivy out of retirement so that the grandparents in the audience have someone to relate to. If so, I think he's misguided. Like, with movies, there seems to be this assumption that men only relate to male characters in a movie, and women only to the female characters, etc. And, well, I don't know. That might be the case for straight, white, middle–class men who have the luxury of plenty of straight, white, middle–class male characters to relate to. But women and gays and hyphenated Americans surely relate to all kinds of characters. Just because we've had to. There's been so few really good (or even halfway decent) female or gay or Hispanic–American or Native American characters, and that's only slowly changing. So we're less likely to see *any* of the characters as The Other.

But, anyway, if Jack Dynes thinks he has to provide a wider range of personas (David says that's personae, and I say huh?) in the wrestling, I'm not going to argue.

Oh, and then I finally get a clue about the signs. About why they were a bit odd. *Matt Malign the comeback king* indeed. My second constructive thought for the night!

If Malign and Ivy's comeback was such a big surprise, how did the audience know to make the signs before the show? Signs that could only be relevant for those two people and some only relevant for that particular comeback match. Huh. Unless the audience members were friends of Malign, and in the know … ? Yeah, that was probably it.

But it still strikes me as odd. So I decide to keep an eye out for other signs that seem a bit too psychic.

The tabloid follows up

The tabloid that's been showing occasional interest in the realities of pro wrestling now runs another piece. I don't know if Jack Dynes will be amused or mad that they run it in the entertainment section rather than the sports pages. Anyway, here's most of it.

> ### Pro Wrestling 'Better' For Being Fake
> *'Well, it has and it hasn't,' says 80–year–old Jeb Brown when I ask him if professional wrestling has changed over the years. 'Things were simpler back when I first went to the travelling shows. You knew who was good and who was bad. They might change from good to bad, or bad to good, but*

*you always knew exactly when it happened. There was no, you know, **grey** areas.'*

But isn't the storyline more interesting if the heroes aren't all wearing white hats, and the villains aren't all in black?

'I guess,' Brown concedes. 'But, yeah, they're telling stories – stories like my wife Bet's daytime soap operas! It's a wonder she doesn't start watching with me. But in my day, all you saw was the match itself. None of this stuff that goes on outside the ring.'

So, you don't like what pro wrestling has become?

'Now, well, I didn't say that. It's just different, is all.' Jeb Brown shifts in his seat, and ruminates for a moment or two. Then he brightens. 'I always knew it was fake, though.'

In what way?

*'See, I always went to every show that ever came through here. Never missed a single show. Then one summer I went up to Springfield to help my cousin when his wife died, God bless and keep her, and I took him to see the wrestling when they came through, cause he hadn't set foot outside the house since the day of the funeral. And it was **the exact same show**. I'd swear it on the Bible! **Exactly** the same.'*

They had all the same matches?

'The same matches, the same results, the same holds, the same throws, the same punches. Everything exactly the same as the show back home. See, they could get away with it back then. The shows weren't on television, they weren't broadcast right across the country. People just went to see the wrestling in their home town, and that was that.'

How did you feel when you found this out?

Brown sighs. 'I'd be lying if I said I was happy. I felt real, uh, dis– uh, dis–

Disillusioned?

Yeah. I didn't go to the next show. Just stayed home, and drove my wife Bet crazy with my moping. But when they came round again, I figured it's still a good show, so why not enjoy it?'

Why not, indeed?

*'Then I figured maybe it's even **better**. Because they think about what will make it a good show, and that's what they do. It's like – yeah, it's like*

they're telling a story. And they're not just making it up as they go along. Which means it's a better story.'

Thank you, Jeb.

The *Sharpshooter* reporter John Gurrie phones us again, and tells us that he's finished writing his long insider's article.

Gurrie   Now I just need to keep it up to date, so I'll be ready when my editor finally gets game.

David   Is he going to, though?

Gurrie   He has to. One day soon, he has to. Did you see that tabloid interview with the old guy?

David   Yeah, we saw it.

Gurrie   If dear old Jeb Brown (whoever he is) can work out that pro wrestling is better for being fake, then we're on the home stretch and the finish line is coming fast.

But David is full of doubts. Even when he drags the dusty laptop out, intending to go on with writing The Great American Novel, he ends up just sitting there and staring morosely at the screen. In all the years I've known him, I've never seen this righteous man so horribly uncertain.

Confrontations

Butch and Sundance have another tag team match against du Lac and the good Bizarro, during which they camp it up for all they're worth. And they take it further than I'd have thought possible. Every move becomes imbued with homoeroticism, but not in a good way. Butch and Sundance drape themselves over their opponents at every opportunity; du Lac and Bizarro squirm away in disgust. Even *my* sense of taste is mildly outraged, and that's saying something. David just watches it all in stony silence.

After the match – which the Good Guys win, natch, by (apparently) pounding their nelly challengers into insensibility – the camera goes backstage to find Homosapien and Millennium in a corridor waiting for the next match. They're up against Fixx and the bad Bizarro. (It occurs to me that we haven't seen Lucifer for a while and I don't know why. I'll have to ask Adam next time he calls.)

Anyway, of course Butch and Sundance walk past Homosapien and M on their way back to the dressing rooms, and of course they are holding each other up in a close embrace, and of course they stop to chat.

Butch   Hey, man. We'll get them next time, I swear it. Third time lucky.

Homosapien glowers. M casts them a cool look.

Butch   I *know* we're good enough. Not as good as you, though.

Sundance   My people have a saying about heroes –

Homosapien   Oh, give me a break! That match was just another farce. You won't win until you start behaving with a bit of dignity.

As before, Butch and Sundance turn woebegone faces up to him, and their hold on each other tightens. As before, Homosapien only gets more righteous.

Homosapien   You won't win until you respect this sport, and your fellow athletes, and the fans out there.

The audience knows a cue when they hear one. They cheer and holler, but then they fall quiet again except for the occasional catcall. I mean, they don't want to be cheering Homosapien right now, do they?

Butch   Hey, we *do* respect you, man.

Sundance   You're, like, our hero.

Butch   Always have been, always will be.

Sundance   You're the bravest man I know, being Out and Proud as you are.

And – get this – Sundance actually breaks away from Butch's embrace, and steps closer to Homosapien, his gaze worshipful. As if mesmerized. As if he hardly knows what he's doing.

Sundance   There's no one like you in any professional sport in all of America. Homosapien – you're truly amazing.

M is smiling now, quirkily, as if half proud for her friend and half amused by this extravagant praise. Homosapien is embarrassed. After all, who wants compliments from someone you're trying to tell off? He barely manages to restrain himself from shuffling his feet.

Homosapien   Now, look –

Sundance   We're gonna think about what you said. Respect and dignity. Of course you're right. We're gonna think about that, long and hard.

And suddenly he blushes, realizing the sexual connotations of such words. Even though he didn't mean them sexually. Or maybe he did, what with his idol standing there before him in little more than purple lycra … Maybe he just totally gave himself away.

Butch gruffly protests, *"Hey!"* and grabs Sundance's arm, drags him back to his side. He is furious. Jealous. He stalks off, still hanging onto his partner. Sundance casts one last glance back at Homosapien and obediently follows Butch. Not that he's given much choice.

Homosapien and Millennium are doing all right in their match against Fixx and Bizarro. Until, speak of the devil and all that, Lucifer storms in and starts laying into Homosapien. The referee calls for the match to be stopped – disqualification due to outside interference – but the bell rings and rings in vain. Lucifer keeps going regardless. And he's just plain mean. I can see that he's not pulling his punches – and he does things like tipping Homosapien over too far before slamming him down on his back, so that he lands badly.

Emma is yelling at him, but Michael Rosen is not listening. It seems as if Adam decides to play dead. He just lies there limply on the mat and takes it. And even Rosen has the pride not to keep laying into a man when he's down. At least, not on national television. So eventually he stalks off, with a worried Fixx and Bizarro in tow.

Which leaves Emma to help Adam back up the ramp.

David is staring at the screen, white–faced, like a deer frozen in the headlamps.

Before heading back to the hotel that evening, Clancy (aka Sundance) visits Adam and Emma's makeshift dressing room. Politely knocks on the door, and lets himself in when invited. "I just wanted you to know that I meant it, Mr. O'Connor. Every word."

"What?" Adam asks, confused. He's taken one punch too many. Plus, as far as he's concerned, Mr. O'Connor was his father.

"You *are* heroic. I really admire what you've been doing as Homosapien."

Adam sighs, and settles back into his seat with an icepack on his nape. "Well, thanks, but – uh. Oh hell, I dunno. It's Adam, by the way."

"Clancy." He steps closer, and they shake hands.

"You know Emma, right?"

"Hello properly," says Emma with her lovely smile.

Clancy returns the smile with interest, and shakes her hand too. Then he turns back to Adam. "I know it hasn't been easy, but I think you were smart to make Homosapien gay."

"Yeah? Did you see what just happened out there?" Adam ruefully adds, "I'm not feeling real *smart* right now."

"They say we should choose a character that doesn't fall too far from the tree."

"Well, yeah, but …"

"I meant it about you being brave," Clancy continues. "You're not making it easy for the fans to take you to their hearts – but you're being true to yourself, and that's gotta get over with them in the long run."

Adam is just looking up at him. Emma tells me later that his expression is an exact copy of the woebegone face Sundance turned on him during the show.

"When Nick and Mr. Dynes started talking about going with these gay characters, I argued against it. I mean, I want to make it in The Big Show, you know? I thought that only someone who's ambivalent about making it would do such a thing. But then I started watching your matches and I realized I was wrong."

"Oh God," Adam says weakly, "maybe not."

"I think the fans respect you for being true. I think they like that raw kind of honesty, that *proud* honesty. And they like creativity. They wanna be entertained. You do *all* of that. Nick and I are just doing half of it. We're going for the creativity and being the most outrageous heels that we can."

A silence stretches. Adam is thinking. Well, he's trying to think over the God–awful pounding in his head.

"Look," says Adam at last, dropping the icepack and standing again, hands on hips and squaring up as if confronting someone much scarier than Clancy. "Look, I just feel like – I feel like I've lost the plot with Homosapien. I don't know what happens next. And there's this move I've been working on – I just can't sort it out. So, uh, if you have any ideas, I'd appreciate hearing them."

"Oh. Of course. Thanks!" Clancy is beaming. "Maybe we could work out together? I'd be honored."

"Sure, we can work out. But, uh – Well, you save the best ideas for yourself. And Nick. Tell me your second–best, if you want. No – tell them to Mr. Dynes. Get the credit for them."

"Yeah, sure," Clancy replies. "That's great! I'll get back to you."

"Thanks."

Clancy nods, and heads for the door. Adam relaxes a bit. But then he straightens up in surprise as Clancy's farewell wink seems to take in him as well as Emma. Adam feels a bit dizzy. Emma just laughs.

The State of the Federation

Terry has his serious Current Issues In The WWW interview with Jack Dynes. And what else would they talk about except whether pro wrestling is real or not.

Terry   Well, Mr. Dynes – is it … ?

Dynes   Is it *real?* I can't believe you're asking me that, Terry. Of course it's real! This is a *real* sport with *real* athletes … I'd like to see *you* try to do what they do, week in and week out.

Terry   Oh, I know that I couldn't.

Dynes   Exactly.

Terry   But – excuse me for persisting, sir – I'm sure you're aware of the newspaper articles claiming that the match results are decided ahead of time, and that the matches themselves are more about telling a story than a real contest between athletes.

Dynes   What would they know?

Terry   Some of the articles even suggest that it's a good thing. Um, I mean – they say it would be a good thing if it were true.

Dynes   Is that really something that the fans could get behind? Would we have the millions of fans we do today if we weren't giving them real contests?

Terry   I don't know, sir.

Dynes   Well, I do.

Dynes nods, as if he's made his point. And they wind up the interview.

Terry   Thank you for your time, sir.

Dynes   My pleasure, Terry.

Once the camera stops rolling, Jack Dynes shakes Terry's hand firmly, genuinely, but he doesn't say anything. As Terry walks away, Sam (the trainer) joins Dynes, and they share a worried look.

Dynes   Well, we raised the question, Sam. Not that we can't still go back, but we're getting pretty close to the point of no return.

Sam   If there's gonna be changes, it's better that we drive them, Mr. Dynes, you said so yourself.

Dynes   Yuh. And there are changes to be made, that's for sure. But doing it in public? I'm still not convinced.

Sam   You've always been two steps ahead of anyone else in this game. You haven't steered us wrong yet.

Dynes   *Yet*. That's what I'm afraid of. God … it's one helluva gamble, ain't it?

Sam   Yes, sir. But you've got the cojones to throw the dice if we have to.

Dynes grins at him, kind of wry.

Dynes   All right, all right – that's enough about my cojones from you.

Sam   Yes, sir.

The two of them walk off together, ready to face whatever comes next. Friends, partners. No matter what.

The Booker and the Writer

Every three weeks, as da Dub Dub Dub swings through its home town of Chicago, the wrestlers assemble for a day at the office and amidst all the paperwork they catch up on, Jack Dynes talks to each of them about the matches to be booked for the coming weeks.

This time, for reasons unknown, the wrestlers are asked to meet with Dynes all together in the conference room, rather than individually or in pairs like usual. There is some unrest and muttering, and suspicious glances – especially in Adam's direction – except of course from his best friend Emma, who sits calmly by his side at the conference table. They all figure something must be wrong. You notice how we human beans tend to assume the Worst Case Scenario if we don't know for sure?

Anyway, they crowd in. All the names we've met so far and all the ones we haven't. There aren't enough chairs, so most of the wrestlers stand around the walls, arms crossed and faces surly.

At last Dynes strides in, and makes his way to the head of the table, accompanied by Sam and some young dude no one knows. Two of the wrestlers there offer their chairs, but Dynes waves them back down. "I'll make this quick, and then we'll get on with business as usual." He clears his throat, glances around at the wrestlers. "I wanna introduce you all to Tim Whitehorse. He'll be part of the booking from now on. It'll be me and Sam and Tim, and you listen to Tim like you listen to us. Any questions?"

An expectant silence. Then one of the older wrestlers – old enough to be Tim Whitehorse's father – is brave enough to ask, "In what capacity, sir?"

Dynes nods. "Tim just graduated with honors in screenwriting. We've been relying on our own ideas for a long time. And we'll still rely on them, cause your character has to sit right with you. But Tim here will be fine–tuning the characters, the stories. If you haven't figured this out yet, I believe in letting an expert do his or her –" with a nod to Emma – "job, and this guy can tell a mean story. So you take his word like you do mine. Or you take it up with me."

There's some muttering and much exchanging of glances.

"Yuh, I know." Dynes cuts across the restlessness. "I know. But things are changing. I'm not a hundred percent sure what pro wrestling will look like in a year from now. I've got my theories – and I guess we've all got our notions of what it *should* be like – but we're just gonna have to go with the changes for a while. Tim's here to help us ride it out."

The older wrestler clears his throat. "I don't mean to doubt you, sir – but a *writer* … ?"

"What we've had opened here is, uh – What d'you call it, Tim?"

"Pandora's box, sir."

"Yuh. Pandora's box has been opened, and everything's changing – and I know you're afraid that the WWW won't weather this storm. *And it won't* – unless we try to go with it. All right?"

Adam notices that Jack Dynes is carefully not looking at him. But a lot of the others are casting him the darkest of looks.

"Now, I don't need to remind you about the clause in your contract that says no unauthorized media comments or interviews, right? This, uh, this *innovation* is gonna put us ahead of the game. We'll just let the other federations follow along as best they can. Plus, that Tad Scott Foster – he'd give us hell. Even though he wouldn't be half as funny without *his* writers making up his jokes for him."

There's some dutiful chuckles, but some of the dark looks aimed at Our Hero are turning deadly.

"All right, we've got a full day ahead." Dynes glances at his clipboard. "Michael Rosen, you're up first."

The others reluctantly leave, the muttering growing to a buzz as they reach the corridors. It's a fair bet to say that every last one of them is dead curious to see what might be different about this booking interview … But all they can do for now is gossip and speculate and wait.

A dramatic reconstruction

As near as Adam and I can figure it, this is what went down that day between Michael Rosen and Jack Dynes. To set the scene – the two of them are sitting up one end of the conference room table along with Sam and Tim Whitehorse, the WWW's new writer. And Tim is pitching his very first idea.

"The audience *loves* Millennium, sir. I mean, they *really* dig her. Well, who wouldn't, right?" Tim is almost foaming at the mouth with excitement, looking from one man to the other for reinforcement.

Dynes nods his agreement. No question about it, everybody loves M.

Rosen just glares.

"What I was thinking was, well, Lucifer can have learned his lesson, yeah? She's forced him to see her as more than just his valet, right? She's no bimbo, she's not just window dressing, she's not even a trophy. And he has to acknowledge that. Yeah?"

"Yuh," Dynes says, indicating that Tim should get to the point.

Rosen is glaring so hard now that he's starting to smolder.

Whitehorse tries in vain not to break out in a sweat. "Uh – so what I was thinking was, uh – well, was that Lucifer can ask Millennium to come back to him. But not as his valet this time. As his partner, his equal. His tag team partner."

But Michael Rosen knows all too well that Emma would say no to such a storyline, that Millennium would refuse. And that would be just *too* humiliating at any time, let alone doing it on national television. Rosen's glare begins to show cracks. He glances at Dynes. Looks down at the table rather than meet Whitehorse's eager gaze again.

Dynes can see Rosen is about to crumble, so comes to his rescue. "Sorry, Tim, that's not gonna work. What else have you got?"

"Um, well …" Whitehorse flicks through the pages of his notepad, frowning over his own scribbles. "There's the gang thing –"

"Mr. Dynes," Rosen interrupts.

"Yuh?"

"I wanted, uh – if you would – uh, I want – I'd like to be released from my contract. If you would. Sir."

Young Tim Whitehorse is looking bug–eyed from one to the other, amazed and aghast at this Real Life drama.

Dynes doesn't seem overly surprised. After a moment, he smoothly says, "I'm truly sorry to hear that, Michael."

"Yeah. I just – uh. Well, you know, what with, uh – with M. And then I'd fit better over there."

"There?" Dynes is watching him with a shrewd expression. "Where's that, Michael?"

"Uh, the EWF." The Extreme Wrestling Federation; no further explanation required.

Dynes nods. He understands. "There's a four week notice period."

Rosen looks up at him with something like hope. Or maybe it's too painful to be called hope, I don't know. "So you would?"

"Yuh. Yuh, all right, on one condition."

The mingled relief and fear is too much. Rosen closes his eyes. "God, anything but that." He juts his chin in Whitehorse's direction. "Anything but that with Emma."

Dynes nods again, and after a long moment he musingly replies, "Yuh, all right. Anything but that."

Glumness

Michael Rosen snags Caesar and Brute as soon as their booking interviews are done, and despite their protests he takes them to the nearest hotel with 24/7 bar service. Soon he is drunkenly singing the praises of the EWF, but they don't humor him – the WWW is *the* federation to which any wrestler aspires. Not much later Rosen's pals have deserted him, and he is sitting at the bar all alone except for a bartender whose smooth professionalism only irritates.

Alone. Always alone.

Actually, right now I have this sneaking pity for Michael Rosen, so I'm not going to draw the obvious moral at his expense. It's kind of ironic – isn't it? – that the one thing we human beans all have in common is our isolation.

More glumness

The news spreads, and eventually reaches Emma and Adam's dressing room. Michael Rosen is giving up on the WWW and going where the violence is. Going where Emma isn't.

"I'm sorry," Adam says to her once they're alone again. "I'm really sorry that all this stuff got in the way."

"All this stuff? What, like my best friend?" Emma casts him a watery smile.

"Yeah, stuff like that."

"Well, Michael is Michael, and I'm me – so it was never going to work." But then her voice cracks – "Was it?"

Adam gets up and goes to hold her. "I'm really sorry," he murmurs helplessly.

There's some dampness and gulping and snuffling, the embarrassing kind of crying that you can only do in your best friend's arms. But then she straightens, and Adam lets go, and Emma starts drying off and then bravely reapplying her make–up. Eventually she says, "Well, I always knew there was more to life. I mean, there's more to life than romance. Right?"

"Yeah," says Adam, turning away to repack the bag that's been packed and waiting for an hour already. "Yeah, there is. Absolutely."

Emma looks at him. Frowns. Watches him for a while before saying with careful casualness, "How's David? Have you called him lately?"

Just as casually, Adam replies, "Not since we all had breakfast together."

"Adam," she says seriously, "I always thought that you and David were really great togeth–"

"Yeah, well," he says, cutting her off. Which usually he just *doesn't*. "Like you said – there's more to life, right?"

A long moment stretches. "Right."

They don't dare meet each other's troubled gaze.

Glumness, glumness, everywhere

David is lower than I've ever seen him and not just due to the fall weather. (I mean, I love the leaves turning gold and I think the crispness in the air is invigorating, but David seems to find the changing season melancholy. Even more so than usual this year.) I guess at least he's not pretending he doesn't even care about Adam any more. It's clear now that he cares. He just can't seem to do anything about it.

He spends a lot of time at the shop doing a whole lot of nothing. Leaving me to manage the stock, the customers, you name it. Not even hauling the laptop out, let alone opening up the Great American Novel. What he *does* do is collapse on the sofas down the back of the shop, and mope. He mopes big time. It's just not like him. Irascible, I can cope with. This is way different.

"I really thought I was Something," he says to me when I happen by. He's sad, as if he's mourning for himself.

(Patrick keeps his mouth shut for once. Tall tales but true. I feel like tartly telling David that he's not dead yet – but who knows if that would help, so I keep my mouth shut.)

"I used to think I was really Something Hot. *Shit* Hot. The cleverest queer in the country. Until …"

(Eyebrows are raised. David doesn't even think he's clever anymore? Now, that's bizarre.)

"Until …" He is lying sprawled there, looking up at the poster of Homosapien. "Until I realized I wasn't," he finishes kind of lamely.

I sigh and leave him to it.

Letter to the editor

Sharpshooter magazine runs a letter in its *Your Turn* column which provides at least one answer to Jack Dynes' question.

> *In The Know*
>
> *Whatever Jack Dynes is doing with pro wrestling these days, whatever he's turning it into – I'm loving it. I'm in the know and I'm loving it more than ever, because now it's not just the same old same old, week in and week out. It's exciting. I can't wait to tune in to the next show to see where they take it. I'm driving the people in my office nuts talking about it all the time.*
>
> *So, I only have one request for everyone at the WWW – keep up the good work!*
>
> *C Smith Akron, OH*

Campness, campness, everywhere

Ah, this is more like it! David and I are drinking white wine so dry it makes my mouth pucker, while watching the wrestling broadcast live from San Francisco. Butch and Sundance are camping it up and the crowd is reacting with plenty of heat.

Homosapien's little fan club have turned up again, all wearing his shade of purple and bearing appropriate signs – including one begging *Marry me, Adam*. The club members are loving every minute of Butch and Sundance, mind you. Far be it from a gay fan club to remain faithful to their one–and–only. A couple of them have even copied Sundance's war paint and one of them is almost hidden under a cowboy hat like Butch's. Ah, well. I can't really knock inclusiveness.

Butch and Sundance's tag team opponents are announced and the match is on. And for a long while our guys are easily on top of the situation. A few lucky breaks and they quickly pummel the opposition into stupors. The crowd are cheering or jeering as is their wont. Butch grins happily, and takes the opportunity to grab Sundance's hand, twirl him around, pull him into a close embrace, and then dip him … If I'd been asked to think up a romantic move, I couldn't have bettered this. Butch draws his partner up slowly … into a kiss … I sigh happily. David burbles a delighted little laugh.

I turn to my favorite old curmudgeon in surprise. "I thought you didn't approve of these guys?"

He shrugs, and smiles at me. "Come here," David says and once we're settled again he has his arm slung round my shoulders. Which is nice.

I've often thought it's not only that friends are the most important thing for gays. Friends are friends are friends indeed. But also gay friends get to be more affectionate with each other than straight guys ever can. Which isn't just nice, it's très cool.

So, David and I sit there snuggled very close together for the rest of the show. And even when Homosapien is announced, David doesn't twitch let alone release me.

A new storyline

Back to the real topic … The San Francisco show.

Homosapien is announced to the rocked–up chords of *Homosapien*. Our Hero still isn't dancing to Our Song like he used to, but at least there's a spring in his step now and he's smiling. As before, he goes out into the audience to acknowledge his little fan club. And they adore him for it. Who wouldn't?

Of course he has a home town victory, though it's only against Louis du Lac, who he's beaten before. But then Millennium joins him in the ring, while du Lac still lies groaning on the ramp, having managed to crawl so far and no further. Homosapien grabs a mike and waits until the audience are quieter and ready to listen.

"Whoever said that San Francisco was a cold place," he calls out, "never had a warm home town welcome like you've given me."

The fans cheer or jeer, according to their loyalties. But there's more cheering than Homosapien usually gets, because a wrestling audience's parochialism overrides most other considerations.

Homosapien lets them quiet down again, and then announces, "You're good people." Millennium is nodding agreement, and smiling at everyone in the whole damned stadium. "*Real* good people."

This of course sets them off all over again and even more so this time.

"So I thought I'd take this opportunity to right a wrong. To balance the books. I thought I'd do that *here*, tonight – in San Francisco, the city of equality. The True Heartland of the Land Of The Free and the Home Of The Brave."

There's still some cheering, but mostly the audience are murmuring restlessly, wondering what's coming next. San Francisco ain't just Castro Street – and this is pro wrestling after all, with its high demographic of rednecks.

Suddenly Homosapien bursts out, "Did you know that I earn *half* of what Lucifer gets paid?" He lets that sink in, then follows up with, "And Millennium here – Millennium, the most exciting thing to happen to pro wrestling in a hundred, in a *thousand* years – she earns *half* of what *I* earn!"

The crowd are still restless, uncertain, though there's a few catcalls, a few supportive hollers. (It's then that I catch sight of a sign reading *Equal Rights = Equal Pay*. A bit too psychic, isn't it?)

"And why is that? Because I'm gay? Because she's a woman? That's not right."

There's a growing swell of noise, as if half the audience are arguing with the other half.

"Tell me!" Homosapien cries out. *"Is that right, San Francisco?!"*

The hollering breaks out into stamping of feet. The crowd seems, ironically, about equally divided.

"Oh yeah?" a male voice breaks in. Homosapien turns to see that du Lac has reached the top of the ramp, and he's gotten a mike from somewhere. "Oh yeah?" The other guy has the audience's attention by now. "You'll get equal pay," he growls out, still bent in half as a result of his injuries, *"when you're equally as good!"*

The crowd go wild. Louis du Lac throws down the microphone, and gimps off backstage. Homosapien and Millennium look at each other, half dumbfounded and the rest determined. We go to a commercial break.

"Well," mutters a certain Serious Gay Rights Dude in my ear, "that was fun, wasn't it?"

Something tells me that if he cared enough, he'd be sarcastic.

The ratings

At last the day dawns on which the quarterly comparative ratings are released with pages of detailed analysis. Jack Dynes is at the office even earlier than usual, in his best suit and tie. Sam waits with him and drinks way too much caffeine.

Finally the executive secretary puts the various charts and statistics into Dynes' hands. He and Sam spread them across the desk and pore over them, hardly daring to believe their first interpretations. But eventually Dynes sits back and heaves a huge sigh of relief. It seems that, after a long slow dip in the figures, the WWW is steadily climbing back to its former levels of popularity – and there's no sign yet of it peaking, though that has to happen soon.

Jack Dynes smiles. Allows himself a moment. And then he gets on with the day's business.

Drawing lines, taking sides

There's a show in Seattle. In between matches, Homosapien is pacing back and forth in the ring, talking about equal rights and equal pay and all that. He's more earnest than righteous. The crowd aren't reacting much, as if it's nothing to get very excited about. I am wondering who thought this storyline was ever gonna get over with the audience.

Finally Homosapien stops ranting, and stops pacing, and just stands there. He lets the silence grow. The crowd belatedly respond with anticipation. Then Homosapien cries out, "I want everyone who's with me – everyone in the WWW who's with me, everyone in the WWW who believes in equality – to come out to the ring right now. Let's show them we mean business."

A long pause. Homosapien is watching the ramp with supreme confidence. Apparently he's expecting half the wrestlers to come pouring out. Any minute now … Any minute …

There's no one. Homosapien's face crumples a little. He's on his own. He sags a bit. Someone in the crowd starts jeering and a few others join in.

But suddenly there's a kerfuffle off to one side, in the middle of the audience. There's a surge towards the centre of it, and cheering breaks out. Homosapien is peering over there, as is the rest of the audience, trying to make out what's going on.

Then Millennium appears in the middle of it, in her street clothes, as if she was running late and just dashed for the nearest entrance to the stadium which happened to be a public one. She makes her way down through the audience towards the ring. Hands reach out to her from beyond the security guards that flank her, and she clasps them on her way past.

She gets to the ring and swings herself in over the top rope. Homosapien grabs her by the hips, lifts her as high as he can, spins around with her while she laughs down at him. Anyone would think they were happy to see each other.

Anyway, finally Homosapien puts her down, and she stands there beside him, his first, best and last ally. Homosapien lifts the microphone again. "Come on! Right now! We can't be the only decent people in the whole damned federation!"

Another pause. And then there's someone dressed all in black clambering into the ring, though I didn't see anyone coming down the ramp. I can't make him out at first, his face is hidden by something he's carrying – but then he puts it down, and I realize he's a cameraman who's been working just outside the ring. An obviously Hispanic cameraman. And I am so used to overlooking these guys, that he seems to have appeared out of nowhere.

Homosapien and Millennium are kind of gaping at him, just as flummoxed as me. The guy walks over to them, offers his hand to Homosapien. "I'm with you, man."

"Thank you," our hero manages, shaking the guy's hand. "That's great. That's *really* great. Thank you."

Millennium shakes his hand too, smiling beautifully, and then she pulls him into a hug. A hug from which he emerges with a broad grin and a whoop. The audience laughs in delight along with him. Who cares about equal pay when *this* is his reward?

"OK," says Homosapien into the mike, looking up the ramp again. "Who else is there? Come on! There's strength in numbers. We can stand together on this."

There's movement from backstage and then Lucifer appears. The crowd welcome him with a roar, but there's some hesitation. Surely he's not going to turn Good? Surely he's the last person to join Homosapien's cause? Lucifer just stands there for a while on the stage at the top of the ramp, waiting for the audience to quieten. Homosapien and Millennium hover there in the ring, confused.

Finally Lucifer lifts his mike and says, "The strength is all on *this* side, faggot."

The crowd cheer and holler. This is more like it!

He mincingly mimics Homosapien's call to arms: "I want everyone who's with me to come out now." He sounds like he's trying to impersonate a little girl. Homosapien is furious. Lucifer shudders, and clears his throat with a retching noise. "Well," he booms in his usual tones, "I want everyone who wants to whup this pussy's ass to join me *here!*"

The crowd go crazy. They love this.

The poor old cameraman is still in the ring, but he's backing away, wondering what the hell he's let himself in for. He cowers against the ropes, but he doesn't quite leave. I bet he *wants* to.

Homosapien and Millennium are still standing there, determined. Hands on hips. Defiant.

There's movement again backstage, and the crowd wait with bated breath to see who'll appear. It's Butch and Sundance. Well, to be exact, it's Sundance dragging Butch along with him. They walk right past Lucifer – though Butch casts him a glance full of regret – and they head down to the ring.

Homosapien welcomes them in, shakes their hands. When he turns to face Lucifer again, Sundance is right there at his shoulder. Butch stands a little way off, sourly grimacing at his partner. OK, so it's five against one, in favor of the faces.

The Bad Bizarro brother appears, and stands by Lucifer. No surprises there. Five against two.

Then Louis du Lac appears, and because he's a Good Guy I expect him to make his way down to the ring to stand by our hero. But he doesn't. He halts by Lucifer, and plants himself there, arms crossed, face disgustedly glowering. And I remember that he always was a bit homophobic.

And then it dawns on me how brilliant this is. Gangs are forming, yes – but it's not simply Good Guys *vs.* Bad Guys. The issues that Homosapien raised have created a fault–line across the usual loyalties. This is very very cool! Anything might happen, and probably will.

The Good Bizarro brother shows up and there's a collective indrawn breath. Maybe the audience haven't consciously worked it out yet, but they're aware that this Bizarro is about to make a significant choice. The two brothers are glaring at each other, full of hatred. The Good Bizarro takes a step down the ramp. Looks again at the alternative in the ring.

And he steps right back onto the stage. Takes his place in Lucifer's gang, though as far away from his brother as he can be. Lord above. Five against four isn't looking so great, especially when one of the five is only a cowering cameraman. And I would bet my life savings – well, I would bet a lot more than *that* pittance that Caesar and Brute will align themselves with their old mate Lucifer.

There's a bustle, and one of the Bad Guy's bimbo valets appears, in all her blond bosomy glory. She makes her way through to the top of the ramp. Of course everyone expects her to Stand By Her Man. But, no, she gives them the flick and totters down the ramp on her high heels. Homosapien is gentleman enough to help her through the ropes and into the ring. Everyone there welcomes her. Great. Six against four. (I suppose if she's on our side now, I'll have to find out her name.)

There's a long pause. Then another stir backstage. And Blue appears. The crowd, already on their feet, welcome him with resounding waves of cheers. He's as well loved as ever.

Blue hovers at the top of the ramp, drinking in the adulation. Surely he'll join our guys. But who knows? Nothing is certain now. He looks about him. Looks at the guys just behind him. Looks at the guys in the ring. Weighs up his options. And begins striding down the ramp.

I holler my joy, I can't help myself. Thank God! What can't we accomplish with Blue on our side?

OK, so now it's seven against four – though only five *vs.* four if you just count the wrestlers. And there's always Caesar and Brute to take into account. (I don't think they're in Seattle, so I guess they'll declare their allegiance during another show.)

Lucifer lifts his microphone. Holds out a hand to ask for a bit of quiet. The crowd start to simmer down, take their seats again. An expectant hush falls. Lucifer lets the anticipation build.

Finally: "I am Lucifer!" he declares. The crowd cheer. "And *we* are The Fallen."

The crowd erupts again. God, this is good stuff! If this is something the new writer dreamed up, then more power to him.

Homosapien is standing there with his compadres around him, but his sagging posture indicates he feels he's been defeated at his own game. After an encouraging word from Millennium, though, he stirs himself, lifts the microphone. "Uh, so, the four of you together earn more than the seven of us –"

He is interrupted by jeers and booing from the crowd. Lucifer and his pals are laughing.

"Uh," Homosapien stumbles on, "equal rights means –"

"No one cares, faggot!" cries Lucifer.

"We'll go on strike, if we can't renegotiate our contracts," Homosapien declares. He's beginning to rouse again. "You guys – The Fallen," he sneers – "you can't put on a show without us."

"Try it, faggot. No one'll miss you. No one'll even notice that you're gone."

Homosapien is standing tall again. "Yeah, they will. And, Lucy – don't call me faggot ever again!"

"I'll call you what I like, faggot. You're nothing but a bunch of politically correct pussies."

Blue has stepped up beside Homosapien, absolutely furious. He grabs the mike, and is about to say some fighting words when the curtain rustles again backstage. The Fallen turn to look. Everyone is staring, wondering who it is and whether they're gonna change the balance of things. There's quiet throughout the stadium, nothing more than a slight murmur from audience members as they turn to their neighbor and say, "Do you think it's … ?"

Another rustle. The curtain lifts. And out steps Jack Dynes!

There's a clamor from the audience. He's not exactly anyone's favorite guy, but why's he there? What's he gonna do? What's he gonna say?

He takes the microphone from Lucifer, and steps to the top of the ramp. Calls for silence. The audience take a long time to settle down again. Finally they fall quiet.

Dynes lifts the mike. And he says to Homosapien, "You're talking about going on strike?"

Homosapien takes the mike back from Blue. He clears his throat. And gamely replies, "Yes, sir."

Dynes nods his head. "Yuh. I'm sorry to hear that." Not that he sounds very surprised, though. He lifts the mike again. "Yuh, well, then … I'm with these guys." And he jerks his thumb at The Fallen.

The crowd go absolutely bananas. There's never been anything like this, not ever before. They love it.

And The Fallen love it. They each shake their boss's hand, gather round him, clap their comrades on the back. They're delighted.

Then the camera cuts back to our guys. Homosapien is looking shocked, but determined. As if this is only gonna stiffen his resolve.

But Blue – Blue, the WWW's Ultimate Good Guy – is looking horrified. He's only ever been on the inside before and now he's well and truly out in the cold. The others in the seven gather round, but he hardly even knows they're there. He's lost. And on a close–up of his horrified face, the show ends.

Phone call

The phone rings, and I pick it up. "Q4 bookstore."

"Hello, Patrick."

"Adam! How the hell are you? God, it's good to hear you. We haven't heard from you for like *forever*, and don't you know how beautiful Boston is in the fall? I really wish you'd –" But I finally manage to stop myself gushing. How uncool was that? Though Adam is chuckling down the line as if he's as pleased to hear me as I am to hear him. I clear my throat and start again, somewhat more nonchalantly. "Hey, gorgeous."

"Hey," he replies.

"David's doing the bank–and–post–office run. Shall I get him to call you?"

"Nah, that's all right, I'll catch up with him later. So, Patrick … What do you think of this new storyline? The equal rights thing?"

"I like the gangs. I like that it's not just Good Guys *vs.* Bad Guys."

"Yeah?"

"Yeah, that was great. Only you guys have to get yourselves a cool name, like The Fallen."

"Any ideas?"

"Lord, I don't know. I'll think about it, if you want."

"Sure."

I ponder for a moment, wondering whether to raise it or not. Of course I do, though. "It's a bit of a serious issue, isn't it? The equal rights thing? Not much fun." There's silence on the other end of the line, but I find myself leaping in with both feet. Story of my life, I suppose. "And I miss the dancing. You never come out dancing any more. There's not enough *dancing* in wrestling these days."

More silence.

"Adam?"

"Yeah. Yeah, uh … Patrick, you'll have to let me think about that."

"Sorry," I say.

"No need," he replies.

"OK." We silently commune for a moment. And then I ask, "So, how have you been?"

"I'm all right." And before I can follow up with any more personal questions, Adam rushes on – "Look, Patrick, I'm gonna be sending you and David something. You have to help me out here."

"Sure," I immediately reply. "What do you mean? What is it?"

"You'll know when you see it. You'll know what to do."

"Sure, OK. I'm your man."

"Thanks, Patrick." But Adam sighs. "Dancing, eh? I think maybe you're right. And I guess Homosapien doesn't have anything left to lose any more." Another sigh. "I guess I don't, either."

I wait, but there's nothing more. "Adam, are you all right?"

"Yeah, I just – Well, do you have a *home*, Patrick? A place that you call home?"

Home? It's my turn to sigh. "Not really. I never meant to stay here in Boston for so long. I was always gonna move on. Heading for San Francisco,

I guess, but taking my time getting there. You know? That was gonna be my home. But I just ended up staying here."

"Is that a bad thing?"

"I don't know." And I realize that I honestly *don't* know any more. Until now I would have said yes, it's a bad thing, and I really have to move on again soon – and then I *would* have, just out of sheer pigheadedness. But now I realize that maybe Boston isn't such an awful place to be. "I don't know. I'll have to get back to you on that."

"It's just – I was thinking that I haven't had a home for years, not really. Tulsa sure isn't. Not anymore. Not that I'd be there a whole lot if I *did*. That's the nature of the beast with this job, we travel so much. But I guess it'd be nice to have a home to go back to when I can."

I am holding my breath, just in case. I don't know what Adam's thinking, but I'm thinking Boston, and more particularly David. Because it's the people that make a place a home, isn't it? Not just the place itself. And here I am, *not* moving on.

Neither of us dares to say anything, mind you. We give our goodbyes in hushed kinds of tones and we carefully hang up. And I figure we're not quite at the end of this story just yet.

Tag team match

There's a tag team match, with Homosapien and Blue (of our gang) against the Bizarro brothers (of The Fallen). Both teams are fraught with tensions, though – Blue is worried about siding with Homosapien against The Boss, and the Bizarro brothers are still very much Good and Bad even if they're supposedly on the same side now – so nothing goes well or easily for either pair.

Homosapien has been in the ring for what seems like forever, taking far more than his share of a beating from first one Bizarro and then the other. When he finally manages to crawl over to his corner, Blue is in too much of a fug to even notice he's there, hand pleadingly reaching out. Sure enough, one of the Bizarros grabs Homosapien's ankle and drags him back into the ring for another beating. Blue belatedly wakes up, but he looks more sour than sorry about the situation.

Eventually the Bizarros start arguing tactics. The heel – who of course thinks nothing of cheating – wants his brother to join in the beating he's giving Homosapien, while the face – who of course disapproves of anything irregular – insists that as he's not legally tagged in, he mustn't get into the ring. Instead of progressing the match, soon they start raining blows on each other.

Now that Homosapien isn't the one being pounded, he starts to slowly crawl back to his corner again. Eventually he gets there, and Blue is actually ready and waiting for him this time. Blue is tagged in. He's fresh and ready to rumble – but the Bizarros are still busy fighting each other. Blue huffs a bit, yells at them. They shrug him off, obviously beyond caring. He runs at them with his arms outstretched, a one–man Double Clothesline, and barrels into them. They tip over the top of the ropes, and fall to sprawl on the floor … where they do nothing more than continue their argument with each other.

Blue is frustrated as hell. He gestures to the referee, indicating that he should do something – but all the referee can do is begin counting down from ten. If one of the Bizarros isn't back in the ring by the time he's done, they forfeit the match.

Which is what happens. The crowd are restless and dissatisfied as Blue's hand is lifted in victory. Usually they'd be cheering him unreservedly, but not tonight. Blue is royally pissed off. Where's the glory gone? He snatches his hand away from the ref and starts helping a sore–and–sorry Homosapien back up the ramp – but when Millennium runs out to support her friend, Blue leaves her to it and stalks off backstage by himself.

No one is happy about this match. No one's happy at all.

Confrontation

The next show opens with Jack Dynes standing in the ring with a microphone. The crowd are anxiously awaiting whatever he has to say, but he's taking his time getting around to it. Eventually he cries out, "Hello, Buffalo!"

The crowd cheer in response. It's a cheap way of drawing heat, but it never fails to work.

"I've got some footage I wanna show you. Some footage of *your heroes*," he sneers. "Well, they don't look so heroic when they're skulking around the basement. Roll that tape!"

The houselights go down, and the big screen fills with static. Then there's a grainy black–and–white image of a boiler room or some such, the camera angle high up in the ceiling. Perhaps the shot was taken by a security camera.

The image speeds up for a moment, and then goes back to normal speed as seven people walk in. And of course it's Homosapien and Millennium, Butch and Sundance, a reluctant Blue, the bimbo and the cameraman. Our gang.

The crowd are murmuring as they watch this, wondering what's gonna happen.

On the security tape, Homosapien is talking to the others, exhorting them. Some are keen and some aren't. He shows them photos, indistinct to us, though they seem to make a big difference to the other gang members. Eventually there's a vote, and everyone raises their hand to vote *yes* with hardly any hesitation even from Blue. Then they all file out again.

"Meeting in basements," Dynes scoffs as the houselights come back up again. "Sneaking around like a pack of rats. Some revolution! What a class act!" He lets that sink in for a moment, then says, "Let's see what the benefits are for loyalty. For putting the *Federation* first. For putting the *fans* first!"

This is, of course, greeted by a loud cheer. How could it not be?

"Roll the tape!" cries Jack Dynes.

Again the houselights go down. The footage this time is in color, and apparently taken on a handheld video camera. There's a lovely rolling stretch of lawn, and trees in their prime, and the sunlight of a balmy day. In the shade of those trees is a large group of picnickers, happily waving at the camera from their chairs and blankets. There's Lucifer and the Bizarro brothers and du Lac – and, yes, Caesar and Brute – all scrubbed up and spruced up. Likewise, an assortment of pretty wives and adorable children. Everything very civilized. Everyone very privileged and, well, *white*.

Whoever is filming this now walks over to a middle–aged lady (dressed casually yet impeccably, coiffed expensively), and turns the camera on himself as he puts his free arm around her waist – and of course it's a grinning Jack Dynes. He swings the camera back around the other happy faces once more, before the picture fades to black.

The crowd are muttering amongst themselves, with an occasional inarticulate yell directed at the ring.

"Yes, there are rewards," Jack Dynes continues, "for putting *you*, the fans, first."

"There are rewards for ass–licking, you mean!" someone cries out.

Confusion, until we realize that Homosapien is on the stage at the top of the ramp.

He lifts his microphone again. "But some things are more important than brown–nosing the boss!"

Dynes glares at him. "You're a fine one to talk," he slowly says. "You'd know all about ass–licking and brown–nosing, wouldn't you?"

The crowd are ooh–ing and aah–ing, laughing and catcalling. Homosapien just shakes his head like he's sorry for the man.

"You owe it to the fans not to go on strike," Dynes says. "You selfish sons–of–bitches."

"Putting our jobs on the line to fight exploitation – that's not selfish. The fans understand. *You exploit the fans too!*"

Dynes tries to override where this is going. "No one liked the baseball players for striking! No one understood that."

"We don't earn an average of over $2 million *each and every year* like the baseball players. Not even Blue or Lucifer get that. The fans know where we're coming from. They've got bosses too."

"You ruin this Federation, and I'll personally see that you –"

Homosapien cuts him off. "Yeah, it *is* all about you, Mr. Dynes, isn't it?" He pauses, looks around the audience to make sure he has their full attention. "Who makes the money here? Who makes the money out of ticket sales? Merchandise? Who gets *the fans'* hard–earned money at the end of the day?" Another dramatic pause. The audience is holding their collective breath. "The owners," Homosapien explains. "In this case, *The* Owner. Singular. And that's you, sir. We just want to share what *you* earn, Mr. Dynes."

"But –" Dynes splutters. "But – Yuh, but who takes the risk? The person who takes the risk should reap –"

It is the wrong thing to say, of course. He meant financial risk, but Homosapien chases down another meaning. "Yeah, we take the risk all right. We put our lives on the line for you, every night. And *this* is how we live."

He points at the screen overhead. The houselights go down again and there's a shot of a ramshackle old weatherboard cottage. (I'm sure this is a gross exaggeration, but who's complaining?) "*This* is all we can afford. And yet *you* live here …" The image changes to a shot of a palatial mansion, pristine white amidst rolling lawns and beautiful trees. In fact the garden looks a lot like the place where The Fallen were enjoying their picnic.

Dynes is horrified. Mortified. As the houselights come back up he is stuttering, trying to string a few words together. "You bastard!" is all he manages.

Then we notice that Homosapien isn't alone. The rest of his gang are standing beside him. And they are all glaring down at Dynes, united at least in this.

"I am Homosapien!" our hero declares. "And *we* are The Righteous."

Signage

Later during that show I notice there's a guy in the audience holding a sign that declares *I'm ITK*. This puzzles me for a long while, though oddly enough I feel that I *should* know what it means. After much racking of brains, I finally manage to translate it. "I'm in the know. That's it! Like that letter they published in *Sharpshooter* a while ago. *I'm In The Know.*"

David scoffs at this. "Then it should be *I'm IK*. You don't include a T for *the* in an acronym."

"Oh," I say, chagrined. A moment later it occurs to me – "But *I* didn't know that, right? And I bet *that guy* doesn't either. Yeah?"

"Yeah." David shrugs. He's given up complaining about The Declining Literacy Of Youth Today, especially when it comes to anything relating to pro wrestling.

Next time the camera cuts to the guy who's In The Know, he looks directly at us and taps his nose, smiling conspiratorially. As if he knows that we're In The Know too. How about that? It's kind of cool that we don't have to feel alone anymore!

The storyline continues

And so the story played on. I don't suppose you need all the details.

The Righteous form a picket line outside a stadium, and end up surrounded by cheering fans (though no one misses the actual show, of course). Terry (the mostly–serious commentator) draws Homosapien aside for an interview.

Terry   You're taking quite a risk, Homosapien, publicly defying your employer, the owner of the WWW. What is it that motivates you?

Homosapien   It's simple, Terry. I want a home I can call my own. A decent home. I want to be able to *afford* a decent home.

Terry   Well, I have to admit that sounds perfectly reasonable to me.

Homosapien   Yeah, it *is* perfectly reasonable. I'm not talking about a 'home' like Mr. Dynes has, I'm not talking about a mansion. Just a regular, decent house. But on the wages I get paid – most of which gets eaten up by all the travelling costs that come with the job – I don't have anywhere I can call my own.

I can't help but remember my last phone conversation with Adam. It seems clear that he's drawing on his own very real yearning for a home.

Anyway, so when Terry heads back into the stadium for that night's show, he immediately gets into an argument with Rumbler (the color commentator). If there are sides to be taken, it's almost guaranteed that the two commentators will be on opposite ones.

Terry   Well, I really think that young man and his friends have a very good point. We should all be able to afford the necessities in life – and if a decent home isn't one of those necessities, I don't know what is.

Rumbler   Oh, *please!* You can't be thinking of going out on strike?

Terry   I might, yes. If that's what Homosapien thinks is best.

Rumbler   Oh, *fine* – so you'll be joining The Politically Correct Pussies, and going out on strike, and betraying the fans –

and betraying Mr. Jack Dynes, without whom you wouldn't even have a job in the first place!

Terry   I happen to believe that Homosapien is a fine young man, and he has a very good point.

Rumbler   I think I'm gonna be ill …

It's an argument that pauses only for the actual commentating of matches.

And once Jay Caesar and Brute have won their tag team match against the lower-ranked heels Butch and Sundance – even while the referee holds their hands in the air to signal their victory – Caesar and Brute pick up on the argument too.

Brute   Hey … So how much do you earn, Jay?

Caesar   I ain't telling you in front of all these people.

Brute   I bet it ain't enough.

Caesar   It's enough.

Brute   How can it be enough? When even Blue and Lucifer, the two biggest names in the Federation – even they don't get enough?

Caesar   You're not thinking of going over to join those pussy-whipped bastards … ?

Brute   Maybe I am. There's some things that are bigger than the both of us.

Caesar   You're gonna join up with those *girls* and those *faggots* … ?

Brute   Yeah, maybe.

Full of resentment and anger, Caesar knocks his long-time partner to the mat and stalks off up the ramp alone.

But when we next see The Righteous all together, they are doing nothing more than arguing amongst themselves, apparently unaware that it's all being televised for the audience on the stadium's big screen.

Blue   I think we should just *talk* with him first. Mr. Dynes is a reasonable man, and –

Sundance   The only 'reasonable man' in the Federation right now is Homosapien. Why won't you *listen* to him before –

Butch   For God's sake – it's all 'Homosapien this' and 'Homosapien that' with you these days. Come on, honey – we were gonna go get a drink together, remember?

Sundance	Not *now*, Butch.
Millennium	Butch, please don't leave yet. We need to get this sorted –
bimbo	Well, all I'm saying is you'd better hurry up. In five minutes I'm due for a manicure, pedicure and facial.
cameraman	You're all talking wages and travel expenses, but no one's mentioned danger money yet. Those fans in the front rows, they're a menace, I tell you, and the VIPs are the worst. The other night I –
Brute	Christ, Jay was right. What's the use of any of you?
Millennium	Brute, *please*. This isn't helping. None of you are helping!
Homosapien	Oh God, this is all too hard …

Lucifer is on the stage at the top of the ramp, watching all this on the big screen along with the audience. He chuckles gleefully into a microphone.

| *Lucifer* | I spy with my little eye … Trouble In Paradise … ! |

OK, I admit that at first I thought this storyline was a bit boring. Not real exciting. But by now I'm intrigued. And, by the way, the WWW's ratings are still steadily climbing, they're higher than ever, and definitely no peaking yet. Tall tales but true. Incredible.

Very Important People

It's a Friday morning, mid October, and I know that the WWW must be in town getting ready for the show that night. The rhythm of our lives has become attuned to da Dub Dub Dub's touring schedule. But Adam hasn't called or anything, and David is moping around like a month of rainy days, so I am left to assume that for the first time since all this started they don't have plans to see each other.

A courier arrives with a flat cardboard envelope and oddly enough it's addressed to me personally rather than to the bookstore. I sign for it, wink at the courier (who promptly exits, flustered) and cast a curious glance over the unexpected delivery.

My heart skips a beat when I see the sender is Adam O'Connor, from the WWW headquarters in Chicago, and that it was specifically scheduled for delivery today. When my heart starts up again, it's racing. I suddenly recall that Adam said he was sending something and he needed my help. In all the subsequent talk of his yearning for a home I'd forgotten to even wonder what it was. Well, I guess I'm about to find out.

I tear the red strip off the courier's envelope, and out slides a regular business envelope with the WWW logo in the top left corner. OK … I reach for the letter opener, and neatly slit it open. Two tickets fall out onto the counter.

I gape down at them. Tickets for tonight's show at the Garden. And, what's more, *front row seats*. The tickets are even marked *VIP*. I am gaping so hard that my mouth may never close properly again. The front rows are reserved for local celebrities (like the town's favorite football players), or friendly reporters (so they get to see the action up close), or the home–town wrestlers' friends and families (as a back–up just in case Jack Dynes can't find anyone more important). I've heard that such tickets are as hard to find as a queer without fashion sense. And Adam went to the trouble of scoring them, and having them delivered to us on the day itself, and …

He wanted my help. He said I'd know what to do. Which means he's afraid that David will shrug this off, this opportunity of a lifetime. This enormous gesture of good will.

I pick up the tickets – carefully as if they might crumble or dissolve or vanish or something – and I go find David. He's perched uncomfortably on the edge of one of the sofas, flipping through one of the new titles with a distinct lack of interest. "You've got a date tonight," I announce.

He looks up, half hoping and half despairing.

"With Adam," I say.

The hope grows for a happy moment, but then is overtaken by panic. "Did he call? I didn't hear the phone." A hearty dash of confusion adds to the mix. "Why didn't he ask me himself? Are you sure he didn't mean you?"

"Look, he sent these," I blurt out, sitting by him and holding out the tickets as if they're holy relics. At this stage I'm not sure that I'm actually helping. "VIP tickets. Front row seats. Any wrestling fan would kill or at least seriously maim for these."

David smiles, kind of weak and watery. "Oh, OK. You go, Patrick. Take whomever you like. I'm no wrestling fan. Not really."

"No," I firmly reply. "No no no, you don't get to do that. The whole deal is that he wants you there. *You*, David Vigil."

"So why'd he send them to you? He addressed them to you, right?"

"Because he was afraid you'd do this. He's afraid you won't be there for him. He wants you there, David, and he's gone to all kinds of trouble to get you the best seat in the house, with your best friend beside you, and you just *have* to go. It's a social obligation. Don't you get it? This isn't an invitation you just turn your back on."

David's smile has kind of quirked, as if he's deeply amused by something *other*. But he doesn't get sidetracked. "How do you know all this?" he asks me. "What did he say?"

I look at him levelly, man to man. "I *just know*." And I don't say anything more.

The words hang there for a long long moment. David looks away, but I can still see the quirked corner of his smile. Eventually he comments, "So, you're my best friend, huh?"

OK, I hadn't meant to let that slip. But I don't muddle the issue like I once would have. I just say, "Yeah."

"And you think I'm obliged to go?"

"Yeah, I do."

He nods, though he looks no better than stoic. "All right."

I grin with relief, and grab him in a hug. *"Yahoo! We're going to the wrestling!"* The two of us lose balance and topple over into the depths of the sofa.

David firmly returns my hug for a moment, but then manages to pick himself up. "So, what time does it start? We'll have to leave directly from here, I guess. Do you want to go home and get changed this afternoon? I'll book a cab to the Garden for eight."

I just lie there sprawled on the sofa where Adam once sang his love for David. I did it! David might have agreed because he feels an obligation to *me* rather than to Adam, but I am certain that all I have to do is get him there. I can trust Adam to do the rest.

My fifteen seconds of fame

And so there we both are at my very first live pro wrestling show! David and I are a few minutes late, but we get ushered to our seats with the utmost courtesy – because of course we're VIPs at least for this one night.

There's a match already started, they're jerking the curtain, but I am too overwhelmed to pay much attention. The buzz is incredible. And what seats! There's nothing but the waist–high padded security barrier between us and the area around the ring. We are just round the corner from the commentator's table, but they're not in place yet. I look around me at the audience, who are already warming up. Wrestling's fan–base is so much broader these days; it's no longer just young guys, it's no longer just rednecks, though there's still plenty of both. On the whole they look a lot more affluent too, and most are wearing the latest t–shirts featuring Blue or Lucifer or The Fallen, so I guess that means the merchandising is doing well. Jack Dynes must be happy. Or maybe he just doesn't quite believe his luck yet.

The first match finishes. David is just sitting there, paying attention but not getting real enthused. As the commentators walk out to take their seats, the ring announcer asks for a wild bout of cheering as he counts down to when the cameras roll and we go out live to homes across America – and, delayed by a few hours, right around the world. I beckon to David and he grimaces (though very mildly) before complying. I go bananas on cue, while he stands and claps politely. Honestly, you'd think we were at the opera or something equally dire.

But I get my reward for playing along – I glimpse myself on the big screen, and turn to find which camera is locked in on me, with that red light on top that means it's The One. Got it. I instinctively do what I must. Still staring down the lens, right into the heart of the machine and through it the whole damned audience, I solemnly tap my nose. *I'm In The Know.*

And then it's over, they've cut to another shot, and then another one. I leap up and punch the air, victorious, and when I land I give my bemused best friend a big hug. I had my chance, and I didn't blow it, not at all.

One really hasn't lived until one appears live on the big screen at a pro wrestling show.

Butch and Sundance

A couple of matches later the sound system blasts out Jimmy Somerville's ever–inspiring *You Make Me Feel (Mighty Real)*. I go bananas, of course, and I get a bonus three seconds of fame as they flash me up on the big screen again. (Hey, maybe the ringside cameraman likes me. I blow him a kiss just in case.)

announcer   Put your hands together for the WWW's most out*raaaaage*ous tag team, founding members of The Righteous, hailing from Blythe in sunny California – Butch and *Sun*–daaaaance!

Of course the audience are mostly booing and jeering, but I am cheering my little heart out. The pair of them jog down the ramp, hand in hand, and slide under the lowest rope into the ring. While the music bounces along, Butch regathers Sundance's hands, and twirls him around, then pulls him into a close embrace and dips him, before drawing him up slowly into a kiss … OK, they've done it before, and they'll do it again, and I know it's all an act, but I melt inside. They are just *too* delicious. And it seems that Sundance is even *more* gorgeous in the flesh than he is on screen. And that's saying something. Incredible tales but true.

Butch and Sundance's old foes Louis du Lac and the good Bizarro brother are announced. These two tag teams used to be divided on Good Guy *vs.* Bad Guy lines, but now it's The Righteous *vs.* The Fallen and it's gotten hard to say exactly who's good and who's bad.

Anyway, while the other two wrestlers are making their way to the ring, an odd little thing happens. David and I lucked out and are sitting directly opposite Butch and Sundance's corner of the ring. They are standing up there on the apron, outside the ropes, waiting for the match to begin. And I slowly become aware that Sundance is looking down at me, watching me. My skin prickles. I glance away, then dare to look back. He's still watching me. So I stare back up at him, doing the whole deer–caught–in–the–headlamps thing. And Sundance winks at me.

I shiver, all goosebumps. Then Butch notices; grabs Sundance's arm and shakes it, demanding his attention, his loyalty; glares at me for daring to distract his partner. And I sit down, shaking like I've just been doused by a bucket of cold water. Of course that was just a set play, part of the whole queer routine. It didn't mean a thing.

"Are you OK?" David asks, confused and clueless.

It wasn't real, I remind myself. Boy, they had me taken in for a moment there! Like I'm some kind of rookie, some kind of greenhorn. Like I'm not

In The Know after all. "Yeah, I'm fine," I reply. The bell rings to signal the start of the match. And I stand up again.

But I haven't been fair – I've been so into the wrestling that I've been ignoring David. I keep one eye on the match, and I cheer when Butch or Sundance do something right, but I also pay a bit more attention to my rather bored best friend. "How are you doing?" I ask.

He shrugs. "I don't get why he wanted us to be here."

"Adam wanted *you* to be here," I counter. "And the night's not over yet." I cheer as Butch tags Sundance in and, for the few seconds that they're both legally in the ring, they execute a particularly clever maneuver on the helpless du Lac.

"You like these guys, don't you?" David observes.

"Sorry. They've grown on me."

"That's all right. It's not like they're competition for Homosapien anymore."

"I really should be booing them."

"Why, if you like them?"

"They're still meant to be heels. At least, I *think* they are – it's all a bit complicated now. But, anyway, bad guys get booed."

David is sadly puzzled.

I explain, "It's all *heat*, whether it's cheering or jeering, and heat's a good thing. Heat is what they want."

As the match winds on, Butch and Sundance's tactics get camper and camper. Finally Bizarro has been beaten into a stupor, and is lying spread–eagled on his back in the middle of the ring. His partner is hollering at him from their corner, but Bizarro is too far gone to hear him. An exhausted Sundance crawls over to his unconscious foe, and collapses across him for the pin. Only, the way he falls (accidentally or not), it's as if they're in the throes of a sixty–niner … The crowd are booing and catcalling in disgust. The referee is grimacing with distaste, and keeps his distance, but he drops and starts the count. One … Two … Bizarro manages to get a shoulder off the mat.

The crowd yell and cheer in relief. But I notice that some of them are actually laughing and shaking their heads in amusement. And it occurs to me that the crowds are free to enjoy Butch and Sundance and their gay antics, because they are now beginning to know or at least guess that it's all scripted. They don't have to be uncomfortable about it, they can just cheer or (preferably, in this case) boo to their hearts' content. How about that? I'm sure David won't approve when I explain this theory to him – but *I* think it's all right, because the mob might just find themselves enjoying all this queerness, and that might just painlessly widen out to an acceptance of real queerness before anyone even notices. (Well, it might!)

Anyway, The Fallen team end the match with a disqualification – which I reckon they force because otherwise they were going to lose – and they stagger back up the ramp, looking mighty pleased with themselves. Sundance scrapes his partner up off the mat, and supports him as best he can. But, just before they leave the ring, and I *swear* I don't just imagine it, Sundance glances back at me. There's no expression on his face, and there's definitely no wink this time, but I swear he deliberately looks for me, meets my gaze. And I break out in goosebumps all over again.

Most likely to!

It's been a long long evening, and there's still been no sign of Our Hero. David has been getting more and more withdrawn, and I fear even disgruntled. But finally it's time for the last match of the show, and therefore the climax of the night's entertainment.

announcer   This championship match is scheduled for one fall only. And the winner of this match will take home the WWW championship belt!
Weighing in at 300 pounds, born and raised in Hell's Kitchen, please welcome the reigning WWW champion, *Lucifer!*

Lucifer appears, bearing the most evil–looking scowl I've ever seen. The crowd go crazy for him, partly in surprise. I don't think anyone knew there was going to be a title match that night. So, anyway, Lucifer reaches the ring, and prowls around it, still scowling, and –

– and that's when the rocked–up *Homosapien* blares from the speakers!

announcer   The challenger, coming to you all the way from San Francisco, weighing in at 243 pounds, is … *Homosapien!*

If I went bananas before, well, I went the whole fruit salad this time. And David's suddenly standing there close beside me, clutching my hand for support. Neither of us know quite what to expect.

But the first thing that happens is an absolute revelation. Homosapien comes out from backstage – and he's *dancing!* He's dancing to the music, just like he used to – thrusting those hips, swaying that butt, showing off all his purple–lycra–molded assets, and smiling with the infectious joy of simply being *alive*. (I am so damned happy for him that it doesn't sink in for ages that this is exactly what I asked him for. "There's not enough dancing in wrestling anymore," I complained. And maybe Adam listened.) Not only that, but Homosapien is also proudly singing along to Our Very Own Anthem. "Homo superior / In my interior / But from the skin out / I'm Homosapien too." Oh yeah! You go, girl! This is glorious.

Homosapien reaches the ring, and walks around it as the music fades, looking out and waving to the audience as if they're just as pleased as he is that he's there. He doesn't once look at me or David, mind you, even when he takes his place in the corner nearest us. There's a few quiet moments, during which he stretches, bounces on the balls of his feet, eyes Lucifer, gets ready for this match. He must have known we were there, though. Even if he didn't catch my few seconds of fame on the monitors backstage, there must have been some way for him to be sure we were there.

The referee beckons them both in closer, and lays down the law. Which of course the audience can't hear, but it all adds to the tension, the seriousness of this championship match. The referee is done and the wrestlers return to their corners. Homosapien is focused on the match itself now and seems totally unaware of the audience let alone we two insignificant members of it. He swings his arms and bounces again, warming up.

David and I are standing there clutching each other's hands like a pair of nelly old dears watching their baby take his first steps out into the cold hard world.

And the referee signals for the bell to sound and the match to start.

I'm glad to see that Homosapien begins well, immediately taking charge of the match. Of course the tide will turn soon enough, but at least he has these few minutes in which to strut his stuff. After raining a series of blows on Lucifer, Homosapien swings him into a corner, where Lucifer dazedly waits for Homosapien to barrel into him, a move promptly followed by a knee to Lucifer's dangly bits. "Ooh, that's gotta hurt," I say as the audience collectively winces. Homosapien grabs Lucifer's arm and spins him out of the corner, flings him onto his back in the centre of the ring, pins him for the count. One … Of course it's too early for a victory, but for once Adam doesn't seem to be in mortal danger from Michael Rosen. Two … Lucifer manages to get a shoulder up, and then rolls up onto his hands and knees while Homosapien stands and regathers.

"Hey!" I exclaim to David during the lull. "This is wonderful!"

But David immediately counters, "No, this is awful." And I notice how tightly he's hanging on to my hand with both of his.

"Why? Why, what's wrong?"

"That bastard is gonna start hurting Adam – for *real* – as soon as he can."

David is right, of course. I turn back to the ring with a sudden terror.

"Why the hell did he want me here to see this?" David mutters.

The tide does indeed turn, and Lucifer takes the lead in the match, and begins laying into Homosapien. David can't bear to watch, but I do – well, I watch with my eyes screwed up so that I can close them at a moment's notice. And after a while I notice something. "David, look. It's OK. Look at this."

He manages to peek. And it slowly dawns on David, as it already has on me, that this is a real pro wrestling match. By which I mean, it isn't a real fight at all. Michael Rosen is actually respecting his opponent enough to pull his punches, to cooperate in his holds and moves. To put him over. Amazing. Truly amazing. Because, of course, in a real pro wrestling match, these two men aren't opponents, but partners, co–stars. And since when did Michael Rosen consider Adam O'Connor as such? This is terrific. More like Homosapien's wonderfully technical matches with Blue, rather than the slugfest his matches with Lucifer have been.

David and I watch, open–mouthed with shock, as Michael Rosen demonstrates as much professionalism as Adam does.

The tide turns again. As Lucifer begins to tire, Homosapien regains the ascendancy. I assume this is simply a way of lengthening the match, which the audience are loving. (They used to appreciate the real fights between these two, but I think they're appreciating this display of technical skill just as much if not more.) This is a title match, so I know there's no way that Homosapien is going to win. Especially since he formed The Righteous and started talking about going out on strike. He hasn't paid his dues yet. Or … maybe he … Hhhmmm. I frown, trying to think this through. That would make one hell of a storyline, letting Homosapien win the championship. It would sure help stoke the fires of resentment in The Fallen.

Anyway, back to the match. Homosapien spins Lucifer into the ropes, and on the rebound drops him with a Clothesline. Excellent. Lucifer is lying face down on the mat, not moving. A near–exhausted Homosapien rolls him over onto his back, and rests an arm on his chest for the pin. The referee starts another count. One … Two …

And suddenly Homosapien is dragged away towards the ropes, the pin broken. Everyone – Homosapien, the referee, the audience, yours truly – stares wildly around, looking for the cause. And it's Jack Dynes! The owner of the federation is there outside the ring, holding up his hands as if to declare his innocence. But he's just interfered in this match! Huh! The plot thickens!

Despite the fact that this is his boss, the referee is furious. He glares at the man and points up the ramp, emphatically gesturing, telling Dynes to get backstage. He has no business being there and certainly no business trying to affect the outcome of this or of any match. Dynes argues, apparently pleading the case for a disqualification, but the referee won't have it. (I smile to myself. Maybe the referee will be the next recruit for The Righteous. After all, if the boss can take sides, why not the referees?)

OK, so the referee is absolutely determined to play this one fairly. Reluctantly, and still arguing, Dynes makes his way back up to the top of the ramp. The referee turns back to the ring and signals for the match to continue.

Lucifer has caught his breath, and rallies for a while, but a thrill runs through me as Homosapien again takes charge. All the momentum is going his way. It would take more interference from Dynes, or some such thing, to get in Homosapien's way – which is perfectly possible, of course. But I am wishing, willing, praying with every part of me, that Homosapien can have this. He's certainly paid his dues with me.

Another surge of effort from Lucifer – but Homosapien ducks under his renewed assault, picks Lucifer up, and dumps him on his back. Before you can say, "I'm the cruiser / You're the loser," Homosapien has him tied up like a pretzel, and is resting his weight on Lucifer in the most provocative tableau I've ever seen –

"Wicked sodomitical!" I'm thinking –

"It's the Homo Superior! It's the Homo Superior!" the commentators are yelling over the crowd's roar –

Homosapien smiles down at his victim, who stares back up at him, almost too befuddled to be humiliated –

Jack Dynes is at the top of the ramp, tearing his hair out –

The referee goes down for the count –

One …

Lucifer colors up, begins to stir –

Two –

Homosapien pushes in closer, as if he's thrusting home –

THREE!

Oh My God! Oh My God! Homosapien has won the match! And not only that – he's the WWW's newest champion!

David and I are jumping up and down, and hugging each other, and hollering, and I'm not ashamed to say there isn't a dry eye between us.

Dynes is on the big screen, gaping in shock, hands on his head, horrified.

The audience is going crazy – cheering or yelling, who cares, it's all heat.

A red–faced Lucifer makes his wounded way up the ramp towards his boss – but is rebuffed. He was meant to win! (At least, that's the way Dynes is playing it.) The two of them, thoroughly mortified, and totally mad at each other, disappear backstage.

Millennium dashes out past them, and runs down to the ring to celebrate Homosapien's victory with a long hug. Homosapien picks her up and swings her around, grinning fit to burst. There ain't any dry eyes up there either.

The referee hands Homosapien the championship belt, and Millennium helps him fasten it around his waist. Then the ref and M, each side of Our Conquering Hero, lift his arms in victory, let him soak in the audience's approval (and who cares if it's a bit muted compared to the roar that Blue would have received under similar circumstances).

David is so happy and so surprised that he grabs me up and plants a kiss on me, right there in the middle of 20,000 screaming fans.

Lord save me, all is chaos and delight.

The day of our love

They don't go to an ad break, they don't end the show yet. They just let Homosapien revel in the good stuff. The ref disappears, and eventually Millennium leaves him alone in the ring, the belt glittering gold under the spotlights. The big screen provides a close–up of Homosapien's ecstatic face as background to the real thing.

Finally, though, the crowd begin to quieten. Homosapien walks over to the ropes and asks for a microphone. A few moments later the Garden is hushed enough for him to use it.

He lifts the mike, he grins and shakes his head as if he can hardly find the words. Then – "Mr. Dynes once said I didn't want it badly enough."

A murmur runs through the crowd.

"Oh man …" Homosapien happily sighs – "I wanted this!"

And the audience is right there with him, right there with his blissful satisfaction, as if both he and they have been seduced and ravished by this unexpected success.

"Thank you, Boston!" he calls out. "Thank you for sharing this with me!"

Of course they cheer him for that.

He waits for them to quieten again. Then he says, "But – call me greedy – there's one other thing I want in my life."

A moment passes. My heart is thudding. I don't dare look at David.

"This is wonderful, don't get me wrong. And I've got my best friend here with me to share it with."

He gestures to Millennium, who grins up at him from near the commentator's table. "You da man," she says. Another murmur of approval ripples through the crowd. Homosapien blows her a kiss.

"But victories can feel pretty hollow if you don't have that Special Someone at your side. That Significant Other. Whoever it is that makes your heart sing. You know what I mean, don't you, Boston?"

There's a surge of deeply felt agreement, but there's also some uneasiness. Because if they haven't all figured by now that Homosapien is really truly gay, most of them at least know enough to suspect it. Fear it.

Homosapien looks around, shifts the microphone in his hand. He still hasn't looked directly at me or David, but David must know by now that this is for him. He is so quiet that I can't even hear him breathe.

That's when Homosapien sings to him once more, sings a line from his song …

And I just hope and pray that the day of our love is at hand.

"If you're out there listening," Homosapien says – still not looking at us, not singling out David, so that David is free to make his own choices. "If you're out there, then I'm hoping and praying that you'll give me a second chance. I know I don't deserve it, but you're man enough to forgive me."

And he says to the crowd, "This is who I am. This is me, Adam O'Connor. This is real. No more bullshit. Maybe you can't respect me for that, or accept me. If you make me a heel because I'm gay, that's OK by me. That would say a lot more about you than me."

There's a swell of mixed response from the audience, but Adam ignores it. Instead he sings again, very quietly, thoughtfully, as if he were alone.

You and I, me and you, we will be one from two, understand?

He takes a long breath, tilts his head back. I suddenly wonder if he's close to weeping.

And the world is so wrong that I hope that we'll be strong enough / For we are on our own and the only thing known is our love.

I finally look at David. He *is* weeping. He says to me, "What do I do?"

"Go to him," I say. "If you want him, he's yours, and for God's sake *go to him.*"

David nods, lets go of me. Props himself up on the barrier and swings a leg over. Suddenly there's a security guard there, blocking his way, but just as suddenly there's Emma, having a word in the guy's ear. I can just hear a comment over the guard's headset too, and then the guy grudgingly nods. Emma takes David's arm, winks at me, and helps my old curmudgeon of a boss up into the wrestling ring itself.

There are no more words, sung or spoken. David just dazedly steps towards Adam, and then they're in each other's arms, desperately hugging each other like there's no tomorrow. And the show is over. The commentators walk away up the ramp, the dull old houselights come up, the audience start filing out. But David and Adam stay right where they are, clinging together for dear life. And they quietly kiss to seal their happy–ever–after.

Emma reaches over the barrier to tug at my hand. "Hey, Patrick," she says. "Come on backstage."

"Really?"

"Yeah, really."

Like any fan–boy, I am dazzled. It's suddenly all too much! I feel like crying, and for the wrong reasons. But Emma smiles, and tugs at my hand again. And then David and Adam are there too, waiting on me. So I clumsily clamber over the barrier, and – oh my god i am actually walking up the actual ramp – the four of us head backstage to Adam and Emma's dressing room.

How it ended

All is confusion for a long while.

At some stage, a saddened Emma quietly explains to me that Michael Rosen is leaving the WWW, and that was his last match, and Jack Dynes had stipulated that Michael could only break his contract if he lost his title to Adam as the result of a real pro wrestling match. And so Michael Rosen swallowed his pride, and put Homosapien over to the crowd, and that's how desperate he was to leave. I almost feel sorry for the guy for a moment or two. I definitely feel sorry for Emma. Not that Rosen was ever good enough for her.

But Emma brightens soon enough when she sees Adam proudly showing the championship belt to an awe–struck Nick and Clancy.

The six of us find ourselves gathered together in a circle, and Adam gives an impromptu thank–you speech, just very honest and simple and heartfelt, in which each of us plays a starring role. But Adam saves a special mention for Clancy. "You *all* had faith in me, more faith than I had in myself," Adam says. "But, I don't know why, it was Clancy's faith that helped me turn a corner and finally start believing I could do this."

Clancy leans in to shake his hand again. "You're the hero, Adam," he says. "I'm just glad I could help." (Ah, yes, Clancy – who I swear was watching me again. Honestly, if I didn't know he was straight, I'd be brimming full of surmises by now.)

Adam gives David another hug, and they stand there together each with an arm slung round the other's waist. "Well," says Adam, "I vote that we take this to Chez Lui."

"Where?" asks Nick.

"The best nightclub in town," Adam replies.

And so we do.

When we get to Chez Lui, the place is full to the rafters and *rocking*. Almost as soon as the six of us step through the door, my friend the DJ puts Homosapien's song on. I am gaping. "Did you script this *entire* night?" I ask Adam. He just winks at me, grinning broadly. I guess so!

Naturally Homosapien is not only our host but also the club's Guest Of Honor for the night. He is kept busy for a while signing autographs, shaking hands, kissing cheeks, deflecting offers, though there is of course supplementary attention paid to the other three wrestlers. Finally they're allowed to join David and me in a booth.

The six of us lift our charged glasses, and David proposes a toast: "To friends."

"Friends!" Down the hatch, and (ah …) that feels better.

During all the hubbub, I am pleased to discover, the confusion and the 'aftermath' feeling have pretty much vanished, and we are all right back in the thrill of Victory Bravely Won and Love Newly Pledged. The six of us are content, though, to sit there together and either silently commune or inanely chat. And smile a lot. We are all smiling a great deal.

In the midst of this, I am chilled by a sudden taste of reality. I spot Mr. Tall, Dark & Intense lurking in the crowd, peering at me. I am careful enough not to look afraid or vulnerable, but I know I lose the smile. Will this damned storyline ever really resolve? I know that if I talk to David about it, he'll insist on him and Adam facing the guy (if not slaying my dragon for me, then at least warning him off) or else he'll say I should report Mr. TDI to the police so they'll definitely have him if he ever assaults anyone else. But, me, I just want it over with. I just don't want to have to think about him anymore.

The thing is, as I go on watching the creep, it occurs to me that *he's* the one looking afraid and vulnerable. *He's* the one whose face has fallen. He's looking around at the people surrounding me, scanning my friends, assessing them. And he knows they're each and every one a threat to him, even if they don't know it. Mr. TDI never thought I had any real friends, but now he can see that he was wrong. And he quails. I actually see him quail and he's no longer so tall or dark or intense at all.

I am still watching him, solemnly, unflinchingly. And Mr. TDI backs off, turns away, threads his way through the crowd to the door, and leaves. And that, God damn it, is that.

Back to the important stuff. Back to the party.

I can see that Nick is still a tad uncomfortable, this being a gay club, and him not being at all gay in the slightest not even in his little pinky finger. He has been sticking close to Emma, but that's all right because they've managed to strike up a real conversation, and they are talking animatedly between themselves, and eventually Nick asks her to dance, and of course she says yes. Soon enough he's grooving on down, and even though he's in the midst of The Other, he's finally realized that this particular Other ain't The Enemy. And that's all well and good.

Adam gets up, and with a gentlemanly flourish offers his hand to David, who happily joins him on the dance floor. They slow–dance, and kiss, and murmur, alone together in the midst of the frenetic music. It is *sweet* to see them finally get it right together.

Eventually I figure I should quit watching and just leave them to it. I smile to myself, and turn away.

And then I realize that I'm sitting there all alone with Clancy. Who's watching me again, with a softness about his mouth and a glint in his eye. He tilts his head towards the dance floor, his long dark hair shifting round his shoulders like a waterfall. "Would you dance?" he asks. "With me?"

"Yes," I say. Though I don't move. We sit there and look at each other some more. God, the man is gorgeous. But … "I thought you were straight."

His smile quirks, though he nods agreement, and half of me dares to hope while the other half is resigned. Clancy leans in very close to say, "Always have been." Then he sits back again, still smiling. He becomes a touch conscious under my gaze and a little bit of the mystery of him melts away. Not much, but just enough. *Always have been*, eh? Which leaves the question begging as to whether he always will be …

I take his hand and the two of us join our friends out on the dance floor.

How it really ended

Delicious, eh? I love a happy ending.

Well, dear reader, I suppose that of all these fledging relationships you mostly care about David and Adam, so I'll just say that they haven't done it easy – but then who ever does? Especially when you're getting on a bit and you're set in your ways and one of you is yearning for a home which the other isn't *quite* ready to share just yet. But, hey, they're still very much together, and they really do love each other, and they're planning to be very much together for a good long while yet. They give me all kinds of hope.

This story began about a year ago, and we've all gone through some changes in that time. Pro wrestling has too. John Gurrie finally got to publish his in–depth article in *Sharpshooter*, and it kind of defined pro wrestling for a long while, until Jack Dynes decided to shake everything up and roll the dice yet again. Despite all this, though, a good third of the fans remain convinced that pro wrestling is real. Not that it matters much either way, in my not–so–humble opinion, when the numbers of bums–on–seats and dollar–takings have blown out beyond Jack Dynes' wildest dreams. The WWW does different things, they play with what David calls the layers of identity, the layers of meaning, and that attracts different people at different times, for different reasons. The rednecks still love it – well, most of them – but the fact that it's *not* real attracts other people as well. As for storylines, Dynes still takes his cues from the movies, even more so now that pro wrestling is officially Sports Entertainment rather than just sport. Wrestling's more than just violence or a soap opera or a parody. It's a postmodern phenomenon!

"It would make a great book," I say. "All the controversy, all the *what's real* now that we know a lot of it isn't. And I'm sure there's another pair of star–crossed lovers waiting in the wings."

"So … *you* write it." David smiles smugly, like he has better things to be doing right now. Which he does.

There's a whole nother story in there … Imagine that. I might have to write a sequel. So, stay tuned. Same bat time, same bat channel. And let's get ready to *rrruuummmbbbllleee … !!!*

About Julie Bozza

Ordinary people are extraordinary. We can all aspire to decency, generosity, respect, honesty – and the power of love (all kinds of love!) can help us grow into our best selves.

I write stories about 'ordinary' people finding their answers in themselves and each other. I write about friends and lovers, and the families we create for ourselves. I explore the depth and the meaning, the fun and the possibilities, in 'everyday' experiences and relationships. I believe that embodying these things is how we can live our lives more fully.

Creative works help us each find our own clarity and our own joy. Readers bring their hearts and souls to reading, just as authors bring their hearts and souls to writing – and together we make a whole.

I read books, lots of books, and watch films. I admire art, and love theatre and music. I try to be an awesome partner, sister, daughter, friend. I live an engaged and examined life. And I strive to write as honestly as I can.

I have lived in two countries – England and Australia – which has helped widen my perspective, and I have travelled as well. I love learning, and have completed courses in all kinds of things. My careers have been in Human Resources, and in eLearning and training, so there has always been a focus on my fellow human beings and on understanding, conveying, sharing information.

Knitting gives me some down time and the chance to craft something with my hands. Coffee gives me stimulation and a certain street cred. My favourite colour has segued from pure blue to dark purple, and seems to be segueing again to marine blues.

I think John Keats is the best person who has ever lived.

And that's me! Julie Bozza. Quirky. Queer. Sincere.

If you want to know more, please do come find me at **juliebozza.com** and **libra-tiger.com**.

Titles by Julie Bozza

The Butterfly Hunter Trilogy:
    Butterfly Hunter
    Of Dreams and Ceremonies
    Like Leaves to a Tree
    The Thousand Smiles of Nicholas Goring

Albert J. Sterne:
    The Definitive Albert J. Sterne
    Albert J. Sterne: Future Bright, Past Imperfect

Novels and Novellas:
    The Apothecary's Garden
    The Fine Point of His Soul
    Homosapien … a fantasy about pro wrestling
    Mitch Rebecki Gets a Life
    A Night with the Knight of the Burning Pestle
    A Threefold Cord
    The 'True Love' Solution
    The Valley of the Shadow of Death

Stories and Anthologies:
    Call to Arms
    A Certain Persuasion
    An English Heaven
    No Holds Bard
    A Pride of Poppies

www.ingramcontent.com/pod-product-compliance
Lightning Source LLC
Chambersburg PA
CBHW071157180726
48291CB00007B/2491